A Dream
Passage

J.D.E. Savill

A catalogue record for this book is available from the National Library of Australia.

Author: Savill, James D. E., author.
Title: A Dream Passage / J.D.E. Savill.
ISBN: 978-0-9923477-5-8 (paperback)
Dewey Number: N A823.4

Target Audience: Young Adult.
Genre: Speculative Fiction.
Copyright © 2018 J.D.E. Savill

Publisher: Scruffy Wuffy
P.O. Box 566
Jamison A.C.T. 2614, Australia
Email: info@scruffywuffy.com
www.scruffywuffy.com

Cover: Jason Moser

For dreams,
And winks and chirps and kisses.

1. Dreaming

Dreaming of Kala is easy. With just one thought of her, I have her cheeky smile in my mind. I imagine her delicate features; her button nose, tender lips, soft skin and the fineness of her blondish-brown hair. The expression on her face is calm and trusting, and even with her eyes closed, she radiates confidence and unfaltering optimism that everything will work out. That's Kala.

Today, I see her standing, then hovering and drifting through knee-length grass, moving effortlessly towards the mound in the park that we know so well. The sky is cloudy and grey except for a single spot, directly above, where the passing sunbeams have created a crisp cylinder of light so pure and perfect that it could only exist in a dream.

Kala's hair is golden and glistens in the brightness. I watch her eyelids open, revealing her gorgeous turquoise eyes.

"Dream with me, Tomas," she says.

"I am with you," I reply and I see the two of us standing together. I have my arms around Kala's waist and we're both sparkling in the magical aura of the sunlight.

Together, we watch the sunlit edge transform to become a window to a forest world appearing around us. I point at the tallest of the trees. Kala shows me a butterfly and we both hear a buzzing bee.

I notice a floral and slightly citrus scent in the air. It's pure and fresh—just like Kala!

"That perfume. Is it from the flowers on that vine?"

"You'll have to see," says Kala, mysteriously.

A pair of rainbow parrots appears beside the flowers, tilting their heads from side to side as they look at us. The one on the left winks at us, then chirps and drinks from the red flower. Then goes the other one; winking and chirping and drinking.

Kala winks at me, chirps like the parrot and playfully pecks me on the cheek, making silly eyes at me.

"You're mad," I say, returning her peck.

"I love this place," says Kala.

"Me too. I wish we could stay."

***

I'm woken by a touch on my shoulder.

It's my mother, Beth. "Morning," I say wearily.

"How were your dreams?" she asks, frowning.

I love my mother, but I don't like her questions.

"I dreamed with Kala," I reply, aware that it isn't what she wants to hear. Honesty is difficult, but it's very important to my parents. I let my parents down in other ways, but not with my honesty.

"You don't have time for those dreams, Tomas," says Beth. "It's only a month until your passage. You can't have your own dreams any more. You need to be responsible. Soon you'll be dreaming for all of us."

She often goes on like that. "How were your dreams?" I ask, trying to move the discussion away from me.

"Busy," she says. "I think we're making progress with the school."

She's always serious about her work. "Will you get consensus?"

"I'm not sure. Maybe you can help us when you've taken your passage."

"I'll try."

For a dream to come true, the system requires a minimum number of people to dream together while wearing their community wristbands. They need to have what they call *consensus* on the action. That's when a majority of people dream for exactly the same thing. After my passage, I'll be able to dream in support of Beth's work. I like the idea of helping her with that.

Beth kisses me on the forehead, then leaves my room. That's my cue to get ready for school. I get out of bed, shower and dress in my navy-blue school shirt and grey trousers. Looking in the mirror as I comb my hair, I see a boy nearly sixteen, around six-feet tall, thin and tanned with brown eyes and wavy brown hair. Kala tells me that I'm handsome but I don't see that. I just see scrawny me.

I join my father, Davis, in the kitchen. He's laid out bread, cereal and starfruit on the kitchen table. It's the dream food breakfast allocation that appears in our cupboard every morning at six a.m. He looks at me and smiles proudly. He has kind eyes. Beth, arriving in the kitchen, shakes her head. Davis checks his smile for a few moments but then it returns.

"Don't worry," says Davis. "I know he will dream well."

"How do you know that?"

"He'll dream well because he's our son," replies Davis, grinning.

Beth stares, disapproving.

"You know, Tomas," continues Davis, "Your mother and I dreamed of a son who was honest and caring. You are that son. And we dreamed that our son would have courage. You have that too."

"You two dreamed together?"

"Yes, we did. Back then we had more freedom."

"But we didn't always have what we needed," adds Beth. "Some people didn't have enough to eat."

I try to imagine what it would be like to be free to dream whatever I wanted, without consequence. "You were lucky," I say.

"It was different back then," says Beth.

"Why did it have to change?"

"It was Zennuta," says Davis. "You've been taught about how he created the dream system, haven't you?"

He knows I have. "Yeah, we've been told about that."

Zennuta, who we call 'The Dreaming One', created the dream technology. What I really want to hear about is the time before that. The problem is that my parents don't like to talk about it.

"What was it like doing physical work?" I ask.

"Best not to try to imagine it," replies Beth. "You don't want those ideas interfering with your dream work."

She didn't answer my question, but that's not unusual. And now, if I don't ask something else, and fast, I'll be getting questions from her. I can already see her thinking.

"Do you think there could ever be consensus on a no food dream?"

"It doesn't work that way," retorts Beth. "We get our food each day because we dream of it. If we don't dream it, it won't be there for us each morning."

"We could grow our own food," I say.

"Grow our own food!" exclaims Beth. "Don't talk of such things."

"Whose idea was that?" asks Davis.

"It was a boy in Kala's dream class."

"So, it was from Kala," scoffs Beth.

"It's okay," says Davis. "We did grow food in the old times."

"Could you tell me more about how it was back then? I'd really like to know."

"Another time," says Beth. "We want you to focus on your training now. Can you do that?"

"How about after my passage? Will you tell me then?"

"You know the Dream Council doesn't like us talking about it."

"How about I ask Grandpata? He likes talking about the old times."

"We'll see," says Beth. "But for now, you need to focus on getting your dreams under control."

I nod in agreement, grateful that she hasn't specifically forbidden me from asking Grandpata.

2. School

It's a school day. I'm sitting on the right-hand side of the third row of the classroom. I always choose the same seat—the one closest to the door.

My teacher, Rexus, is a serious man and probably the most boring person I know. He repeats the same things over and over again.

"You must pay attention now," he says. "Your passage is only weeks away and you have so much to learn."

He teaches us about law, science and mathematics. Every morning though, we have our dream lesson. We learn about the dream rules and techniques to use when we're not dreaming well.

For this morning's lesson, Rexus wants us to practice our dreaming. He's asked us to imagine that we want an apple for lunch. "It's not just any apple," he says. "It's a shiny red apple."

I don't find it difficult to imagine. Every dream apple that I've eaten is shiny and red. They're perfectly round and every one tastes exactly the same. The only other apples I know are the sour and lumpy ones from the old tree at the front of my grandparents' house.

I decide to dream of a cross between a dream apple and one of my grandparents' sour apples. I'll dream it to be red and perfectly round in shape, but tart in taste. No one else is going to dream of my kind of apple, but that won't matter—this is just a training exercise.

"Dream well," says Rexus. "Remember that it's the details that make it work. And remember that your dream will only work if the majority of you have exactly the same dream. And you'll need to dream of the precise time and location for the apple to appear."

He usually tells us the time and place. This time though, he seems to have left it for us to decide. Again, it hardly matters. This is just practice.

"And remember," he repeats. "It's not just any apple. It's a shiny red apple."

I relax, close my eyes and think about my apple. It's medium sized, shiny and perfect in shape. It's vivid red and I've just taken it from our cupboard at home. I imagine the crisp, serrating sound I hear as I bite into the juicy apple flesh.

"Eeewww!" I say, shuddering. It's really sour, but I really like the idea of it. Kala would like it too. I imagine the two of us together, sharing this apple. Kala takes a large, confident bite and chews a few times before stopping, shivering and contorting her face.

"Your turn," she says, smiling and holding the apple out for me.

I'm about to take my bite, but suddenly I'm aware of a presence next to me. There's someone there beside me. And now they're shaking my hand. "Tomas," I hear. "Wake up, Tomas."

Opening my eyes, I see Rexus hovering over me. "Oh," I mumble, realising my entire class is staring at me.

A Dream Passage

"I think you should explain your dream," says Rexus tersely.

"My dream?"

"You fell asleep, Tomas. Tell us what happened."

My brain is in the zone between sleep and consciousness. It's difficult to focus, but I remember my training and use it, the way I've been taught, to focus, search my memory, and recall my dream.

"I was thinking about an apple," I say. "It was a medium sized, shiny red apple that appeared in the food cupboard at home. I started to dream about how it might taste. It was crisp and juicy—and ... ah ... delicious." I manage to check myself, stopping short of mentioning the sourness, or Kala.

Rexus appears satisfied. "That's not too bad Tomas," he says. "Except that you weren't meant to fall asleep."

I don't mind his comment. In fact, it's virtually praise from Rexus, but then I see him pause, glancing ever so slightly towards a particular student in the front row. Titus is a model student: punctual, studious and always saying the things that Rexus wants to hear.

"What was the key thing that Tomas missed?" asks Rexus.

Titus eagerly raises his hand.

"Titus," says Rexus.

"He didn't specify the time he wanted the apple to appear."

"That's right, Titus. Tomas should have imagined the specific time for the apple to appear. You must remember the details, Tomas."

I nod in agreement, happy that Rexus has moved around to another student. He isn't making too much fuss over my mistake—this time.

"Your turn, Bella," says Rexus. "Tell us about your dream."

***

The afternoon lesson is about our justice system. We've learnt many of the laws over the last few weeks and now we're covering the criminal trial process. It starts with a prosecutor presenting the case against the accused. The accused or defendant responds to the issues raised. They go back and forth until both sides have no more to add. After that, the Dream Council gives its recommendation and then we all dream for the justice we want.

I should pay attention to these lessons but the only thing on my mind is meeting with Kala. We have two hours together on school days and they're the best hours of my life. As three p.m. approaches, I focus on my community wristband, anxious to hear the melody that marks the end of the school day.

It's now close to three and Rexus is summing up the lesson. *Do da, de da*, chimes my wristband. *Beep, beep, beep.*

I pack up with speed and intent. Rexus sometimes comments on my enthusiasm for leaving, but not today. I think it's because of the attention he gave me this morning. He probably has a rule about not hassling a student twice in one day. It's just the kind of rule he'd have—structured and boring.

My thoughts on Rexus and his rules evaporate as I leave the school yard. My focus is on meeting Kala at the park that's between our schools; about a twenty-minute walk for me and about fifteen minutes for her. It's one of the few parks that hasn't been redeveloped. If it had, it would have a blue swing set, wooden balance beams and a spongy green, soft landing floor—the same equipment that's in all the dream parks. We like our park because it's grassy and unkempt, and we usually have it all to ourselves; just the way we like it.

I walk quickly and it's not long before I pass the last house and look expectantly for Kala. And yes! There she is, standing proudly on top of the mound at the centre of the park.

"What kept you?" she asks, grinning.

"I must have been dreaming," I reply, just before we take hold of each other.

Immediately, I'm excited by my grasp on Kala's warm and contoured body, and reassured by the tightness of her hold on mine. I love this feeling and I'm always amazed by the way that the reality and presence of our touch is better in every way than the memories I have from our last time together.

It's a similar thing with Kala's scent. I absorb the smell of her crisp, floral and slightly citrus perfume. It's like the distilled essence of Kala's spirit that we noticed in our dream; only this is better. I must tell her that.

We linger, holding each other tightly without speaking. We often stay like this for ages. Sometimes I wonder if we're having a competition to see who will be first to release. Today it's Kala, although her hands remain firmly around my waist. "What a fantastic dream," she says.

"Yeah," I say. "You were so beautiful in that sunlight."

"Thanks! And you looked good with your shirt off. I could see the muscles in your arms."

I like her looking at my body. I wish I actually had the muscles she imagined.

"How'd I get the muscles?"

"You got them from working in the fields. You've been working hard, tending our crops."

"That sounds good. I'd like work like that. We'd grow our own food and the work would make us strong."

"I'd like it too," says Kala. "We'll both be strong and muscular one day."

She always talks like that. She thinks anything is possible if we dream it. I guess it's kind of true. The problem is that we'd need dream consensus for us to have big muscles. Kala and I would be the only ones to dream of that!

"Let's lie in the sun," I say.

We often lie side by side on the mound when it's sunny.

"What should we dream of tonight?" asks Kala.

"Let's dream that we're having a picnic together. We can sit on a rug and be completely surrounded by a thick green rainforest."

"What's a rainforest?"

"Grandpata said they were places full of trees, vines and decaying leaf litter. In some places the growth was so thick that the canopy of the trees blocked out most of the sun, making it hard to see. He said the rainforest was full of all kinds of animals. Some of them were small and timid. Others were large and aggressive."

"That sounds wonderful."

"It sounded a little scary to me," I say, remembering the feeling I had when Grandpata told me about it. "Maybe we should make it somewhere with more light and just the nice animals."

"It's only a dream, though," notes Kala, facing me and caressing my hand. "Let's dream of that rainforest and all those animals tonight."

"Okay, then," I say and I'm about to kiss Kala's hand, but I stop short of it after remembering what my mother said about my dreaming.

"What's wrong?" asks Kala.

"It's Beth. She hassled me again this morning."

"Again!"

"Don't your parents worry about you?"

"No, they're not worried. I'm lucky they don't work on that side of the dream business."

She's referring to the Dream Council policy work. She is lucky. Kala's parents are some of the few adults I know who don't work on dream policy. Their job is to maintain the broadcast network.

Kala told me that they have all sorts of electronic equipment at home. The item that interests me most is an electronic book with tales from the old times. The only things

I hear about from back then are from my grandparents. Grandpata tells me his stories again and again. He talks about the long hours he spent fixing old cars, the wonderful food that Grandmata cooked, and all the singing and dancing they did.

Kala can talk about anything with her parents. She's lucky to have that. "I like your parents," I say.

"They like you too," says Kala, squeezing my hand.

I like it when she says that. It makes me feel that anything is possible. For a while, I feel warm, lying there beside Kala in the sun. But then a cloud passes above and I remember the reality of our situation. My parents don't like Kala and we both have reputations for being undisciplined. There's no way that we'll be allowed to be together as adults.

***

I remember the day, two years ago, that I met Kala. I'd had a bad day at school. Rexus had been lecturing me about something. I don't remember exactly what it was. Maybe it was my messy handwriting. He often goes on about that, as if someone's life could depend upon it. And it's not just me and my writing either—he hassles everyone in my class. It's like he has a roster to ensure he covers the entire class. Even Titus gets it on his day.

It had been one of those days when it was my turn for Rexus' attention. After school, I felt like time on my own. I went for a walk and wandered, paying little attention to where I was going. Somehow, I ended up down at Fox Creek. I stood by the creek, watching the glistening sun on the flowing water, noting the variations in the trickling sounds that come from what appears to be such small changes in the water movement. I stood there, mesmerised.

I thought I'd be there alone and there was a good reason for that. Two months earlier there had been a storm upstream that caused a flash flood at Fox Creek. Two children were swept away and, tragically, they died. I remembered Beth saying how outrageous it was to have children dying from accidents in a community that could make dreams come true. After that incident, the Dream Council made a rule that children were not allowed to go to Fox Creek, even if it hadn't been raining.

So, there I was at Fox Creek, a place I wasn't supposed to be. I stood watching the water until my vision changed, the water became clear and I saw small, dark things near the bottom of the creek. When one of the larger ones moved, I realised it was a fish.

As I moved closer, the fish moved away. I followed it upstream to a wide pool with a large protruding rock at the centre. I lost sight of it there. When I looked up, I noticed something odd on the sand beside the creek. As I walked closer, the thing on the sand took shape. It was a person!

"Oh no!" I said aloud, distraught at the thought that it might be another drowned child.

I walked towards it, but about halfway there, I thought it would be best if I left immediately and told no one what I'd seen. That way no one would know about my visit to the creek. After all, there was nothing that I could do for whoever it was.

But I didn't leave. I couldn't leave that body there. It was a person. It was someone's son or daughter. They deserved to be found, despite what trouble it might cause me. Nearing the body, I guessed, based on the length of the hair, that it was probably a girl. And from her size, she could be around my age. I could even know her! She was lying face down with her arm over her face. In a way, she looked at peace.

"Who is it?" said a voice.

I jumped.

"Oh," I said.

"Who is that?" she said, raising her head ever so slightly to look at me.

She was alive!

"I'm Tomas," I said.

"I'm Kala."

"I thought you were dead."

"You were wrong."

"You're not supposed to be here, you know," I said.

"Neither are you," she replied and we shared a smile.

For a while I just stood there awkwardly, gawking at what I had thought was a corpse.

"You're standing in my sun," she said. "Why don't you sit down?"

I looked at her again, noting how comfortable she was lying there, barely looking at me.

"Are you going to sit?"

I sat down and we started to talk. I asked her why she was at Fox Creek. She said that she found it peaceful.

"What about you?" she asked.

I told her about Rexus lecturing me. She told me about her teacher and her school. I told her about my parents and she told me about hers. We talked and we talked.

Kala was different to anyone I'd met before. Like me, she wanted to have her own dreams. That surprised me, but the thing that amazed me most was her confidence. She said that everything would turn out, not only for her, but also for me.

"You'll find a way," she said.

I'd never met anyone with such faith before.

That was about when the patrol officer found us. He told us that we had to go with him and he was going to take each of us to our parents and tell them that we'd been at Fox Creek. For once, I didn't care.

Kala and I sat together in the patrol car, looking silently towards each other. I remember thinking how pretty and different she was. She was her own person and she was able to do as she pleased, with the support of her parents.

The officer chose to take me home first. Arriving there, I said goodbye to Kala and we gave each other the gentle touch of foreheads that's used between good friends.

My parents weren't happy about me being caught at Fox Creek, but accepted my story about wandering there. Beth seemed more concerned about the girl I had met and why she was at the creek. I suppose she was right to worry. I already felt close to Kala and for some reason I knew my life would change from knowing her. I will always remember that day.

The next day I couldn't wait to get out of school. And of course, I went straight back to the creek. We hadn't discussed meeting there, but there was Kala, already waiting for me. "What kept you?" she said.

It was the same patrol officer that caught us there at the creek the second time. He told my parents that I was undisciplined and said he would be making notes on a file. My parents were furious and banned me from seeing Kala.

The following day we met near the creek again, but not wanting to risk a third incident, we walked away from it. We walked and we talked and we ended up at this park.

Now, even though we've stopped going to Fox Creek, no matter what we do, we're seen as rule breakers and my parents won't allow us to be together. We could ask for community approval, but there's no way we'd get consensus to overrule my parents, given what has happened and the notes on the Dream Patrol file.

***

Kala is lying still and close, beside me. Sometimes I'm glad that she can't read my thoughts. I don't want her to know of my doubts. I wish I could be strong and believe, the way she does, that everything will work out for us. She is certain that we can find a way. She has that sort of faith with all things and she doesn't mind that people consider her different. That's part of what I love about her.

I try to move my thoughts to another topic. I even use my dream training. The trick is to focus on the details as if it is a real vision. It's difficult, but my will succeeds and the unwanted doubts subside.

"Let's dream that the rainforest is here," I say. "Our mound here is covered in a soft leaf litter. And there's a huge tree just there. It's a hundred metres tall! And there's another tree there and another just there. And they're all covered in vines with those red and yellow flowers. And there's a parrot clinging onto that vine."

"It's that pair of rainbow parrots we saw last night and they're singing," adds Kala. "I'll meet you there. Don't you be late."

Kala is smiling warmly. I know she likes my descriptions. I seem to have a knack for making up imaginary places. Most of them are based on my grandparents' stories.

With our dream plan in place, we move on to talk about other things. I tell Kala more about my day and what happened in my dream lesson.

"That Titus is a real dream job," says Kala.

That's what she calls people who do what they're told and dream what they're asked to dream.

"How was your day?" I ask.

"It was a standard school day from the Dream Council book of standard days," she says. "I sat and talked and nodded and ate and breathed as I was supposed to do. If it wasn't for you, I'd be having the same standard day as every other girl."

"Trust me, you're not the same as any other girl," I tell her, lifting her hand and admiring it.

I can't help but move on to appreciate the rest of her. In some ways Kala is almost plain. She could be just another healthy looking blondish-brown haired girl. But she is different. She has a cheeky spark and she's confident in her faith that all things are possible.

There's not another girl like her and when my body is close to her, it awakens parts of me that hadn't been stirred before. I can't stop that. Sometimes it embarrasses me. Kala says she doesn't mind. She says it's natural and that she trusts me.

***

The time for us to leave each other is always the best and worst part of our meetings. We hold each other tightly and silently. I feel the honesty and faith of her hold on me. I return it with commitment and desire. I hide my doubt. "It feels as if we are one person," I tell her.

"I know," she says.

As we part, I use the words that my parents said to me when I was younger. "Sweet dreams, my love."

"Sweet dreams, my love," says Kala.

3. Dream work

Our house is one of the older dream houses. It has five bedrooms and two bathrooms. We call one of the spare bedrooms our guest room even though it's only been used a couple of times by my grandparents. My parents use another of the rooms for their work and the other one is used as a store room for old furniture and other things that we rarely use.

The latest dream houses have only two bedrooms. It's been that way since the Dream Council decided that families should only have one child. It's a shame about that rule—I would have liked a brother or sister.

I'm nearing our front door and can hear talking. I skip up the three steps to the house, taking care to slow up at the door to open it quietly. Inside, I can hear my parents' conversation.

"A hand is too much," says Davis. "I'm going to dream for a finger."

"But she stole a printing press. If she got away with it, who knows what might have happened," says Beth.

"She might have printed something?"

"Very funny," says Beth. "They could have printed anything they liked. We know she's from a subversive group."

They must be discussing a criminal case. I enter the kitchen, quietly stopping just inside the door.

Seeing me, they stop talking.

"Tomas," says Davis. "How was your day?"

21

I hesitate. I don't want to tell them about my dream lesson and I dare not mention Kala. Not much else happened today.

"What's a subversive group?" I ask.

"You weren't meant to hear that," says Beth.

"Who's the woman you were talking about?"

"That discussion was between your father and me."

"Sorry," I say and I turn to leave for my room.

"He's going to be sixteen soon," says Davis. "It's probably the right time to include him in these discussions. Besides, he's going to hear about it in the broadcast."

Davis often supports me. He likes openness as well as honesty. And he's right—I will hear about it in the broadcast. I've been listening to the broadcasts for the last three months as part of the preparation for my passage.

Beth looks at me, then nods her head. "Okay then. It won't be long before you'll be dreaming on these issues."

Deep down, she shares the same ideas about openness and honesty. I think it's one of the things that brought my parents together.

"We could start with Origins," says Davis.

"Origins?" I query.

"Origins is a group from the South," concedes Beth. "They're a small number of farmers who want to challenge the Dream Council. The woman who stole the printing press is from that group. They would have used the press to print information in opposition to the Dream Council."

"What do they want?"

"Some people say they want more land for themselves," says Beth.

"Others say that they want us to stop our dream work," says Davis.

"Why?" I ask.

"They think we've become slaves to the Dream Council," says Davis. "They want us to return to the life of the old times."

"They're crazy," adds Beth.

I stay focused on Davis who is looking back at me. I want to know more about this Origins group but I know that Beth doesn't want me to. I'll ask Davis more about it when we're by ourselves.

***

I have my opportunity when Beth goes to her room.

"The woman who stole the press. Will she really lose her hand?"

"We don't know yet," replies Davis. "We've got to hear the case first. Then we'll decide if she's innocent or guilty."

"It sounded to me as if you'd made up your mind."

"Well, from what I've heard so far, it sounds like she's guilty. I'd prefer that she just lost a finger but the Dream Council wants us to be tough with this group. They'll probably get consensus on the hand."

"That's so extreme."

"They want us to set an example with this woman."

"Why?"

"The Dream Council is worried that the Origins group has been more active in the last few months."

"Should we be worried?"

"No. There's only a hundred people in the South and they're a long way from here."

"Does the Dream Council know who they are?"

"I think so. From what I know it's just about everyone in the South."

"Why don't they arrest them?"

"They've committed no crime. They've just chosen not to be part of the dream system. Besides, we can't exactly round them up and keep them all in prison."

At school we were told of a southern region that hadn't been developed. Rexus said it was full of derelict farms. I just assumed it hadn't been developed because there was more urgent dream work to do. Sounds like there's a lot more to it than that.

In my head, I imagine a group of people meeting in an old farmhouse. I see a woman there, who, although missing a hand, continues to argue for action against our city, Norden.

"Have you ever been to the South?" I ask.

"No, I've had no reason to go there."

"What about curiosity?" I ask, but just as I've said it Beth enters the room, glares at Davis, then makes a show of pressing the orange button on her wristband which activates the small orange light at the centre of our communication quadrant. The quadrant itself is just a silver coloured thin metal frame. It's in our living room and that's where the three of us go for the broadcast.

Davis stares at me before pressing the orange button on his band. I nod and press my wristband button too. We then move to the couch beside the quadrant and sit in anticipation of the light pulsing at six p.m.

The broadcast begins with a welcome from the Dream Council leader, Krakus. He's been in charge ever since Zennuta's passing.

In the beginning, Krakus was Zennuta's deputy. People sometimes talk about the pictures of the two of them together. Zennuta's free spirit was easily recognisable from his long, wiry, grey hair and beard. Krakus, on the other hand, is completely bald. They say that Zennuta had the ideas and Krakus had the discipline and organisation to make things happen.

Krakus' image is projected onto our wall. He appears comfortable and confident in front of the camera. He speaks quietly and calmly. We listen to his welcome and his summary of the program for the broadcast. There are standing items such as food, housing, education and justice, then a special topic for the day, and after that there is a summary of the dream plan for the night.

Krakus returns for the very last part of each broadcast. That's his time to emphasise the things he wants us to remember. At the end of his speech, he gives us his final message. We all listen attentively. People say that he's never ever said the same thing twice. Yesterday, his advice was to

'Dream well, but not for yourself. Dream well, for your children.' It's always something simple like that.

His final words are always, 'Dream well, good people.' Our reply is, 'Dream well, good leader.'

Despite his wholesome advice, there's something odd-looking about Krakus and I don't trust him. It's not his baldness. It's his eyes that get to me. They're white and glazed as if they've turned around in their sockets. I sometimes wonder if he was born that way or if he got it from some kind of sickness. Kala and I sometimes joke around, turning our eyes inward, pretending to be Krakus. We give each other advice, 'dream me some new hair' or something like that.

One of the first times I watched the broadcast I made a comment about not trusting Krakus. Davis asked why and I answered honestly, that it was because of his creepy eyes. Davis said he respected my right to express my opinion but didn't agree with judging people by how they looked.

Beth wasn't so gracious. She said she was ashamed of my prejudice. I sometimes think about that, and now, when I see Krakus on the broadcast, I'm torn between trying to give him a chance and my gut feeling that tells me that I shouldn't trust him.

The broadcast continues with the standing topics. So far they've covered food and housing. We take notice when they get to education. Beth moves to the seat at the centre of our quadrant and gazes patiently towards the camera/projector that's wired at eye level between two of the quadrant poles.

She's one of the two presenters arguing the case for a new school.

Our quadrant light turns green, indicating that our camera is activated and it's Beth's turn to speak. Her image is projected brightly against the white wall beside our communication quadrant. Everyone in Norden will be seeing her on their broadcast screens, now talking about the number of children who would attend the new school.

I sometimes think about how astoundingly clever Zennuta was to come up with the broadcast technology that supports the dream system. Co-ordinating the dream work would have been very difficult without it.

It's an odd feeling knowing that Kala's parents are part of the team that maintains the network. Kala told me that they're often rostered on to support the broadcast and fix any technical problems. I wonder if they're working tonight.

Another person, a man called Giro, speaks against the school. He works for a section of the Dream Council on transport planning. Giro is concerned about the location. He argues that the site is in the way of a new road they have planned to the South.

I feel sorry for Beth when she has to argue against another section of the Dream Council. It sounds like she's going to have to come up with a different location for this school to get the support she needs.

The next topic is justice. There are two cases for community trial today. The first is the case of a man called Cello. He was charged with consorting and fighting.

The prosecutor, a man called Hector, says that Cello was caught in bed with a woman called Jilla without the agreement of her parents or community consensus, and that Cello fought with Jilla's father. Cello's defence is that he was seeing the woman he loves and that Jilla's father started the fight and he only defended himself. The prosecutor says that the father had every right to be forceful, given the situation, and that Cello should not have fought back.

Cello says that Jilla's mother had given the couple consent. The prosecutor says that Cello and Jilla needed consent from both parents and recommends a punishment of one year of exile on the Island of Contemplation. Cello says that a year is too long. He suggests one month, if people thought him guilty of a crime. That's the end of the case. It's now up to the community to dream for the justice they want.

Beth is looking at me and I know why. She's worried that I'm going to end up like Cello. For a moment I imagine myself on trial for being with Kala. My stomach churns. Quickly, I adjust my thoughts, searching for a vision of something good. I imagine myself lying peacefully beside Kala on the mound in our park.

The next case is introduced. It's the case of the woman who stole the printing press. Her name is Dana. The prosecutor says that the press went missing from the Dream Council office and that Dana was a visitor to the office on the day it disappeared.

The Dream Patrol found the press at the house where Dana was staying and the press had Dana's fingerprints all over it. They also found printed leaflets that criticised Zennuta and the Dream Council.

Dana is defiant. She says the whole thing is a set up. She says that she was asked to go to the Dream Council office to talk about the South. She had a meeting with Krakus and then the next day she found the printing press outside the house where she was staying. She brought the press inside and was wondering what to do. A few minutes later some patrol officers arrived and arrested her. She says that she's never seen the leaflets before.

The prosecutor asks her if she is a member of Origins. Dana looks straight back at him and says, "Yes."

Beth raises her eyebrows. Davis shakes his head.

The prosecutor asks Dana about the fingerprints that the Dream Patrol found on one of the leaflets. She says she can't explain them and says again, that she was set up. The prosecutor says that she's a member of Origins and she's guilty, and should lose her hand.

Dana is horrified. She says she is innocent of the crime and that is the last we see of her on the broadcast.

There's no special topic today and so that's the end of the broadcast business. There is a brief summary of the dream issues for the day and Krakus gives his recommendations. He recommends a month on the Island of Contemplation for Cello and the loss of a hand for Dana. He says that Origins is becoming more active and it's time to get tough on them. He wants us to punish Dana to show Origins that we won't tolerate their subversion.

The last thing is Krakus' message.

"Dream well, but not for yourself. Dream well for your future," he says.

That's just one word different from yesterday!

He says his farewell, "Dream well, good people."

We all respond, "Dream well, good leader." A few moments later the screen projection stops and the orange light goes off.

Beth and Davis go to their room. I think it's to talk where I can't hear them. It's a shame because I'd like to know what they thought about Cello and Dana.

***

I arrive at our kitchen for dinner at five minutes before seven. That's unusually early for me. Beth and Davis aren't there and so I gather the dinner allocation of the food that appeared in our cupboard this morning and place it on our dinner table. Today we have fish, carrots, green spinach, beetroot, potato salad, lychees and macadamia nuts.

The food selection is based on advice from the Dream Council's health experts. They only vary one or two foods each week—it's easier to remember in dream work when there are fewer changes. The two changes from last week are a fruit item, which went from apples to lychees, and the protein item, which changed from crumbed chicken to a boneless fish.

A Dream Passage

Beth and Davis join me just after seven p.m. Beth is quiet. Almost certainly it's because of what happened with the school.

"Will Dana lose her hand?" I ask Davis, quietly.

"Probably," says Davis, looking down. Beth says nothing. It's clear that they don't want to talk. I eat the rest of my fish silently. Sometimes it's like this.

"Lychees!" I say, breaking the silence and loading them into my bowl. I get a smile from each of them but it is not enough to make them talk.

As I eat my lychees I think about what it would be like to lose a hand. I imagine the pain and the shock of waking up and finding it truly gone. And I wonder how it would happen. Would I wake up during the amputation? And would it hurt? Surely it would. It seems like such an extreme punishment for stealing a printing press.

4. The usual dreams

I feel a tickle on my foot. Or did I dream it?

Itch! There it is again! It's annoying. I'm not ready to wake up. "Stop that!" I say. It has to be Davis.

"Good morning, Tomas," he says, grinning warmly.

"Morning," I say, drowsily. I'm glad it's Davis. He won't ask about my dreams.

"Come and have breakfast," he says brightly. "Your mother wants to talk to you."

Gloom enters my head. I had my sixteenth birthday last week. My passage ceremony is booked and only one week away. She must want to talk about something to do with that.

I need a few minutes to recall my dream. If I don't embed it into my consciousness now, I'll lose all memory of it and then I won't be able to discuss it with Kala. "Can I have five minutes?"

Davis nods and leaves my room. He's good like that. I focus on recalling my dream. Kala and I have been enjoying our rainforest dreams. I remember a tree canopy, hanging vines and a fruit that Kala picked and fed to me. It was small, round and yellow; a bit like a lychee but lemon in flavour. Delicious!

And that smell was there again. The scent of the flowers on the fruit trees which matched Kala's perfume. It was as if the entire forest, the flowers and the fruit, were a fragrant and delicious extension of Kala. That's what I told Kala as we lay side by side on the forest floor.

A Dream Passage

We watched the birds that chattered and jumped, and we saw that winking and chirping pair of rainbow parrots again. This time they seemed to be watching us just as much as we were watching them.

"Tomas!" I hear. "Tomas!"

It's Davis again. "Time for breakfast," he says.

My images of Kala and the rainforest disappear.

I shower and dress in my school clothes, then meet my parents in the kitchen. Beth has finished eating and is sipping tea. That's unusual for her. She usually eats and goes. She has papers in her hand. Davis is next to her, also drinking tea.

"We have the instructions for your passage," says Davis.

"Oh," I say. What I'm actually thinking is "Oh, no!" My passage will mean the end of school. I'll be allocated some kind of dream job and I'll have to dream responsibly. Worst of all, my parents will start to suggest 'dream job' girlfriends for me. They won't be Kala.

"Your passage booking has been confirmed," says Beth, clearly excited by the news.

"How do you feel?" asks Davis.

"I'm nervous," I say. It's the only thing I can think of that's true and doesn't refer to Kala.

"Don't worry, you'll be fine," says Beth. "Here are your instructions."

She hands me some of the papers. I can tell that they want to go over the details but it's the last thing I want to do right now. My heart is throbbing. I've got to get away.

"Thanks," I say, getting up from my seat. "Let's go over it later. I've got to get to school early today. I have a test."

I take a banana and withdraw to my room. I can see their disappointment but they don't protest. I managed to defer the discussion but it won't be for long. They'll be waiting for me at dinner tonight.

***

School today was a chore. I did have a test—a maths test. It's a subject that I usually do well in but today I didn't care. What's the point in trying when my life is already mapped out?

At the park I hold onto Kala longer than ever before.

"What's wrong?" asks Kala.

"My parents got the passage instructions this morning."

"Mine too," says Kala, unconcerned.

"Why aren't you worried? It's only one week from now!"

"I know. But it's not all bad. We'll finally be treated as adults. We'll be able to make our own choices."

"Our own choices? All I can imagine is a job that I don't want, dreaming other people's dreams, and seeing less of you. I don't see many choices in that."

"Don't worry," she says, taking my hand. "We'll be okay."

I can see the belief in her eyes. I even feel a small transfer of assurance from her to me. If only my doubts weren't so strong.

"Let's talk about our dreams," says Kala.

"Okay," I say. "There was something about the rainforest that was unusual," I say. "Do you remember the lemon taste of the fruit you gave me and the slightly citrus smell of the flowers? It was the same as your perfume. It's like it's all part of you."

"Yeah," says Kala. "That was amazing! And do you remember that pair of rainbow parrots perched in the tree?"

"Yes, and the way they winked and chirped, and looked straight back at us?"

"Yes, that's it!" says Kala. "They really were looking at us. It was as if they were you and me."

"What do you think they were saying to each other?" I ask.

"They were telling each other how good it was to be free."

I smile at Kala, wishing I remembered more of our dream. "Let's dream of the rainforest one more time tonight," I say. "I'd like to know more about those parrots."

"Me too."

We spend the rest of our time trying to think of other animals we might find in the rainforest. I remember my grandfather talking about an animal that hung upside down from the trees. He called it a bat. He said that it ate the fruit from the trees. Kala talks about a bear-like animal that once lived in the forest canopy and ate leaves. She calls it a sloth and says that they moved very slowly and slept most of the day.

All too soon it's time to part. We hold each other, say our farewells and I'm alone again, stuck with my doubts.

I won't be able to avoid the passage discussion at dinner time. I decide that I might as well give into it. I guess I owe that to my parents. They mean well and they're good to me. I'll be as enthusiastic as I can.

***

The passage discussion goes well but afterwards I question my actions. I didn't lie about anything, but should I have been more honest with them? Should I have told them about my dreams and how I'd like to do something other than dream work? Should I have told them how strongly I feel for Kala?

If I really had a choice I would defer my passage for another year. There have been a few cases of young people doing that but I guess they were sick or injured, or had some other 'good' reason. I don't have any injury or excuse. All I have is doubt.

I consider it again and again throughout the week, but I come to the same answer every time. I just can't see the point in telling my parents how I feel unless it can somehow change what I'm going to have to do.

5. The passage

I feel a hand on my shoulder. Who is that?

"Good morning, Tomas," says Beth, enthusiastically.

"Good morning," I mumble, feeling tired. I didn't sleep well. I remember being awake for hours. I don't recall dreaming.

Oh, no! It's Passage Day! No wonder my mother is smiling. My gut starts to churn.

Beth has already laid out the ceremonial outfit at the end of my bed: pants and a hooded shirt. They're all baggy because they're designed to fit a person of almost any size or shape. The celestial blue shirt is decorated with tiny diamonds, patterned to represent star constellations.

We're supposed to dream with the wisdom of stars—knowledge spaning eons or something like that. That seems a bit far-fetched. I'm only sixteen. How much wisdom can I possibly be expected to have? I suppose it's more of an aspiration. It's one of the many symbolic aspects of the passage ceremony.

"It's the outfit that your father wore," notes Beth.

"Really?" I say in a way that doesn't require an answer. I really can't imagine Davis wearing these clothes. He's not into symbolism.

I step into the pants and double tie the drawstring. The shirt slides on easily and sits very loosely on me. Surely, these ill-fitting clothes are a sign that I shouldn't take the passage!

I could say, 'Sorry, I couldn't go ahead. The poorly fitting shirt was a bad omen.' If only Beth would go along with that.

Then I notice the belt that goes with the shirt has fallen to the floor. I slowly collect it and tie it around my waist, gathering in the surplus shirt material. I barely recognise my reflection in my bedroom mirror. I look like I'm wearing oversized pyjamas. And I'll be wearing this *all* day!

I join my parents for breakfast and we sit together quietly for a while. It's as if Beth and Davis are waiting for my permission to show their pleasure.

"Your ceremony was different, wasn't it?" I ask solemnly.

"We didn't get to travel along the river," notes Beth.

"And we were older and married," adds Davis. "We did our passage together."

"That would have been nice."

I would have liked to have shared my passage with Kala. Sadly, though, she'll be travelling on a different creek today. We'll both end up on the same river and we'll both arrive at the Passage Hall, but we won't be together.

I see the parental instructions laid out on the table in front of Davis. "Do you know where to go?"

"Yes," replies Davis. "Your entry point is at Fox Creek. It's about a twenty-minute walk. We'll need to leave at around quarter past three."

It's ironic that the starting point for my passage is the place where I first met Kala and yet this trip is going to take me away from her.

"Have you read your instructions?" asks Beth.

She knows I have. "I'll go over the lines again this morning," I say. That's what she wants to hear.

I ask a few more questions about their passage ceremony. Beth likes talking about it. Their ceremony was the first one ever. Although I've heard much of it before, I welcome the distraction and listen attentively. It occurs to me that today will be more their day than mine. After breakfast I return to my room to go over the instructions and my lines. I read, again, how the ceremony is symbolic of people joining together to dream for all.

I've been designated as a 'canoe joiner'. My parents are to have me at Fox Creek by four p.m. There I will board a canoe with another sixteen-year-old boy, a 'canoe starter' who will have begun paddling further upstream.

My parents will send me off with their blessing. The canoe starter and I will paddle two kilometres downstream to where Fox Creek meets the Zennuta River. As we travel, we'll be joined by other sixteen-year-olds, starters and joiners, all paddling together in their canoes.

From the river junction, we'll canoe a further three kilometres down river to the Passage Hall jetty. We've been instructed to enter the Passage Hall quietly and to go directly to our allocated positions on one of the three coloured lines that encircle the central stage. Mine is position seventeen on the orange line.

The ceremony will begin with us chanting and singing the dream songs we learned at school. As we sing and chant we'll be joined by an outer group consisting of our parents, Dream Council leaders and community elders.

One of the parents, a council leader and an elder will be chosen to offer us encouragement and advice. One of our group will be asked to respond.

The speakers are selected randomly. That means that every person at the ceremony must be prepared to speak. It's considered a great honour to be a speaker. I've prepared something I can say if I am chosen: "Thank you all for your good advice. We will strive to dream with the experience of our leaders, the kindness of our parents, and with the wisdom of our dream father, Zennuta."

I think the last bit about Zennuta is the kind of thing they'll want to hear. I can even imagine a cheer.

But what if I'm chosen and I fumble in the emotion of it all? I could easily say the wrong thing or speak without conviction in my voice. And what if I saw Kala from where I stood to speak and I stood frozen, staring at her? The honour of being selected could easily become humiliating for me and an enduring embarrassment to my parents.

After the advice and our response comes the main point of the ceremony. We'll all, jointly and harmoniously, pledge our commitment to dream well, to follow the instructions of the Dream Council, and to abide by the Dream Rules. These are the lines I've been learning.

After our pledge we will officially become part of the dream community. The outer group will cheer and congratulate us. Beth and Davis will be so very pleased. It will mean they have successfully seen me through to adulthood.

The parents and elders will return to their homes to dream for us. We will stay at the hall and sing our dream songs again. At just before six p.m. they'll turn on the communication grid and we'll be part of a special broadcast, dedicated to our passage. Part of the dream plan for tonight will be for everyone to dream that our group of new adults assembled in the Passage Hall has the strength and wisdom to dream well. If we have consensus, I guess it will become so.

After the broadcast our group will eat together and then we have something called 'bonding' scheduled. I'm not sure what that is, but it continues until the curfew time of ten p.m. when we'll move to the rows of mats arranged at the edge of the Passage Hall, where we'll sleep and dream together.

***

I've spent most of the day alone in my room. Time is passing slowly. At times I've been visualising myself already on the river, sitting motionless in the canoe as the canoe starter paddles me inevitably towards the Passage Hall.

***

Just after three p.m., Davis comes to my room.

"Are you ready?" he asks.

I think of some of the things I'd like to say, but it's no use. I'll be taking the passage. "Yes, I'm ready."

Beth comes to my door.

"He's ready," says Davis.

"Let's go, then," says Beth.

***

Passage Day is a public holiday. As we walk along our road we see many people out the front of their houses. "Dream well," they say, as is the custom. I know many of them. Thankfully, I don't have to respond. I'm only obliged to nod graciously.

We turn a corner and walk for a further ten minutes along the road. We're now midway along a grassy path that leads directly to Fox Creek. I notice patches of delicate snowdrops scattered along the mown edge. Kala would like them.

I see Davis tread on a few of the flowers. Was that an accident? The snowdrops represent the stars and the stars represent the eons of wisdom we should try to use in our dream work. The flowers are symbols of the symbols. Davis probably didn't walk on them intentionally, but I fully approve of his carelessness.

Now we're at the creek. I recognise the stream and the sound, although it feels so different this time. I don't see any canoes yet—we must be early.

"Look at the lilies," says Beth, pointing to three pairs of white flowers floating on the surface.

"More stars," notes Davis, unimpressed.

The trickling of the creek and looking out for more flowers is nicely capturing my attention. I'm even starting to forget why I'm here.

A Dream Passage

"Tomas," says Davis. "We have a gift for you."

I'm surprised by this. It isn't customary to give gifts. He has something in his hands. He lowers my hood, then moves his hands slowly from the front of my neck to the back. I feel the weight of the thing he's left behind.

"What is it?" I ask, but I soon see that it's my father's own leather necklace and diamond pendant.

"This was your Grandpata's," says Davis. "He gave it to me and I am giving it to you."

I've touched the necklace before. As a child I'd play with the diamond around Davis' neck when he carried me.

"It's heavy," I note.

"The diamond represents strength and toughness. Wearing it will give you strength and courage to make good choices."

That's symbolism, I note, but Davis is being serious with this.

"Thank you," I say. "I'll do my best." I really hope that I can make them proud. I hug each of them in turn.

"Look," says Beth, pointing up the creek.

There is a canoe approaching. The paddler is wearing the same hooded outfit as mine. It could even be someone I know, but I can't tell who it is behind the hood.

"You have my blessing. Sweet dreams, my love," says Beth. She has a tear in her eye.

"You have my blessing. Sweet dreams, my love," repeats Davis with glistening eyes.

After today, I'll technically be an adult. I guess they're sad because it means that I'm no longer their child.

"Thank you," I reply, adding, "Sweet dreams," as I hug them both together. They're good people and I know they want the best for me.

I replace my hood before stepping into the water to meet the canoe in the shallows, stopping its movement with both my hands. I know that there's nothing I can do now. I might as well get on board. Our next stop will be the Passage Hall.

I lift one leg over and lift myself into the front of the canoe. The canoe rocks, but by sitting quickly I restore its balance. And we're away, at first drifting with the creek current, and then powered by the paddling of my hooded companion.

I pick up the paddle that's been left for me and make a couple of easy strokes. I'm in no hurry to move but it seems unfair to my co-traveller that he should do all the work.

As we approach the centre of the creek I'm suddenly distracted. What's that smell? It's only a waft, but one whiff is enough. I know that fragrance!

"Kala!" I gasp, turning around. The canoe wobbles but I don't care. I look into the canoeist's eyes and see her.

"Paddle, Tomas," she says, with a tone more serious than I've ever heard from her before.

I look back to my parents, realising that they will have heard us.

"Tomas, no!" shouts Beth but Kala is paddling hard and we're moving quickly. There's nothing Beth, Davis nor I can do. My thoughts are jumbled and I'm barely paddling.

"Paddle, Tomas," repeats Kala.

I start to paddle, moving my arms faster and faster to match Kala's speed. We're soon travelling quickly and heading towards a bend in the creek.

Beth yells again but the rushing creek water is loud. I can't understand what she's saying. I look back again as we round the bend. Beth and Davis are walking alongside the creek but they're a long way behind our canoe. I can't see the expression on their faces but I can imagine how alarmed they're feeling. I continue paddling and watch them until the trees beside the creek obscure them from my sight.

"What's going on?"

"Just keep paddling," says Kala assertively.

I continue paddling and start to think about how far it is to the river junction. My mind skips beyond the river to the Passage Hall. It suddenly occurs to me that that we won't be welcomed there—not the two of us together like this. It will be seen as dissent. I doubt that we'll even be allowed to take the passage.

"Aren't you worried? Do you really think they'll let us take the passage, side by side?"

Kala doesn't answer. When I turn around, I see a look of disdain on her face. I've never seen that before. She stares intently at me for a few moments but then resumes gazing ahead, paddling even more strongly. Further along, we change direction. I look back and see that Kala is directing us towards the left edge of the creek.

"Where'd you get the necklace?" asks Kala.

"From Davis," I reply, turning to show her the gem.

"Nice diamond."

"Yeah. It was Grandpata's. It's supposed to give me courage."

"You're going to need that."

She's right. I'm still thinking about what's going to happen at the Passage Hall.

"Where are we going?" I ask.

"I don't have time to explain now. Just trust me. You will need that courage."

We're fast approaching the gravel at the creek edge and still travelling at pace. I lurch forward, grabbing hold of the rim on either side of the canoe just before the canoe stops abruptly.

"What's going on?" I ask as I'm regaining my balance.

Kala is already out of the canoe.

"Quick, Tomas. Let's go."

I see two people coming toward us. My chest is throbbing. I'm panting. We'll need to move quickly to avoid them.

"What's going on?" I ask again, as I watch Kala move towards them.

"It's okay," says Kala.

And then I see why. It's Kala's parents, Paros and Neros. They're soon with us and hugging Kala. When they release each other, they both turn to me.

"Hello, Tomas," says Neros.

He greets me with the customary gentle touch of our foreheads. This is normal, but his strong embrace takes me by surprise.

"Hello," I say, squeezing out the words.

Paros greets and hugs me too, but releases me quickly, handing me a bag of clothes.

"We need to go," says Paros.

"Where are we going?" I ask.

"The South," says Kala.

I instinctively look back at the canoe.

"We can be together," says Kala.

"It's up to you," says Neros. "It's a matter of whose dreams you want to dream."

I'm overwhelmed and have no sense of what to do. I see the canoe and I see Kala. My mind clouds with the weight of what is such a difficult choice. I want to be with Kala but up until now it's just been an idea. All of this is happening so quickly.

I know how much I want to be with Kala but I can't stop thinking about my parents. My leaving would devastate them. They've just given me their blessing and Davis gave me his necklace which meant so much to him.

I touch the necklace as if that is going to give me clarity. I feel the hardness and texture of the diamond. It's supposed to give me courage but I don't feel courageous at all. I feel torn and deeply confused. Would it be more courageous to flee with Kala or to go on in the canoe alone?

I again look at Kala. She's the girl of my dreams. She's an amazing person and she's done this for me. Kala is my dream! Again, I feel the diamond. I start to feel a glimmer of courage.

I reach out for Kala. "I'm with you," I say, holding her tightly and I feel her kiss my neck.

"This feels like a dream," I say.

"It is. It's our dream," she says, squeezing me.

"Sorry, you two," says Neros. "We really have to go now."

"You need to get changed," adds Paros.

Kala and I stand closely together, exposing ourselves to each other and the creek. As we're dressing, Paros and Neros carry the canoe to the scrub beyond the edge of the sand.

Another canoe emerges from the creek bend as we're bagging our passage outfits.

"Let's go," says Kala, smiling after gently pecking me on my cheek.

"This way!" says Neros, directing us beyond the sand and onto a track overgrown with shrubs and blocked in places with fallen trees. We walk, moving as quickly as the trail allows. So many questions enter my head but I ignore them, focusing as much as I can on staying on my feet and keeping up with Kala.

After about five minutes we reach a clearing. Paros and Neros slow a little.

"It's along this road," says Neros, pointing to a dirt road on the other side of the clearing. "Not much further."

Just along the road we come to a car; a wheeled car from the old times. It's the oldest car I have ever seen, maybe even fifty years old if I had to guess. Neros opens the back door for us. Kala gets in and I follow, collapsing onto the worn leather seat.

I'm grateful for the rest, although my mind is racing with questions. Where are we going? What are we going to do? What will happen to us? How will we survive? I don't know where to begin.

Neros starts the car, revs the engine and soon has the old car moving roughly along the dirt road. Kala takes my hand just as I'm about to ask one of my questions.

"Are you okay?" she asks.

"Yes," I reply instinctively. I'm trying to believe that I am okay. "I am trying to believe that this is real. It feels like a dream."

"Sorry, you haven't had much choice in all of this. We had to keep it secret. This is the only way we can be together."

"This isn't the passage I thought I would take today," I say whimsically.

"This is our passage to a new world," says Kala.

"In the South?"

"Yes, in the South."

This is truly incredible. Kala and I, in the South. Together. I touch my diamond again. "This is an amazing dream," I say. "And it's real. Don't wake me." I kiss Kala's hand beside her wristband.

"Oh, that reminds me," says Kala. We'll need to get rid of these," she adds, pointing to her band.

I glance at mine as Kala pulls a penknife from her bag, cuts through her band and hands the knife to me. This seems like the very last chance I have to change my mind. I look at Kala, then at my wristband.

"Second thoughts?"

"No," I say. "I just want to slow down for a minute. Cutting the band seems like a big thing."

"It's just a wristband."

Looking again at the band, I realise that she's right. It is just a band. I nod in agreement and cut my band.

Kala passes the bands to Paros who, without hesitation, winds down her window and throws them out of the car window.

The littering shocks me, but that's a minor ripple of a thought compared to the waves of questions flowing through my head.

Paros closes her window and Neros seems to take that as a cue to accelerate the wheeled vehicle to a speed I've never experienced before. The contact between the wheels and the uneven ground jerks the car up and down and from side to side. I brace myself with my hands on the car roof, trying to remain stable.

It's smoother when we reach the paved road. Kala and I take the opportunity to nestle together tightly. Neros, however, uses the same opportunity to drive at a speed way beyond the normal speed of a regular wheel-less car. I wonder why he's going so fast. We're going to look conspicuous in this old, wheeled car, driving faster than the regular, wheel-less cars that hover just above the road.

But there aren't any other cars.

"Oh!" I say aloud, realising that my mind isn't working well. There aren't any other cars because everyone is either at home or walking to the Passage Hall. It's Passage Day!

"How are you doing?" asks Paros, turning around and smiling at the sight of Kala and I holding each other. Paros nudges Neros, who turns briefly and looks satisfied.

"We're okay," says Kala.

"I think I'll feel better once we're out of Norden," I add. "How long will it take?"

"About twenty minutes," replies Paros.

"And a nine hour drive to your new home," adds Neros. "We'll stop for a rest though, and arrive there in the morning."

The car speed and movement is unnerving, but I daren't ask Neros to slow down. I trust him and Paros. After all, they arranged this for us.

**

After about half an hour, we've left Norden behind and Neros slows the car to a more regular pace. I relax a little.

"How did you arrange all this?" I ask.

"We believe in freedom," answers Paros. "There are others who feel the same way."

"Are you talking about the Origins group?" I ask.

"Yes, that's our group," says Paros.

"You're a member of Origins?"

"Yes, we are."

"My parents told me about them. They said they were a subversive group."

"Well, I guess we are, but not in a destructive way. What else did they tell you?"

"They said it was a small group."

"There are over a thousand people in the South," says Paros. "And they are almost all part of Origins."

"That's a tenth of the entire population," I note. "That's not small!"

"You have to remember though that Origins is a loose affiliation," says Paros. "The only rules we have are that you are free to make your own choices and to dream as you like."

"The Dream Council doesn't want people to know the real numbers," adds Neros. "All they worry about is getting consensus for their dream work."

My parents would be surprised to know the actual number of people in the South. My parents! Arrrghhh! They would have gone to the Passage Hall. They'll be looking for me. They must be so worried.

"Could you get a message to my parents?" I ask. "I want them to know that I'm okay."

"Of course," say Paros. "We should be able to get them a message tomorrow."

"That quick?"

"Yes, that quick," says Paros, grinning. "We work in communications, you know."

"Thanks! And thank you for what you're doing for us. You're amazing."

"That's okay, Tomas," replies Paros. "We just hope we're doing the right thing for you." She pauses thoughtfully. "Your new life isn't going to be easy."

"But you've given us a chance to have our own lives," I say.

Kala grips my hand. Paros nods and we're all silent for a while. I can't think of any more questions for now. I settle back with Kala.

"Why don't you get some rest?" suggests Paros.

"Okay," says Kala, cuddling into me.

It isn't long before she's sleeping.

"Paros," I say. "Are you and Neros moving to the South as well?"

I see Paros hesitate.

"No, not yet," answers Paros.

"You're not staying with us?"

"You and Kala will live on a farm with a woman Kala knows. And you'll have support from the Origins group. You'll be okay. Neros and I will stay in Norden until we have someone to take over our work there."

"Do you mean Origins' work?" I say.

"Yes, it's our job to warn the South, should anything big happen."

"What kind of thing?"

"Anything, I suppose."

I start trying think of a situations that might require a warning from Paros and Neros, but I can't seem to think straight.

My thoughts seem to be wandering with the car vibration and bumps, drifting between the angst I have about what I've done to my parents and the excitement I feel about my new life with Kala. Eventually the monotonous movement has dulled my mind and I'm dozing dreamlets of my future with Kala between glimpses of a vast grassy plain.

6. The South

As I wake, I feel movement. We're still in the wheeled car. Looking about, I see that we're now on a dusty dirt road and moving much slower than we did yesterday. Beside the road are greenish-yellow fields—some sort of farming crop, I guess. We must be a long way south now.

Kala is sprawled across my lap, facing me with one arm around me. She's beautiful and warm and so relaxed that I feel her confidence and trust radiating even as she's sleeping.

I can't believe we're here in the South. At age sixteen we're moving to a new place and committing to a life together! My stomach is churning. I think I'm feeling pressure. After all, how can we be sure it will work out for us? Looking at Kala though, I know I want to be with her. I just don't know if I'll be able to do the things we'll need to do to live here.

***

Kala is stirring now. She opens her eyes, looks at me, smiles slightly, and then closes her eyes again. I gently tighten my hold on her.

"Good morning," I whisper.

"Good morning, you two," says Paros from the driver's seat. Neros is asleep.

"Good morning," Kala and I reply simultaneously, giving us a laugh. Kala rises to look out the window. The sun isn't far above the horizon.

"Where are we?" I ask, although after saying it, I realise it's a stupid question—Paros could say any place name and I won't know it.

"We're nearly there," replies Paros.

"Nearly at the farm?" asks Kala.

"You should be able to see it soon," says Paros, also nudging Neros' arm to wake him.

Looking into the distance I see a house. It's wooden, unpainted and small—perhaps only large enough for two people.

As we draw near I see a veranda at the front and three cultivated plots not far from the house. Beyond that is a smaller building and more of the same greenish-yellow crop that's growing beside the road.

"Good morning," says Neros, stretching. He kisses Paros on the cheek, and then looks back to Kala and me.

"Good morning," we reply, again, simultaneously. Paros laughs.

"What did I miss?" asks Neros.

"Nothing. I'm just enjoying having Tomas and Kala with us."

Paros parks the car beside the house. "We have someone for you to meet," she says, opening her car door.

Neros follows. Kala nods to assure me. As we step onto the veranda the front door of the farm house opens and a woman steps out.

I stop there. I know this woman. It's the woman from the broadcast! The one who was sentenced to lose her hand! I even remember her name, Dana.

Paros, Neros, Kala and Dana greet each other, touching foreheads and following with a tight embrace.

"And you must be Tomas," says Dana, leaning her head towards me.

"Good to meet you," I say hesitantly as we touch foreheads.

Moving back, I find myself staring at Dana and her hands.

"I still have them," says Dana, smiling.

"What happened? How did you get away?"

"Paros rescued me," replies Dana, patting Paros on the back. "All it took was Paros and her big hat."

"Big hat?"

"Yes. It seems so funny now," says Paros. "We found out they were holding Dana at the Dream Council offices. That was good news because it's where we have our weekly communications meetings. We got a message to Dana explaining the plan. I went to our next meeting wearing a big, old style hat, and I carried with me a set of clothes identical to what I was wearing.

"Dana met me at the office toilet at the time we said. It was just a matter of giving her my hat and the clothes and she walked out of the toilet, past several patrol officers, and straight out the front door.

"And a few minutes later, I walked out of the toilet and complained that someone had stolen my hat."

"And they believed you?"

"Sure, they believed me. The Dream Council is not used to people escaping. I even got angry with them about losing my hat. I told them off for their lack of security."

"You might have overdone that," notes Neros.

"You should have seen the look on the faces of the patrol officers," says Paros, laughing. "And they apologised so many times."

"What about your punishment?" I ask, again staring at Dana's hands.

"Well, they can't punish me if they don't have me," replies Dana.

"Of course," I say, slightly embarrassed. If I was at school now Rexus would be chastising me for forgetting the most important dream rule. For a dream to come true, you have to be specific about a time and a place. They can't punish Dana if they don't know where she is.

"Let's go inside," says Dana and we follow her in.

The house is bigger than it looks from the outside, but tiny in comparison to a dream house. There are three internal doors leading off the central kitchen and eating area. I guess they are two bedrooms and a bathroom.

"What's that?" I whisper to Kala, pointing at a metal container with a funnel at the top that extends all the way to the ceiling.

"I'm not sure," whispers Kala.

"It's your wood stove," says Dana

A Dream Passage

I've heard Grandpata talk of wood stoves. People used to cook with them in the old times but this is the first time I've seen one.

"Why is it *our* stove?" asks Kala.

"This place is now your place," says Dana, looking directly at me and Kala. "I'm giving it to you."

"What?! Are you serious?" Kala asks.

"Yes," answers Dana.

"What about you? Where will you live?" asks Kala.

"I'll be moving around from farm to farm."

"On Origins' business?"

"Yes. Having you here will free me up for my other work."

"It's yours if you want it," says Neros.

Our own place! I'm stunned.

"Yes, please," says Kala.

"It's yours then," confirms Dana.

"Thank you," I say, though I'm struggling to comprehend Kala and I living here at all, let alone on our own.

Dana stands up and fills a metal container with water and places it on the stove.

"Will we grow our own food?" I ask.

"Yes, you'll have to," says Dana. "There's no dream food here."

"Will you show us how?"

"Yes, of course. I'll stay with you for a few weeks to teach you."

A few weeks!

"How long can you stay?" asks Kala, looking to her parents.

"Not long," replies Neros. "We need to be back before we're missed."

"I'll miss you," says Kala, putting her arms around both Neros and Paros.

"You'll be fine," says Paros. "You and Tomas have each other."

I try to muster a reassuring look while Kala remains as calm and as confident as ever. I feel for my diamond.

***

Dana serves us tea and small round cakes that she's placed in the middle of the table. The little cakes have bits of something in them, possibly sultanas. She hands Paros a plastic container, full of a thick, yellow substance.

"Funny little cakes," notes Kala.

"They're fruit scones, made with flour ground from our wheat, butter from our own milk, and sultanas that I got from a wheat trade," says Dana. "They taste good with butter."

"Is that the butter?" I ask.

"Yes, it's churned from the cream from our cow's milk."

I don't understand the words 'churned' or 'cream' but I decide not to ask.

Paros uses a blunt knife to spread the butter on her scone and then hands the knife to me.

"Whoa!" I say, shocked by the intense, yet differing flavours and textures: the dense, bread-like taste of the scone, the oily butter, and the juicy, sweet little sultanas. Yet it all goes so well together.

"Good?" asks Dana.

"Yes," I reply. "It's not like anything I've had before."

"It's rich farm food. You'll need it to fuel all the physical work you'll be doing."

Dana seems to be watching me.

"When do we start working?" I ask.

Dana smiles at my question. "We'll start tomorrow in the vegetable garden. Today, I'll show you around the farm."

After eating, Kala and I wash the dishes. I feel good, standing with Kala and doing something useful.

"Shall I show you around now?" asks Dana.

We nod and follow her out the door. Outside, it's sunny except for a few white clouds above the very distant hills. The area immediately surrounding the house is covered in short grass. I see the road we drove along and the small building and cultivated plots I noticed earlier. Everywhere else, as far as I can see, is covered in the greenish-yellow, grassy looking crop that appears to flow like creek water in the slight breeze.

Dana walks us towards the small building.

"You're going to like this," says Paros.

"This is the shed," says Dana, opening the door.

Inside and to the left is a group of birds that I assume are chickens and on the right are three cows. The chickens make short repetitive sounds as they walk around, nervously pecking at the ground as they move past us. The cows follow, slowly.

"Three cows and ten chickens," says Dana. "The big one is Brutus, the bull. The middle size one with the udders is Cowsy, the milk cow. The small one is their calf. I call him Bru Junior."

On the left side of the shed are shelves with various sized boxes and on the right side are implements. I recognise a shovel and a rake. The function of the other tools is a mystery to me. At the back are several rows of bags, stacked evenly. Beside the front door are two metal containers, one with water in it and the other with what appears to be decaying vegetable scraps.

Dana empties the scone crumbs onto the grass. The chickens let out an excited, *bock, bock, bockah* as they run to the spot and peck the ground enthusiastically, missing and tossing just as many crumbs as they gather.

Next, Dana shows us the garden plots. "These are your vegetables," she says. "In this one we have potatoes, carrots, peas, lettuce and beans. In that one, we're growing beetroot and corn. And in the one over there, there are cucumbers, tomatoes and pumpkins."

I think I see the lettuce and the tomatoes, though they look different to the dream food that we get from the cupboard at home.

"Is that the corn?" I ask. "And are they beans?"

"Yes," says Dana. "You're right about the corn and beans. The potatoes and carrots are there," she says, pointing. "They grow underground. And the peas are growing along the wire there."

"This is fantastic," says Kala, snapping off a bean and biting into it. "Try it," she says, passing me another one. "It's the crispiest, juiciest bean I've ever tasted."

I munch on it. She's right. It's crisp and sweet and fresh— better than any bean I've tasted before. "I had no idea beans could be this tasty!"

"Two inquisitive beans," whispers Dana to Paros and Neros, though Kala and I easily hear it.

"That's them," says Neros, proudly.

"Now, this way," says Dana.

She takes us over to the edge of the grassy crop that dominates the landscape.

"See the seed at the top of the stem?" says Dana, breaking off a few of the grass tops. "Take it in your hand and rub your other hand over the tip."

Kala and I do as she says and the rubbing releases small, diamond shaped seeds.

"That's our wheat," says Dana. "We grind it into flour using the flour mill on the next farm. With flour we can make bread, scones and pasta, and we trade it for the other things we need."

I try eating the seeds. They're hard and don't have much flavour. If anything, they taste like grass.

"They're still green," says Dana. "They won't be ready to harvest for another eight weeks."

"Can we help with the harvest?" I ask.

"You'll be more than helping," says Dana. "It will be your harvest."

I'm not exactly sure what she means, but I'm guessing it's that Kala and I will be working hard. It's a huge field of wheat.

"Tomas," says Dana. "Can you get a tomato from the plot over there?"

"Sure," I say.

"I'll help," says Kala.

We review each tomato. There are eight, but five of them are small. I pick the largest and hold it up to my nose. I've never actually noticed the smell of a tomato before.

"Smell this," I say to Kala, handing her the tomato.

"Fresh and juicy," says Kala. "This is going to be fabulous." She takes my hand as we start for the house.

"Our new home," I say, admiring the cute little house and veranda.

"I know," she says, taking my hand and then pulling us hard enough to swing us both around. "This is amazing."

Kala's enthusiasm moves through her arms into me. I pull her into me, holding her tightly and kiss her tenderly.

Back at the table, Dana serves us another cup of tea.

"Are you two going to be okay here?" asks Paros.

"Yes, this place is fantastic," says Kala. She takes my hand under the table. I squeeze her hand in agreement.

"And you Tomas?" asks Paros.

"I think we'll be okay," I reply.

"We'll get going once we've finished our tea," announces Neros.

"Okay," says Kala.

I guess that every minute that they are away adds to the risk of their absence being noticed.

"You won't forget about the message for my parents, will you?"

"They'll get it later today," says Neros.

"Thank you."

"I'll give you a sandwich for the road," says Dana. "And how about some vegetables?"

"Thanks," replies Paros. "But there are three of you now. You're going to need your vegetables. We'll just take the sandwich today."

It's not long before we're all standing beside the wheeled car farewelling Paros and Neros. In turn, they give all of us a gentle forehead touch and a warm embrace. I'm both happy and sad and conscious of how big this moment is for all of us. I'm certain that Kala and her parents feel the same.

"Catch you on the radio," says Paros, before closing the car door.

"Okay," says Dana, and Kala nods too.

Neros gives us a wave from the driver's seat and then they're gone. We stand waving until all we can see is their dust. It's then that I see Kala's tears. I put my arms around her, giving her all of the reassurance I can muster.

***

I soon notice the quietness of the farm. The only sound is the regular *bock, bock, bock* from the chickens and the gentle whistle of the breeze touching the top of the wheat.

"What was that about the radio?" I ask.

"We use it for Origins' communications."

"But won't the Dream Council listen?"

"We use coded messages," says Dana. "Paros and Neros set that up. Without them and the radio, I think Origins would still just be a small fragmented group of farmers holding rakes."

"So, we can keep in contact with Paros and Neros?"

"It's not meant for personal messages, but we can tell them you're okay. You can't be too specific about people or places though. We use code names if specifics are necessary."

"You could say the kids love the beans," I say.

"What does that mean?" asks Kala.

"I don't know. I guess it means we like the farm."

Kala and Dana laugh.

"Okay, Tomas. You're in charge of coded messages."

"Okay," I agree, not entirely sure that she's joking.

***

It's now just the three of us and Dana said she'll only be with us for a few weeks. In that time we'll have to learn farming and everything else we'll need to know to support ourselves. I'm feeling anxious at the thought of this. Kala and I weren't the most disciplined dreamers. We'll have to do a better job with this. Our lives will depend on it.

Dana tells us we have some spare time before lunch.

"Come on," says Kala, taking my hand, "Let's check out the house."

We walk into the first room. It's small, tightly packed with a double bed, a cupboard and a desk. The furniture is made of rough cut timber. It looks old and used. On the desk is a metal case with knobs and cables.

"Is that the radio?" I ask, and Kala nods.

This must be Dana's room. It's going to be cosy in here for Dana and Kala.

We move to the other room, which is similar, but with only a bed and a cupboard, made in the same, rough cut style as the other furniture. It's not much to look at, but at least I'll have a place to sleep.

Back in the eating area I take the opportunity to go to the bookshelf that I noticed earlier. The ten or so books are similar to the ones I've seen at my grandparents'.

I start reading the back covers. The first book is a story of a woman called Jane who liberates her clan from slavery. The next is about a man called Alex who creates an empire through war.

"They're stories from the old times," says Dana.

I make a mental note to read them.

"Have a look at the green book with the picture of beetroot on the cover."

I soon find the book she's talking about.

"It's about growing vegetables," I say to Kala, showing her the thick book. "It's a bit like one I saw at my grandparents'."

"That's going to take a while to read," notes Kala.

"I wish we'd learnt about vegetables at school instead of all the dream stuff."

"You'd be a veggie brain!" says Kala.

That's corny, I think, but it lightens my mood. "And you'd be my fruity friend," I add, using a silly voice.

Dana shakes her head. I guess she thinks we're immature but I don't mind. We are only sixteen.

***

Dana has gathered lunch items on the table: a loaf of bread on a board with a knife for cutting, butter, the tomato we picked, cucumber, cheese, and lettuce leaves that she collected and washed.

We watch Dana slice the bread, cut the tomato, cucumber and cheese, and assemble her sandwich. I follow, making mine the same, and I can't wait to bite into it.

Again, the flavour explodes in my mouth. I look to Kala and see that she's also bitten into her sandwich and her eyes are open as wide as I imagine mine to be.

"The veggies are so much better than the ones in Norden," I say.

"That's right," says Dana. "The vegetables they dream of have lost their flavour over the years. No one in Norden has any knowledge of how crisp and juicy a lettuce leaf can be. That knowledge has been lost. People are just dreaming of the physical aspects of the vegetables they want in their cupboards. They've forgotten about the texture, the taste, and even the smell."

"And smell this cheese," adds Dana, passing me the cheese that's uncut. "You don't get that in Norden."

She's right. The smell is strong and slightly pungent. I'm not actually sure I like it but Dana has made her point. The cheese in Norden have no scent and very little flavour.

"Are you saying that we have to keep experiencing real things so that we know what is possible in our dreams?"

"Yes, that is exactly what I am saying," says Dana. "You learn fast Tomas."

"If only my parents knew this," I say.

"Everyone in Norden should know it," adds Kala.

"I agree," says Dana. "We sometimes discuss it at Origins meetings. People are missing a whole lot more than lettuce and tomato. We need a way of letting people know what they're missing."

"Can we go to one of the Origins' meetings?" asks Kala.

"Yes, you can. There's a meeting here next week. I'd like you both to be part of it."

"Good," says Kala.

"I should warn you, though, everyone's going to want to meet you two. You're the youngest people we've ever liberated."

"You've saved others?" I query.

"A few."

I'm trying to remember the name of the man from the broadcast. "There was a man in trouble," I say. "He was tried in the same broadcast as you."

"You mean Cello?" says Kala.

"Oh, Cello," says Dana. "Yes, I talked with his girlfriend Jilla. In fact, that was why I was in Norden. I think the Dream

Council worked out what was going on and set up their Dream Patrol to find me with that printer."

"What did Jilla say?" asks Kala.

"She didn't want us to intervene. She didn't want to move away from her family."

"Was Cello sent to the Island of Contemplation?" I ask.

"Island of Contemplation, my raspberries!" exclaims Dana.

"What do you mean?"

"There is no Island of Contemplation. All they have is a prison. He'll just be thrown in prison for a month. At the end of the month, they'll drug him and tell him he's been on an island."

"No Island? Really?"

"They lie about many things," says Dana. "You can't just dream people from one place to another."

"Why not?" I ask.

"Remember that for a dream to work, it has to be specific. How can people dream of a person going to the Island of Contemplation when no-one knows where it is?"

She's right. It's that basic dream rule again.

"I can't believe they're lying about that," I say.

"People around here know the truth," continues Dana. "And some of them have been to Dream Patrol prisons. Not one of them has been to an island."

***

Kala and I finish washing the dishes.

"What should we do now?" I ask.

"Take a break this afternoon," says Dana. "Have some rest. You can work on the veggie garden tomorrow."

"Sounds good," I say.

I go to the bookshelf and pick out the vegetable book. Kala chooses the story about the woman that saved her clan. I'm about to go to the veranda, but I hesitate. It occurs to me that the Dream Patrol might be looking for us.

"Is it okay to be out in the open? Will they come here to look for us?"

"Don't worry," replies Dana without hesitation. "You're both sixteen. They can't make you go back."

Dana is right. It's one of the Dream Council rules. Once a person is sixteen, they are free to live where they want.

"Do they ever come here?" I ask.

"Just once, so far. About two years ago, they came south looking for a woman called Zara."

"What happened?" I ask.

"Zara and her partner Lego were living on a farm. They hid in the field when they saw the patrol car."

"So, nothing happened then?" queries Kala.

"Once the patrol officers had gone, we asked Zara and Lego what was going on. It turned out that Lego had brought Zara here against her will. We didn't know that.

"The thing was that, once here, Zara thought she might even prefer to stay. We suggested that she go back and think about it there and she agreed to that. We didn't want someone brought here against their will. We told her she was welcome to return whenever she liked."

"And did she return?" asks Kala.

"No, not yet."

"Are you sure they won't be looking for me? After all, Kala did kidnap me," I ask.

"You didn't exactly kick and scream," notes Kala. "They're going to assume that you were in on the whole thing."

In my head, I start to understand how it would have appeared to my parents. They will think I was lying to them and that I never intended to take my passage. If only I had known what was coming. I feel my heart racing. I wonder if there could have been another way which would have been easier for my parents. Did they really have to do it with my parents watching? Looking at Kala, though, some of my angst abates and I realise just how lucky I am.

"I think I'll read on the veranda," I say with an uneven tone.

It's not long before Kala joins me. "Are you okay?" she asks, gently touching my shoulder. My mood melts at her touch, although Beth and Davis remain on my mind. I can only hope that the message from Paros and Neros will include some explanation.

"Yes, I'll be fine," I say softly.

We start to read but I find myself frequently distracted by our new surroundings. I notice Kala looking at me. "Shall we look around?" I ask.

Kala nods as if she's saying 'about time' and pulls me up from my chair. We walk past the vegetable plots and foraging chickens and into the shed.

I walk past the tools and through to the end of the shed to investigate the stacked bags. There must be a hundred. I untie one and, looking in, see that it contains seeds, a bit like the wheat grains that Dana showed us, only dried and yellow.

"It must be the wheat," I say, showing Kala.

"What's that?" asks Kala, pointing to the ground at the end of the shed. Just below a table is a tiny little grey animal with a short snout and a long, narrow tail.

"It's a mouse," I say confidently. "I saw a picture of one in a book at my grandparents' house."

"Can we eat them?" asks Kala.

"I don't know. I can remember the book saying they were some kind of pest, but I don't know why. They look harmless enough to me. Let's ask Dana later."

"I think they're cute," says Kala.

"You're funny," I say. "First you ask if we can eat it and then you say it's cute."

"I'm just being practical. We might have to eat them to survive here."

Kala might be right. I realise just how much we have to learn. We have Dana here now but in a few weeks it will just be the two of us.

"Will you eat the mouse?" asks Kala, taking my hand.

It's like she's asking if I'm committed. "Yeah, I'll eat that yummy little mouse," I reply, nibbling on her hand.

We further explore the shed. There's a tool with a long handle and also a long, curved blade. I pick it up and feel its weight. "This might for cutting the wheat."

"Hey, let's walk to the end of the wheat field," suggests Kala. "I want to know how big it is."

***

"Dinner time," yells Dana from the veranda.

The afternoon went quickly. We walked around the entire wheat field. That took over an hour and a half. When we returned, we read in the sun on the veranda. I remember feeling sleepy. Kala woke me to show me a ball that she found in the shed and we started throwing it between us. At first we threw it gently but it soon became a competition, our throwing and catching getting faster and faster, each of us trying to surprise the other with a super quick pass.

"Crumbed chicken, potatoes and vegetables," says Dana, as Kala and I take our seats.

The food on the table is steaming. "Smells great," I say, salivating.

"Yum," says Kala.

"Eat up," says Dana.

I start with the chicken and again, I'm shocked. What an amazing taste. On the outside the breadcrumbs are crispy, brown, and slightly oily, and inside the chicken is moist and tender.

Next, I try a potato. It's also crispy on the outside but soft and steaming hot in the middle. Dana says it's been baked in the oven. I follow with the carrots, broccoli and beans.

"This is the best food I've ever had," I say.

"I can tell," says Dana.

"Thank you," I add.

"That's okay. It's a simple meal. You can make it for me sometime."

"Sure," I say, but I doubt I could cook something so tasty.

I'm feeling an immense debt to Dana. She's taken me in without knowing me at all. I'm eager to do something in return. I guess though, the only thing I can do is to learn the farm work as quickly as I can. That will free up Dana for her Origins' work.

"What time should we get up tomorrow?" I ask.

"Any time you like," says Dana. "It's now up to you."

"Okay. But, what time do you get up?"

Dana laughs. "I'll get up when I want to."

"What time do you normally like to get up?" joins Kala.

"Okay, you've got me," says Dana. "I normally get up at seven."

After dinner, Kala and I take our books and settle on the couch together. Dana emerges from her room holding a pair of pants. She resumes her seat and I see her picking at the pants with a piece of thread.

"What are you doing?" I ask.

"I'm fixing a hole."

"Oh."

"It's different here in the South. We have to fix things when they get broken."

Things really are different here. In Norden, broken things are fixed or replaced through dream work.

"Oh, I almost forgot," says Dana, going to her room. "I have some things for you."

She returns and hands Kala a bag that contains clothes, a watch each, and toiletries such as soap and a tooth brush. The items are the same types we had in Norden.

I take one of the watches and set the alarm for six-thirty a.m. "Where'd you get these?" I ask.

"Oh, we find them here and there," replies Dana.

I look to Kala. "Are they stolen?" I ask.

Dana smiles. "They're not exactly stolen. They're things that people threw away. That watch you are wearing works perfectly but someone in Norden got a new watch and threw that one out. We just collected the garbage."

"Okay," I say.

Dana goes on, telling us about some of the other things they've collected. The most surprising thing is old houses. Dana says that they've completely pulled down two houses and reassembled them in the South.

"Didn't they stop you?" asked Kala.

"No, they said to help ourselves. There have been a few instances like that, where a few people from Norden and the South have co-operated. It just isn't organised or publicised."

"That's fantastic," I say.

"What else could be done if we co-operated?" asks Kala.

"A lot more," says Dana.

After some more discussion, Dana says goodnight and goes to her room. Kala and I nestle on the couch.

"What a day," I say. "I still don't believe what's happened. Is this real?"

"I know what you mean," says Kala. "It's all real though. As real as you and me on the couch together."

That is real. We hold each other tightly, cuddling and whispering until I look at my 'new' watch and see that it's past ten p.m. I'm torn between staying up with Kala and getting a good sleep so that we're ready to start work tomorrow. I really should be strong here.

"Sweet dreams, my love," I say.

"Sweet dreams, my love," replies Kala.

I take my toothbrush to the bathroom. Kala joins me. We exchange exaggerated smiles as we brush, then Kala sticks her tongue out. That's my Kala. I return the gesture, adding a goofy look.

"Sweet dreams," I say one last time as I go to my room. Kala blows me a kiss.

Lying in bed, I listen to the night sounds of our new home. There's a buzzing noise outside. It seems to cycle up and down in intensity. I'll ask Dana about it tomorrow.

Now I'm hearing water running in the bathroom. I guess that's Kala. The door squeaks.

"Is that you?" I ask, but there's no reply.

The floor boards creak. I feel the bed move and the sheet lift, a slight brush of skin and then I get a wonderful whiff of floral and slightly citrus perfume.

For a few moments, we lie side by side and silent as if we're on our mound in the park.

We're not in our park though. We're here together. I take Kala's hand and squeeze it slightly. She's a little cold. I should warm her. I turn, place my arms around her and draw her towards me until we're nestled close. Kala is only wearing underpants; just as I am. Her skin is soft, her body warming and her smell is so good.

My hands move easily to her hips and her bum. I'm clearly aroused. I think about touching her, perhaps even in places I haven't touched before. Maybe we're ready for that. "Is this okay?" I whisper, placing my hand there.

Kala's reply is to gently kiss me on the neck, then place her hand onto mine, gently pressing it down on her, before relaxing back beside me. I'm smiling inside. She's as confident as ever and she wants me to touch her. This is better than anything I could have dreamed.

7. On the farm

I'm startled by the alarm. It's dark. Where am I? I fumble for the watch and finding it, push buttons until the alarm stops. My mind races through the last two days as if they were a dream. Kala, parents, passage, farm, Dana, work, food.

Kala! I nestle into her. She barely stirred at the alarm. She's sleeping here with me, putting her faith in us. I guess we really are free. Maybe we can sleep in after all. I guess we can if we want to.

She's smart and brave and beautiful. I owe her so much. I want to be the man she thinks I am. I know that she doesn't see it like that. She doesn't want me to owe her or repay her. She wants us both to be free. I want that too.

The thing is that I've done nothing. I don't feel like I've earned this freedom. I've been given a great gift that I must pay for in some way.

Now she's stirring.

"Good morning, my love," I whisper. She takes my arm and holds it into her chest. Birds outside are singing. Kala smiles but her eyes stay closed. I think she heard them. It's a wonderful morning.

***

We sit down for breakfast with Dana. The clock says eight thirty. That's later than I thought. Dana has boiled eggs, toasted bread and butter for us. She even pours our tea. I hope she doesn't mind that Kala and I stayed together.

"How'd you sleep?" she asks.

"Well," says Kala and she puts her hand on my leg.

Kala's smile is as sheepish as I imagine mine is.

"What was the buzzing noise?" I ask.

"Oh, that would be the cicadas," replies Dana. "They're little insects."

"Why do they make so much noise?" I ask.

"I don't know," says Dana. "I guess they're talking to each other."

"What are they saying?" asks Kala.

Dana laughs. "I'm not sure."

I watch Dana cut her egg neatly into two halves with her knife and then gently spoon the steaming egg onto her toast. She adds salt and pepper and then looks at me.

I accept the cue, tapping the egg with my knife. It cracks with the impact but it doesn't break. I push harder and it crushes into a mess of large and small pieces mixed up with the runny yolk.

Kala giggles as I tediously extract the eggshell fragments.

"Your turn," I say.

"Okay," says Kala, then she neatly cuts through the top of her egg and easily spoons the contents onto her toast.

"Where'd you learn that?"

"Dana showed me," says Kala, smugly.

"How long have you known each other?"

"A year or so. Dana stayed with us for a few days last year."

"I've known your parents for a long time," adds Dana. "Ten years I think."

I pile my egg bits thickly on my toast, then add salt and pepper, and eagerly bite into it. The soft egg white contrasts beautifully with the grainy texture of the toast and the richness of the butter, and the pepper buzzes on the top of my tongue.

"This is fantastic," I say. "I can't believe the taste."

"It's just a boiled egg," says Dana. "I'll have to make you something really tasty."

"It gets better than this?" I ask.

"Much better," says Dana, sincerely. "I'll make a spicy chicken dish tonight. See if you like it."

"What is spicy?" I ask.

"Spicy means tasty, I guess. The taste comes from crushed seeds and cut up herbs. The spices are small, but full of flavour."

"Can you teach us this cooking?" asks Kala.

"I'll be happy to show you."

Again, I'm thinking about Dana's generosity. "What are we doing with the vegetable garden?"

"Ah yes, the new vegetable garden," says Dana. "This farm has been supporting me well enough, but now that there will be two of you here, you'll need more food. I was thinking that you could work on making a new vegetable plot today."

"Okay," I say.

"You'll need more chickens too and perhaps another cow. We can see some people about that next week."

"Which vegetables will we plant?"

"I was thinking of root vegetables: potatoes, carrots, onions and garlic," replies Dana. "They're the main vegetables I use."

"Will we use the tools in the shed?"

"Yes, you'll need the shovel and the mattock," says Dana. "I'll show you."

"Thanks," I say, gulping the last of my tea and wondering if I'll be strong enough to properly use the tools.

**

Dana shows us the place for the new vegetable plot and then takes us to get the tools from the shed.

"You'll need to cut the grass and dig into the soil with this mattock. Then, turn over the soil with this shovel, and remove the grass and roots with that rake."

She gives us a short demonstration with the mattock for cutting and digging, and the shovel for moving the soil. Kala takes the shovel and the rake and I grab the mattock. Dana then directs us to a smelly pile of decaying muck beside the shed.

"This is a compost heap. Put the grass and roots you take out here and they'll break down into something we can use on the garden."

I nod, although I don't really understand how the stinking pile will be useful. I make a mental note to look it up in the veggie book later.

"Are you okay to start?"

"Yes, please," says Kala and I nod in agreement.

A Dream Passage

***

The mattock is heavy. It takes almost all my strength to raise it and hang on as it crashes into the turf. My first blows do nothing more than cut the top of the grass. It's clear that I need to do more than lifting and dropping. I change my grip, placing my stronger right hand further down the handle. From the top of the lift, I hang on to the mattock with my left hand and drive it downwards with my right hand.

That's better! The mattock slices through the grass and deep into the earth below. From there, it works as a lever, loosening the soil.

Kala begins shovelling. I can see the strain on her face but she keeps going until the earth I cut has been turned over. I mattock and Kala shovels.

We're soon sweating and panting but we keep going: mattock, mattock; shovel, shovel, repeat.

***

We must have been working for an hour or two. The sun is directly above us. I'm feeling uncomfortably hot and our work rate has slowed. We're now in a work pattern of three heaves and thrusts with the mattock, six shovels to turn over the soil, and then a break to catch our breath. Heave, thrust, hit. Heave, thrust, hit. Heave, thrust, hit. Shovel, shovel, shovel, shovel, shovel, shovel, Rest!

"Lunch time," yells Dana from the veranda.

I'm relieved to hear it. Looking down, I see that my arms are red and sweaty. My hands are numbed except for an odd, tight feeling in my skin. I have small red sores on my palms.

"It feels like my arms have stretched," I say. "Do they look longer?"

"They look good to me," says Kala, smiling as she feels my bicep.

I place my sweaty arm around her, pulling her into me and kissing her. Kala is as wet with sweat as I am. I don't mind, though. She's my Kala and I love the feel of her, even like this.

"Hey, you're all salty!" I note.

"Really," she says, licking my sweaty arm.

"Yuck," I say.

Dana has sandwiches and water waiting for us on the veranda.

"Best water ever," I say, finishing the glass.

"What did you put in it?" asks Kala.

"It's just cold water with lemon," says Dana. "It's the work, you know. Your body needs the water. That's why it tastes so good."

"Makes sense," I note.

"You've done a good job," says Dana. "I think you'll have it done today."

Looking across, the area we've been working on looks a lot different to how it looked up close. We're only a metre or so short of turning over the entire plot. Dana is right. We will get it done this afternoon. My muscles and mind seem to relax a little.

Dana's sandwiches are just bread, butter, cheese, tomato, cucumber, salt and pepper but they taste amazingly good. I think they're even better than the ones we had yesterday. It must be what Dana said about the work making things taste better. Dana knows many things. She knows about the farming, and cooking and, from what she's said, she also knows a lot about Norden.

"Did you grow up here?" I ask.

"No, I lived in Norden."

"How did you come to live here?"

Dana pauses. "My story is a bit like yours," she says, looking at Kala. "I had my own dreams and someone I loved."

"Who?" asks Kala.

"His name was Harrop. He was tall, strong and smart. I loved him and he loved me."

"What happened?" I ask. "Where is he?"

"He's in Norden. It's a long story, but in the end, he decided to stay there. The terrible thing is that they made him become a patrol officer. I'm sure he hates that. It's just not him."

"What happened?" asks Kala.

"It wasn't long after the Dream Council was formed," says Dana. "When my father died, I had to choose between taking the passage and living in Norden or moving south and following my own dreams. Like you, I was only sixteen."

Dana is staring straight ahead.

"I chose to move south," continues Dana. "It was the only way I could be true to myself."

"And Harrop stayed behind?" I ask.

"They made it very hard for him. He had little choice but to stay behind."

Dana leaves her story there. She looks sad. I don't feel right asking any more questions. We sit there quietly in the sun for a while. It seems so unfair that Dana, who has been so good to us, is not with the person she loves.

"I'll take care of these," Dana says, taking our plates.

It's clear that she wants time alone.

"Thanks for lunch," says Kala quietly. I thank Dana too.

***

Back on the mattock, I notice that my muscles have stiffened. My arms are pulsing after each blow. We continue our rhythm: Heave, thrust, hit. Heave, thrust, hit. Heave, thrust, hit. Shovel, shovel, shovel, shovel, shovel, shovel; Rest! Repeat.

***

We're now so close to the end of the digging that I decide to keep going, making an extra effort to deliver the blows needed to dig out the last part of the garden.

"Yay," I say when I'm done, collapsing onto the grass.

"Ahhh!" exclaims Kala after turning the last of the dirt. She stages a dramatic fall to the ground beside me. We rest there for a while: two slabs of sweaty tiredness.

I don't want to move but we're not finished yet. "Time for raking," I say, patting Kala gently on the leg. She nods, although the look on her face says, 'Really?'

Raking is easier. The rake is light and we're using different muscles. Also, there's only one rake, so we take turns while the other collects the grass and roots and throws them on the compost heap. We work the entire plot once and then a second time to ensure we've cleared the soil of debris.

With the final rake, the hard work is done! Kala again dramatises her collapse. I join her, but I exaggerate my fall a bit too much—it hurts when I hit the ground.

We lie there in the sun for a while. Again, it's a bit like we're on the mound in our park. But it's different now. We're lying here, together, exhausted. I'm no longer thinking of our future. I'm almost too tired to think. We're just here, together.

The sun is low in the sky, but still warming. My watch says two fifty-five p.m. The new plot looks good: the dirt is smooth and tidy from our raking. The height of the soil catches my notice. "Have a look at the dirt," I say. "It's still the same height as the grass around it. Isn't that strange? We took out the grass and the roots. I thought there'd be less of it."

"I see what you mean," says Kala, screwing her face up like she's looking at something ugly.

"Yeah!" I say, contorting my face. Kala returns with another face and we exchange increasingly silly looks until I notice Dana leaving the house. We watch her go to the shed, emerging a few minutes later with four small containers.

"Here you go," says Dana, quietly placing the containers on the ground. "Potato eyes in that one, carrot seeds there, garlic cloves there, and onion seeds in that one."

I sense a change in Dana's mood. She seems withdrawn and slightly abrupt. This isn't the Dana I met yesterday. I wonder if it's about Harrop.

We need to know more about planting but we're too slow. Dana has already turned for the house.

"What do you think?" I ask. "How should we plant them?"

"Let's look at the other plots," says Kala, standing.

We observe the plots differently now, measuring the distances between the rows and between each vegetable.

"How deep do you think?"

"I don't know," says Kala. "I think we're going to have to ask her."

"I'll go," I say, already moving towards the house.

I knock before entering and inside I see Dana sitting at the table. She's drinking tea and I see a framed picture on the other side of the table. It's a photo of a boy about my age.

"Is that Harrop?" I ask.

"Yes, that's him. Though he'll be older now of course."

He looks like a regular boy of about my height. He doesn't seem much different to me.

"Do you have a question?" asks Dana.

"We're wondering how deep to plant the seeds?"

"Oh, sorry. It's one centimetre for the carrots and the onions, and ten centimetres for the garlic cloves and potato eyes."

"Thanks."

I pause on the veranda when I see Kala working in our new dirt. She squats and stands, then darts from one place to another, marking out the row spacing with the rake. She's bright and chirpy, just like those parrots from our dream. And she's more than that—she's beautiful and the shape of her hips has me wanting her.

"Hello," I say, smiling, pulling her gently into me.

Kala returns a cheeky smile. It's as if she knows what I've been thinking. I slide my hands down to her hips. Now she'll know exactly what I'm thinking. She places her hands over mine. I'm reassured by that. We stay there, quiet and tight for a while.

"Did she tell you the depth?" whispers Kala, breaking the spell.

"The depth? Yes, one centimetre for the carrots and onion and ten centimetres for the garlic and potatoes."

The lines that Kala engraved are a good depth for the onions and carrots. We distribute the seeds at intervals along each row, planting four rows of carrots and four rows of onions.

I use my finger to sink the holes for the potatoes and garlic. Kala follows with the garlic cloves and potato eyes, and then we both cover over the seeds with soil. It's not long before we have the entire plot planted.

"I guess it just needs sun and water now," I say.

"Let's give them some water," says Kala. "I saw a container in the shed."

We fill it at the water tank. I hope it's okay to use the water for this. It takes us ten fills to water the entire plot, but then we're done. We stand there for a while, proudly viewing our work.

"Our first plot," I say, putting my arms around Kala. I'm tired, but I feel good about the work we've done. "I hope it grows."

"It'll grow," says Kala.

There's her confidence again.

We check in with Dana. She says we've earned a rest. We settle on the veranda and enjoy the remaining sun of the day. I look at my vegetable book for a while but I'm distracted. I keep thinking about our work on the plot. It could be the best work I've ever done. Thinking about it further, I realise that it could be the *only* real work that I've ever done. That thought levels me. Am I going to be any good as a farmer?

"What's up?" asks Kala.

I'm not sure how to answer. I want to be honest, but also, I want to be strong for Kala. I'm not sure how to explain my concern about my own ability. Dana emerges from the house as I'm forming words.

"Try this," says Dana, showing us a small plate with three thin strips of red matter on it that I guess to be some kind of vegetable.

Kala and I take a piece each.

"You first," says Kala.

I bite into it and chew. Immediately, I get a tingle on my tongue. I've not felt that before! It quickly becomes a hot spot. It's becoming too hot—not nice. I chew quickly and swallow to get rid of it but the burning continues even after it's gone. My whole mouth is burning.

"What is it?" I gasp.

"It's chilli," says Dana. "You must have got the seeds. Have some water."

I gulp down a cup of water but it does nothing to relieve the uncomfortable heat in my mouth.

"It's too strong," I say.

"That's why you only use a little bit," says Dana. "And you avoid the seeds," she adds, smiling.

Kala takes a small bite of her sliver and that appears a good strategy until I see her face go red and she gasps in the same way I did. She spits out what she can.

"Too hot!" she says.

"You'll get used to it," says Dana. "Come and I'll show you how to use it."

We follow her into the house, wash our hands and join her in the kitchen. Dana has prepared a chicken and cut it into pieces. She shows us how to grind the dried seeds, cut the chillies, and prepare the herbs. She adds oil, salt, pepper and lemon juice, and rubs the mix into the chicken skin.

"We'll leave that there while we do the vegetables."

Kala and I watch Dana thinly cut the carrots and wash the beans.

"Now we cook the chicken," Dana says, pouring oil into a pan and adding the spiced chicken. "You cook it until it turns brown."

Steam spreads throughout the room, carrying with it an enticing aroma. I've never smelt anything like it before. It's chicken and spice, heat and colour all mixed up together—wonderful!

***

I bite into the spiced chicken. It's abundantly fragrant, tender and juicy, and the intense mix of exotic flavour lingers with the warmth and buzz of the chilli.

"Whoa!" I say. "This is good."

"It's amazing!" adds Kala.

"Thank you," I say.

"You're welcome," replies Dana.

Our thanks don't seem enough to me. "And thanks for having us stay at your farm," I add.

"It's your farm now."

"You're doing so much for us."

"It really is okay. I like having you two here."

"Really?" I ask.

"I mean it. I like watching you try new things, even watching you eat this food. It's like I'm tasting it for the first time myself. It's great having you here and seeing you together."

I don't say it, but it seems unfair that Dana, who is such a generous person, doesn't have the man whom she loves here with her. I almost feel guilty that things are working out for Kala and me.

***

Kala and I wash up and then wish Dana a goodnight. I'm sure I'm smiling as we go to our room. Our room!

Kala is quickly under the sheets. In the dim light, I think I spot her cheeky grin as she lifts the sheet, flashing her naked breasts and from what I can figure from the quick glimpse, could be more. I make the most of the opportunity, moving beside the bed where the light is dull, lowering my pants below my excited torso and quickly meeting Kala under our sheet.

***

I wake to the feel of Kala. She's cuddling me from behind. Nice. It's early and even with our morning cuddle and touching, we're in the kitchen to meet Dana at seven.

Dana shows us her morning routine of farm chores. Letting out the cows and chickens and giving them water is easy enough, but there is a real knack to milking Cowsy. Dana teaches us how to extract the cream from the top of the milk and how to churn it into butter. In the afternoon we tend to the vegetable plots, removing the weeds, thinning the rows of carrots, and selecting the vegetables for our dinner.

The next day, after the morning chores, Dana teaches us how to make yogurt. The day after that, she shows us how to kill, pluck and clean a chicken. Neither Kala nor I like the idea of killing, but we both want to eat it. Dana says we have a choice: we can elect to live without eating meat if we wish, but we'll have to make sure we get enough protein.

That night, Dana lets us cook. We spice the chicken the way that Dana showed us and we cook the chicken until brown. Some of the pieces burn a little. Dana said we had the pan too hot. Our cooking certainly isn't as good as Dana's, but it tastes more than okay to me.

***

Lying in bed, I notice a tear in Kala's eye. "Are you okay?" I ask.

"Yes, I'm okay. I was just thinking about my parents."

"You're missing them?"

"Yes, but I hadn't given them any thought yesterday or today. That made me a little sad."

I hold Kala tightly. I know what she means.

"We're busy with the farm and busy together. We haven't had much time for thinking about them."

"I know," says Kala.

"Good night, Beth," I say. "Good night, Davis. Good night, Paros. Good night, Neros."

Kala smiles and says the same good nights, adding "Good night, Tomas, my love," at the end.

"Good night, Kala, my love."

8. Seamus

We've made breakfast for Dana. It's eggs on toast and we've done a reasonable job, although our eggs are less runny than Dana made them. I make a note to reduce the boiling period next time.

"What shall we work on today?" I ask.

"I was thinking you could make bread," replies Dana.

"Aren't we running low on flour?" queries Kala.

"Yes, you'll need to grind some wheat. It's time you met Seamus."

"Seamus?" I ask.

"Seamus is our neighbour. He has a flour mill. You'll need to take one of the wheat bags from the shed and our flour container. I'll show you the track to his farm."

"Won't you come with us?" asks Kala.

"You'll be fine on your own."

"Will he mind?" I ask. "He won't know we're coming."

"He'll be okay. Just don't expect much conversation. Seamus isn't much of a talker."

***

We're soon on the track to Seamus' farm. The wheat bag is large, heavy and awkward to carry. We try various ways to share the weight. The only method that seems to work is for each of us to take it in turns to carrying it slung over one shoulder. We take our time.

We stop to rest at a lavender patch growing beside the track.

"I like the sun," says Kala. "It's lovely and warm on my back."

"I like it on my elbow," I joke.

"I like it on your muscles," says Kala, raising her eyebrows.

"I like it on your bum," I say.

We go on with that for a while with the places the sun infiltrating becoming more and more ridiculous.

After an hour of walking, stopping and sunshine, we reach Seamus' farm. His house looks similar in size and design to ours, but Seamus' house is unpainted and there are gaps in the cladding. There's an old, wheeled car with a large cabin and cargo space parked beside the shed. I notice rusting tools scattered on the ground. The vegetables in his plot are scrappy and overgrown with weeds. Even Seamus' chickens look different—they're skinny and their feathers are dry and sparse.

"Pssst," I say, pointing towards the veranda where I've spotted an aged man sitting on a wooden chair with a blanket over his waist and legs. I then notice that he's sharing the blanket with a small, short-haired dog.

"Hello," says Kala.

The man doesn't reply. He just stares.

The dog jumps off the blanket and barks at us as we walk up the veranda steps although its tail is wagging.

"Hello, cutie," says Kala, lowering her hand to allow it to smell her. The little dog responds with more tail wagging and licks Kala's hand. I offer my hand and it sniffs. No lick for me though.

The man is skinny with a wrinkled face and scruffy white hair. I'd guess that he's older than my grandparents.

"Hello," I say. "I'm Tomas and this is Kala."

"You the newens from Norden?"

"Yes, that's us," I say.

"You 'ere for the mill?"

"Yes," says Kala.

"All right then. I'll show ya to the shed," he says and he gets up.

He walks much faster than I expected. His dog follows him closely. We follow him past the old car and into the open shed. Inside, it's messy with rusting tools and torn bags scattered on the ground. He continues to the far end of the shed where he removes a large, dusty blanket from an object half as tall as me; a strange looking thing—one large circular stone centred above another, even larger circular stone.

"That's ya mill," he says, pointing. "Ya pour yer wheat in the hole there, spin the wheel with that there lever, and yer flour comes out there at the bottom."

Kala finds a brush and cleans the base of the mill while I untie the wheat bag, raise the open end towards the hole and begin pouring. It's difficult to hold the heavy bag steady. Some of the wheat misses the hole.

"Is there a trick to this?"

"Nah. Yer just 'ave ter hold it right. I'll show ya."

He takes the bag from me, holding it with one hand as if it's weightless, then places one foot on the lever and pushes it forward, simultaneously pouring the wheat and moving the lever. The top stone moves slowly at first, but with each press of the lever it moves faster and faster.

"Try it," he says to me, removing his foot.

I comply, stepping in quickly to move the lever with my right foot while Seamus continues to feed in the wheat.

"It's working," says Kala, squatting near the base.

"Want to have a go?" I ask.

"Yes!" says Kala, taking over.

The flour is accumulating in the tray below the stone.

"How long have you been here?" I ask.

"Years," answers Seamus, volunteering no further information.

"Your car. Is it for moving animals?"

"Yes," he says, then hands me the wheat bag and walks away.

I raise my eyebrows.

"Dana warned us," whispers Kala.

"I wonder how he gets by on his own?"

"Maybe he likes it."

I find it hard to imagine someone choosing to be on their own here in the South. In Norden older people on their own live together in extra-large dream homes.

We stop and gather the flour every few minutes. It's a slow process and takes us an entire hour to completely fill our container.

"Let's go," says Kala, picking up the container. I grab our much lighter wheat bag. It's now less than a quarter full.

"Thank you," I say as we walk past Seamus sitting on his chair on the veranda. He raises his hand.

"Bye, bye, doggie," says Kala.

"See ya at the meeting," says Seamus.

He's coming to the Origins' meeting? I find it hard to imagine him saying much there. "See you then," I reply.

***

"How was Seamus?" asks Dana as we enter the house.

"Just like you said," I say. "He didn't say much."

"That's Seamus. But he let you use the mill?"

"Yes, here's the flour," says Kala, placing the container on the table.

"Time to make bread," says Dana.

The bread is made with the flour we milled, some older dough mix, sugar, milk and butter. Dana says the older dough is important—it provides a thing called 'yeast' and that is essential for the bread to expand. She shows us how to knead and rest the dough and says that we can each make our own loaf. Kala jokes about it being a bread making contest.

Remembering Dana's delicious fruit scones, I decide to make a loaf of fruit bread. I whisper my idea to Dana and she smiles and nods, and then shows me to the sultanas, walnuts and cinnamon.

"Hey, that's not fair," says Kala. "Dana's helping you."

"It was Tomas' idea," says Dana.

"I have ideas too," says Kala.

"Okay, let's have your ideas," I say.

Kala pauses to think, but soon raises her finger. "I'll make vegetable bread," she says.

"Veggie bread?" I query.

"What vegetable?" asks Dana.

"Pumpkin," says Kala, perhaps more as a question.

"All right," says Dana. "Go and get the pumpkin. You'll need to cook it first."

***

Our dinner is chicken and vegetable soup accompanied by Kala's pumpkin bread. Dana makes the soup by boiling chicken bones in water, straining out the bones, adding vegetables, and boiling until the vegetables are soft. The last thing she adds is salt and pepper.

"The soup is delicious," I say. "And so is the pumpkin bread."

"It's a bit soft in the middle," says Kala.

"Yeah, but it tastes great," I say. "And it goes well with the soup. I think it's the best pumpkin bread ever."

"What would you know?!" notes Kala, grinning.

She's right, but I stand by my comment.

I admire the colourful cross section on my fruit bread as I slice it. It smells like hot nuts. The only blemish is that it is slightly burnt. I serve two pieces each for us to have with our tea.

"What do you think?" I ask.

"It's awful," says Kala mischievously as she takes her second piece.

"Well, maybe you should leave it for the chickens."

"I think both breads are delicious," says Dana. "I've never had anyone cook something so tasty for me. I'll miss you two when I go."

"It's still a few weeks yet, isn't it?" queries Kala.

"Two weeks," says Dana.

Two weeks! That's not long. We've learned a few things, but there must be so much more we'll need to know.

"Don't worry," says Dana. "You'll be fine. And you have Seamus not far away."

"It looked like Seamus could do with some help himself," I suggest.

"Don't underestimate Seamus," says Dana. "He does okay."

"His farm is so messy, though." I say. "And his veggies didn't look too good."

"That's just the way he has his things."

"Do you think we could help him?" I ask. "We could fix up his vegetable garden or something like that?"

"That's a great idea," says Kala.

"Do you think he'd let us do it?" I ask.

"He's had offers of help before. He always says no. I think he prefers to keep to himself."

"Maybe we could do it anyway," says Kala. "How about tomorrow?"

That's my Kala.

"Would that be okay with you?" I ask.

Dana pauses for a few moments, thinking.

"I guess you could do it. Just don't expect to be thanked."

"Yay," says Kala.

"Is tomorrow okay?" I check.

"Yes, that's fine. The only thing I had planned was to talk to Jessup. I want to trade some wheat bags for some of his chickens."

"Should we stay for that?" I ask.

"No, I'll catch Jessup on the radio. It's a matter of bargaining and I don't need you for that. He'll bring the chickens when he's here for the meeting."

"How many bags for how many chickens?" I ask.

"Last time it was one bag of wheat for each chicken. If he agrees to that, I'll ask for five chickens."

"Seems fair," I note.

"How many chickens does he have?" asks Kala.

"Oh, hundreds, I suppose. Chickens are his specialty. He doesn't grow vegetables or wheat. He trades his chickens for everything he needs."

"I'd like to see his farm," I say.

"I'm sure he'd like to show you. You can ask him."

***

It's morning and it's cold. I'm sorry to leave our warm bed, but this morning we're excited by the idea of fixing up Seamus' vegetable plot.

A Dream Passage

We eat breakfast quickly, sitting closely together but not talking very much. Kala seems to be watching me.

"Let's go," I say.

Kala nods and now she's smiling at me. I guess she's amused by my hurrying. I guess it is a bit silly to be rushing the way I am, but the idea of doing something useful is pushing me. We take the shovel, the rake and some seeds, and we're away. It's not yet seven a.m.

We walk quickly along the route to Seamus' farm. The tools aren't heavy so it's much easier than when we had to carry the wheat bag. It's probably only fifteen or twenty minutes before we arrive.

We move silently past the farm house and over to the vegetable plot. All is quiet. The little dog must be asleep.

"Weeds?" queries Kala, whispering.

I nod in agreement and we start pulling them out, one by one. The smaller varieties are easy to extract with our hands. We use the shovel for the larger clumps. There's no obvious place to stack them so we make a pile beside the shed.

We work quickly. I find myself regularly checking back towards the house—as yet there's no sign of Seamus or his dog.

"Turn the soil over?" asks Kala.

"Yes," I whisper, picking up the shovel. Kala takes the rake, smiling at me again. I turn over the soil with the shovel and Kala follows with the rake. We're working in a hurry. It's like we're doing something naughty and we're rushing not to be caught.

After a while we swap over. Shovel and rake, shovel and rake. Soon, my arms are aching. I suppose they're not yet recovered from the work we did on our own vegetable plot. At least we don't have to cut through grass here, and Seamus' soil seems lighter than ours. We keep going and going. Now we're sweating.

Kala is also checking back towards the farmhouse. Maybe we'll get it done without seeing him.

The turning over and raking is complete. Now it's time for the seeding. This time we know exactly what to do. Kala makes the row tracks with the rake handle. I sprinkle the seeds and Kala rakes the soil over the seeds.

Our work seems to get faster and faster. Avoiding Seamus seems possible. We've finished seeding.

"Water?" I ask quietly.

"Bucket?" returns Kala.

"Shed?" I suggest.

I find an old rusting bucket beside the flour mill, although it has a small hole at the base. I plug it with grass and a rock I find beside the shed.

The water tank is next to the house. We're as quiet as we can be but the water filling the bucket is noisy. Surely this can be heard from the house.

I pour the water through Kala's hands in an attempt to apply the water gently over the seeds. The water is absorbed by the soil as quickly as we feed it.

Back and forth we go from the tank to the garden. After what I guess to be around fifteen buckets, we've covered the garden, although I think it could do with more.

"More?" I whisper.

"He might need the water," replies Kala.

"Then we're done," I whisper, lowering the bucket and my shoulders, and pausing to admire our work. The restored soil bed is neat and fresh—quite a contrast to the rest of Seamus' farm.

I take Kala's hand. I'm happy we did this. It's my second worthwhile thing! Kala kisses me on the cheek. I'm about to give her a hug but something on the veranda catches my eye.

It's Seamus' dog. It's now beside us, wagging its tail and looking up at us expectantly. My attention moves to the door. And yes, he's there. Seamus is looking right at us and he doesn't look happy. He glances up and looks over my shoulder to towards the veggie garden we replanted. His face is at best expressionless and at worst angry. All the positivity I had for our work has suddenly drained from me.

"We're about to be told off," I whisper.

"I don't care," returns Kala.

We approach the veranda.

"Good morning, Seamus," says Kala.

He doesn't reply. We stand there looking at him before he does offer something. "You two lick some bee?"

"What?" I say.

"Yes, we'd like some tea," says Kala, nudging me with her elbow.

Oh. He's offering us tea.

We follow Seamus into his house. I cautiously look around, careful not to be seen as prying. It's similar in design to our house, but just as it was outside, everything in Seamus' house is in poor condition. In particular, I notice chipped cups and cracked plates sprawled over the kitchen bench.

The other thing I notice is that I feel cold. Perhaps it's from air getting through the cracks in the cladding. There are even some holes. I wonder if he was watching us through them.

The kettle is boiling on the stove. Seamus wipes three cups with a towel that doesn't look very clean. I daren't say anything. The old man's hospitality is genuine and he's offering us tea.

Seamus gives us each a cup of tea and serves us bread on a cracked plate. I sip the tea and I'm surprised by the taste. It's different but not in the dirty way I expected.

"The tea is nice. What's in it?" I ask.

"Rosemary," says Seamus, looking at me as if I should have known.

"Rosemary?"

"It's a plant. I put it in yer tea … Ya 'aven't 'ad it before?"

"No," I reply.

"Yer were too long in Norden."

"I agree," says Kala. "But we're here now."

Yes, we are here now and I have Kala and her parents to thank for that. I look at Seamus who is an old man now living on his own. How has it been for him living in the South I wonder. Has he had a good life?

"The seeds will need water," says Kala. "Do you mind if we come back and water?"

"Suit yourself."

We'll take that as a yes. He really is a hard old man.

The bread he gave us is darker than Dana's. It's hard and tastes slightly bitter but I don't mind it.

"What do you think of me bread?" he asks.

"Oh, it's good," I say. "Can I have another slice?"

"Ya must be hungry. No one ever asks for more of me bread. Help yerself."

Kala gives me a funny look as I take a second slice.

"Do you like it here?" I ask.

"Where?"

"On the farm."

"Of course I does," he replies. "It's just me and Spike here: nice and simple. Besides, where else would we go?"

Spike must be the dog.

"You could go to Norden," I say, thinking of how much easier it would be to live in one of the larger, dream houses they have for older people.

"Norden!" he says, apparently alarmed.

"You could have an easier life," adds Kala.

I'm surprised she said that.

"Na," says Seamus, getting up from his chair. "I'm not into all that dream stuff. It's better here; just me and Spike."

"Can we wash up?" I ask.

"No, you best be on yer way. Thank yer for ya work on me garden."

"Thank you for the tea," says Kala.

We collect our shovel and rake and slowly walk along the trail towards home, talking mostly about Seamus.

Again, we stop at the lavender, which exudes a lovely perfume when we examine the flowers.

"Did you really like the bread?" asks Kala, smelling the purple flowers.

"Yes, I liked the texture. It was just like Seamus—tough and crusty. Didn't you like it?"

"No. It was tough and bitter. It was nice of him to make us tea, though."

"That surprised me."

"I think he appreciated what we did," adds Kala, nestling into me and pecking me on the neck. "We did a good thing today."

"Yes, we did," I reply, satisfied and easily distracted by Kala's cuddle.

9. Origins

It's now three days since we worked on Seamus' plot. Kala, Dana and I are having breakfast. This time I made the toast and tea and Kala boiled the eggs. I'm just about to cut open my boiled egg. I think I know the trick. This time I won't hesitate. I'll cut straight through it.

I carefully place my knife at the middle of the egg. Then I cut. There's a little resistance from the shell but I follow through.

There, I did it! It's all about confidence, belief and follow through. Maybe there's something in that idea. I wonder if I can start to trust my other ideas a little more. I guess it's just like walking. When you know you can do it you walk easily, but if you start thinking about it and you hesitate, your movements feel awkward and you don't walk freely.

Dana cuts her egg in half neatly, barely looking at it. She did it easily while she was talking. I suppose she's done it so many times. She's lived here on the farm alone for who knows how long. She's smart and organised. She has her Origins' work and she's been to Norden and casually escaped from the Dream Patrol. She has every reason to be confident and trust her ideas. Who am I kidding? I've done two good things and opened my egg nicely. It's not exactly a platform for confidence as big and as broad as Dana's.

We start talking about the Origins' meeting we're having here tomorrow.

"Will many people attend?" asks Kala.

"Anyone can attend," replies Dana. "But most people don't want to travel. I expect that tomorrow it will be the area leaders—just over twenty people, but each of them will represent the fifty or so people in their area."

"Are you the representative for this area?" I ask.

"No, that's Seamus. He's been the leader of this area for a long time. I'm the group leader."

"You're the Origins' leader?"

"I thought you knew," says Kala.

"Sorry," I say, embarrassed. "You said you were doing Origins' work. I didn't realise you were the leader."

"That's okay," offers Dana but, I do feel stupid. Why wouldn't Dana be the leader? She's more capable than anyone I've ever known. I should have worked that out.

"What will you discuss tomorrow?" I ask.

"We usually start with an update on issues to do with Norden and then we have an update on our own issues, mostly farming matters. After that we discuss requests from members and we finish up with proposed actions. Most meetings go for around two hours."

"I don't think we'll fit twenty people in here," notes Kala.

"We'll use the shed. Could you two clean it up and set up the table and chairs? You'll have to move the tools outside and move all those wheat bags. And I have a favour to ask."

"Sure," says Kala.

"What can we do?" I ask.

"I have to prepare some notes as we have a radio hook up this afternoon. While I'm doing that, I wonder if you two

110

would like to make some food for the meeting. I was thinking of your breads. Your pumpkin bread and fruit bread would be perfect."

"We'd be happy to help," I say.

"And we'll make dinner tonight," says Kala.

"Thanks. That would be a great help. I have a lot to get through."

I start to wonder how much Kala and I have been distracting Dana from her Origins' work.

"Can I ask a favour too?" asks Kala.

"Sure, what is it?" says Dana.

"Could you pass on a radio message to my parents?"

"Yes, what do you want to say?"

"Tell them the kids love the beans."

Dana and I laugh. It doesn't make any more sense than when I said it. I'm glad that Kala is happy though, and that she wants to tell her parents that. I kiss her gently on the forehead.

***

Kala and I have taken an hour to clear the shed and sweep up the chicken and cow poo. The inside stinks, even after we've swept and cleaned.

"I guess they're all farmers," I say. "They'll be used to the smell."

"I have an idea," says Kala. "How about we soften the smell with some of the lavender we saw on the track to Seamus' house. We could get it in the morning."

"Great idea," I say. "We're going to need a lot of it though."

***

In the afternoon we make our bread—three loaves each. I keep watch on mine in the oven to make sure it doesn't burn, taking it out as soon as it's brown on top.

"That smells fantastic," says Dana, emerging for dinner.

"We should have made another one to go with our soup," says Kala.

"A slice each won't hurt," says Dana, taking one of Kala's loaves. "There'll be plenty left for the meeting."

She cuts three large slices.

"Mmmm …!" says Dana.

Kala's pumpkin bread is warm, moist and cooked through. Perfect!

***

The meeting is at ten-thirty. Kala and I get up at eight, have our breakfast alone, and leave to collect the lavender, which is ten minutes away. The bushes are on our side of what seems to be a break in the wheat fields that marks the border with Seamus' property. It kind of makes sense—I just can't imagine Seamus having pretty scents on his land.

Back at the house, we move the kitchen table and the chairs out to the shed. Kala finds some twine and we tie bunches of the lavender around the four legs of the table.

A Dream Passage

At around ten a.m., people start arriving in their wheeled cars; some the same model as Seamus' car, although all of them look in better condition. A few people arrive on foot and one man, who looks even older than Seamus, arrives on a horse.

Dana is introducing Kala and me to every new arrival. We greet them with the touch of our foreheads. Everyone seems to know us already. Some of them say, "Oh, you're the kids from Norden. How do you like it here?"

Kala and I sit tightly. "We like it here," we say.

"We love the farm," says Kala.

"I like the food," I say.

"Yes, it's much better than that dream food," they say.

We get a few comments on the lavender. "What a lovely idea," says a woman with red hair.

"What's that awful smell?" says the old man who rode in on the horse.

Dana rings a bell that sits in a square frame. "Let's get started," she says, taking her seat at the table.

Kala and I move to the side of the table, but back away to the edge. It seems a good place to watch.

"It's great to have such a good turnout," says Dana. "Thank you for coming everyone. Please pass on my best wishes to the people in your areas."

"I'll start with the report on Norden issues," continues Dana. "As you can see, I'm back; although, as most of you will know, I had a bit of an ordeal.

"As we discussed at our last meeting, I went to Norden to try to assist Cello and Jilla who were accused of consorting. Cello was in custody but I managed to talk with Jilla and offered for her to move here.

"She thanked us for the offer but said that she wanted to stay with her family. Her mother is aging and she didn't want to leave her. That's a shame for Cello and Jilla, but we've got to respect their decision.

"Now to my situation. It's apparent that the Dream Patrol are monitoring our activity in Norden. I was aware that I was followed and then they set me up, accused me of stealing a printing press, and detained me."

"Liars," says a large man with a bushy beard standing on the opposite side to us.

"I agree with you, Hollis," says Dana. "And the alarming thing is that they weren't just manipulating the truth this time. They planted the printing press at the front door of the house, made up the story about me stealing it, and said I was printing subversive material. This is worse than anything they've done before."

"We've got to do somethin'," says Hollis.

"We can discuss that," says Dana. "The rest of the story is that I went through a dream trial, they found me guilty, and they dreamed for me to lose a hand.

"I'm happy to report that that didn't happen," continues Dana, smirking but also serious. "I was rescued by Paros and Neros, and they were also successful with the liberation of Tomas and Kala, who you see here. I'm happy to report that they are well suited to farm life and I think they will become strong contributors to our community."

"They already is," says a voice from the back.

I look to see who it is.

"Seamus," whispers Kala.

He speaks!

"We were lucky with these rescues," continues Dana. "But the Dream Council is going to be on guard from now on. Paros said that they reported Tomas as a stolen child and made something of him being taken on his Passage day. They're now calling for our entire Origins' group to be brought to justice."

"They're dreamin'," says Hollis.

"They're continuing their development towards us," continues Dana. "It's a dream road here, a house there and a school to follow."

"How long do we have?" asks the scruffy woman in a blue shirt sitting next to Dana.

"I'm not sure, Anita," says Dana. "My best guess is twelve months before they reach our northerly farms."

I'm surprised to hear that Norden is moving so fast.

"They're headin' towards my gun barrel," says Hollis.

"Settle down, Hollis," says another man. "We don't want yer violence."

"Don't worry," returns Hollis. "I'll tell them I'm not from Origins—just before I shoot 'em."

He seems to be half-serious. I've never been at such an informal meeting before. People are saying whatever they want.

"No violence," says Dana. "We need to come up with other ways."

"Let's hear yer other ways," says Hollis.

"We need to convince them to leave us alone," says Dana.

"How?" asks Hollis. "You're kiddin' yerself if you think Krakus will make a deal with us."

"Let's leave the action discussion for later in the meeting," says Dana.

Hollis nods in agreement, but he seems annoyed.

"Now for the local report," says Dana. "Anita?"

"Thank you, Dana," says Anita. "I'll start with the stock report. Stock levels are good. Farms are reporting increases in cattle, sheep and chickens over the last three months. The biggest increase has been in sheep. Most farms are reporting a good lambing season. The increase in cattle and chickens is small but promising. Farms are also reporting good pasture growth as a result of consistent rains."

"That's good news," says Dana. "But how about our crops?"

I hear a few murmurs, but can't locate the source.

"Tell them," says the man next to Anita.

"Vegetables, oats and barley are good, but we have problems with wheat," says Anita. "At our last meeting, I reported that ten farms were showing signs of rust in their wheat crops. That number has increased dramatically. We now have nearly one hundred paddocks showing rust in their wheat. That's nearly one third of our wheat crops."

"That's serious," says Dana.

"Yes, it is. And, as you all know, the only treatment we have is to burn the affected area. We're doing that, but it doesn't seem to be stopping the rust."

"Any other ideas?" asks Dana.

There is a serious silence throughout the shed until Seamus speaks. "It's no good," he says. "We'll end up losing it all; just like last time."

This is all news to me. I thought you just planted crops and they kept growing until you harvested. I had no idea you could lose a crop from something called rust.

"We'll hav' ter burn the lot," says Hollis.

"Settle down, Hollis," says another man from the back.

"I think Hollis is right," says Dana. "We've got to try something more extreme this time."

"Okay, I'll relay the instruction to burn the entire infected field," says Anita. "Problem is, no one wants to burn their fields. How do we make people do it?"

"You need to convince them with good reasoning," says Dana.

"I'll see how that goes," says Anita.

"Some won't do it," says Hollis.

"Well, we're not going to threaten them," says Anita.

"Let's take a break now," says Dana.

That's our cue to serve our warmed breads and tea. Kala takes the breads, warmed in the oven as I make the tea.

I've never poured so many cups before. It's one cup for each of the area leaders and a cup for Dana, Kala and me— that's twenty-three cups!

I soon find out that our kettle only holds enough water for eight. It's going to take me three boils to make all this tea.

I hand out what should be the last cup to Anita. She thanks me for the tea and says our breads are 'Southern Standard'. I'm not sure what she means by that but from her expression I assume it's a good thing. Anita says we should enter the bread making contest at the annual Produce Fest.

I'm about to ask about that, but notice Hollis standing on his own and looking straight at me. He's raising his hand. What could he possibly want with me? Oh, I see! He has no tea. How could I have missed him?

"I'll get you a cup," I say.

"Thanks," he says.

Kala joins me as I'm pouring the additional cup.

"I can't believe I miscounted the cups of tea," I say.

"Never mind," says Kala.

"And it was Hollis who missed out, of all people."

"He'll probably shoot you for that."

"Ha, ha," I say, adding, "Not if I tell him it was your fault."

"Ha, ha."

"Thanks," says Hollis as I give him his tea.

"Sorry, I must have miscounted the cups."

"No worries. I like ya bread. Yer could enter the bread comp at the festival."

"Thanks." Great, I think. I'm now talking with the guy that wants to shoot everyone. I'm really paying for my mistake. "When is the Produce Fest?" I ask.

"The first week of summer. Comes along and I'll teach ya how to shoot."

"There's shooting at the Produce Fest?"

"Of course there's shootin'. This isn't Norden, you know."

It sure isn't Norden!

"Thanks," I say. "I'd like to learn. What do you shoot at?"

"It's a target at the festival. I prefer shootin' rabbits though."

"You shoot rabbits?"

"Sure. Shooting rabbits is as easy as making tea. Ya just got to shine a light in their eyes and they sit as still as a cup on yer table waiting for boilin' water."

Interesting analogy. What a strange man, I think, as Kala joins us.

"Hollis is offering to teach me how to shoot," I say.

"That sounds like fun. Can you show me too?"

"Sure," says Hollis, obviously happy with Kala's interest.

The bell rings. "Okay everyone," says Dana. "Let's get back to it."

"Nice to meet you, Hollis," I say.

"You too."

Kala and I resume our place, standing adjacent to Dana's table.

"It's time to discuss actions," says Dana. "Let's start with our issues with Norden. Does anyone have any proposals for action?"

"I have," says a middle-aged man from the middle left.

"Go ahead, Laros," says Dana.

"I have one of the most northern farms and every year Norden is getting closer and closer. I am a peaceful man, as you know, but I have children to think of. I don't want them to lose their home. I think we need to take action to stop Norden moving further south."

"We all agree with you, Laros," says Dana. "It's just a matter of what action. I'd like to negotiate a border with Norden."

"But they're liars," says Hollis. "How can we trust 'em?"

"We need to stop their dream roads," says Laros.

"We could sabotage the broadcast network?" suggests Kala.

Kala speaking surprises me. I thought we were here to watch! Everyone is staring. They must know that Kala's parents, Paros and Neros, are the communication experts. They'll be thinking that Kala knows something about it too.

"What do you have in mind?" asks Dana.

"I'm talking about destroying the central broadcast transmitter. I've heard my parents talk about it."

"Wouldn't they just replace it with a new transmitter?" asks Anita.

"Yes, but it would delay the move south," replies Kala.

"There's a problem with that kind of action," notes Dana. "It's likely to provoke them to take stronger action against us and make their move south a priority."

"Yes, you're right," says Kala, looking slightly deflated.

"Thanks, for the suggestion though," says Dana and Kala nods. "Any other ideas?" continues Dana.

"Talking won't work," says Laros. "We need to be in a strong position before they'll negotiate with us."

"I agree," says Dana. "The question is how we improve our position. Anyone have any ideas on that?"

There is silence initially and then general chatter.

"Let's move onto local matters," yells Dana. "Are there any proposals for actions here?"

"Just the action to burn entire fields," says Anita.

"Does anyone want to speak against that?"

Silence.

"We won't need a vote then. Please relay that decision."

"Any other business?" asks Dana.

"I've been asked to bring up trading arrangements," says a thin man near the front.

"What ya wantin' this time?" says Hollis.

The meeting from that point seems to become a discussion about chicken prices. Dana lets the discussion go on. Some people are arguing for fixed prices. Others argue for prices negotiated according to quality. The man, who I soon realise is Jessup, is asking for chicken to be sold based on weight. Dana seems to have withdrawn.

The two big issues were the rust in the wheat and Norden moving further south. I think again about the books at my grandparents' place. Maybe they would have some information on rust treatment. And Norden—if only the people there knew that the people in the South just want to be left to farm in peace.

And what about the number of teas? How could I get the number of teas wrong? I start counting people, but it isn't easy because everyone is now moving and having multiple conversations. I count twenty-four, including myself, but I can't be sure. I decide to try again as they leave the shed.

"Okay, let's wrap it up," says Dana. "I don't think we have agreement on chicken prices. Let's leave the prices as negotiated for now. If there is no other business, then I'll call this meeting closed."

More chatter follows.

"Thank you, everyone," says Dana. "See you next month. Dream well, everyone."

"Dream well," is the mumbled reply.

Funny that they say 'Dream Well' here, just like they do in Norden. I don't let it distract me though, moving quickly to the door.

"What are you doing?" asks Kala.

"Counting," I reply.

"Oh, I see … The teas."

Kala takes the lead with the goodbyes, allowing me to count.

"Twenty-four people," I say. "There were twenty-four people here."

"One more than we expected," notes Kala. "I wonder who the extra was?"

Perhaps I am being paranoid. I know Dana said anyone could attend, but she was only expecting twenty area representatives. Adding Kala, Dana and me makes twenty-three. I wonder if the Dream Council would send someone.

"Dream Council?" I suggest to Kala, raising my eyebrows.

"Could be," says Kala. "Let's ask Dana."

I'm keen to ask Dana as soon as possible but a few people have lingered outside the shed to talk with her. Kala and I start to clean up.

Dana enters the house as Kala and I are washing cups and talking about Hollis' offer to teach us how to shoot.

"Hey, you two," says Dana. "Thanks for your help."

"That's all right," I say.

"Sorry about the transmitter idea," says Kala.

"No, it was a good idea. I'm glad you spoke. It's useful to bring these things up. It really went to the heart of why it's not a good idea to take stronger action. We're worried about the Dream Council taking further action against us. And that's what these meetings are all about—discussing things and making the best choices."

"I've got a question," I say. "I counted the people at the meeting. There were twenty-four of us there. You said that you expected twenty representatives. With the three of us, that's only twenty-three."

Dana smiles. "You two are good with numbers. Next time I'll get you to deal with Jessup."

"We're wondering if you knew everyone at the meeting?" checks Kala. "Is it possible that the Dream Council sent someone?"

"That's quite a theory," says Dana, smiling.

"Did you know everyone?" I repeat.

"Okay then, let me think," says Dana, a little more seriously now. "Yes, I think I did know everyone and I didn't notice any extra people. It may have been a former area leader or someone's partner or something like that."

"So, you don't think it could have been someone from the Dream Council?" I say.

"I suppose it could have been, but that would be okay by me. In fact, I wish they would attend our meetings. Then they may understand us better and come to know about our issues and what we want. I think we'll invite them to our next meeting. That could be the best idea coming out of today!"

"You'd invite the people that want to remove your hand?" I query. "Are you serious?"

"Totally," replies Dana, with an assuring smile.

"Okay then," I concede.

She does seem serious. I really did provide an idea, even if it was by accident. I can't help but admire Dana and her ability to view things in a slightly different way to other people. I guess that's what makes her a good leader.

"I see that you made friends with Hollis," says Dana.

"He offered to teach us how to shoot," says Kala.

"What's the story with Hollis?" I ask.

"Hollis … We'll he's a farmer. He has one of the larger properties in our Northern area. I guess that's why he feels he wants to have more of a say in what goes on. He would be one of the first affected by Norden extending further south. He grows some wheat, vegetables and keeps a few cows. He could do a lot more on his land, but I suppose he'd need help to do it.

"His father died when he was young and he had to take on the farm work. He also looked after his mother until she passed away last year."

"Sounds like a tough life," I say.

"Like many around here; he has had it tough. He's okay, Hollis. It's the ones that don't speak their mind who worry me more."

"Are there many of them?" asks Kala.

"I don't know," says Dana. "You can never know exactly what people are thinking."

"One more question," I say.

Kala feigns a frown, but it quickly turns into a smile.

"Sure," says Dana.

"Why do you say 'Dream well' at the end of your meeting?"

"Oh that? That was something I started," offers Dana, clearly amused. "I wanted to remind people here that we're not that different to the people of Norden. We need to dream of the things that we want and we need to follow our dreams. Just like the two of you."

"Makes sense," I say.

"There wasn't much enthusiasm for it today. That rust is a big problem."

10. Rescue from the old times

It's four-thirty a.m. Kala's breathing has a steady pitch. I suppose she's dreaming. I've hardly slept. My mind seems stuck on the two issues from yesterday: Norden moving south and the rust in the crops.

The people in Norden will be dreaming now. They could even be extending one of their roads towards the South. My thoughts move south along the road to where I imagine Hollis and many of the other people from the meeting have their farms. What will these farmers do if they lose their crops? And what will we do if our own wheat becomes infected by the rust? We'll have to burn entire fields. If we lose our wheat, we'll have nothing to trade for chickens. And are our vegetables safe?

I feel for my diamond. I'm now thinking about Grandpata and his books. They could have information in them on treating rust. If only we could go there and look at the books. We've got to do something.

I put my hand on Kala's shoulder and pat her gently. "Kala," I whisper near her ear. "Wake up."

She stirs, slightly opening one eye. Cute! On another day, I'd snuggle into that, but not today. I pat her a little harder. "Wake up," I whisper.

"What is it?" she asks, pulling my hand across her waist.

"Sorry." I kiss her on the cheek.

"What is it?" she repeats.

"We need to go to my grandparents' place."

"Why?"

"I want to look at their books. They could have information on the rust."

"Talk about it in the morning," she says, kisses my arm and turns. The regular pitch of her breathing returns.

I leave it there for a while, but I can't stop thinking about it. We're lying here while the rust is spreading and the roads are moving south. Soon, I can't take any more of these thoughts. I get up, dress and I'm out the door.

The twin moons are in their half-moon phase, giving just enough light for me to make out the track. I'm soon past the lavender. Will Seamus let me?

The beginnings of daylight illuminate the cracks in the cladding on Seamus' house. There's nothing else I can do but walk straight to the door and give it a well measured knock.

I wait and listen. Nothing. I imagine Seamus and Spike nestled together under a tattered blanket on a creaky old bed. His room is only metres from where I'm standing.

"Spike!" I whisper. "Wake up, Spike."

Then I hear a thud.

"Grrr. Grrrrrrr. Wruff! Wruff!"

"Seamus! It's me, Tomas."

I hear some rustling. He must have heard. But, now I'm nervous. What am I going to say?

"What's goin' on?" asks Seamus, opening the door. "What do ya want with Spike?"

"I was after you. I want to ask you a favour."

"Come in with ya, then. Get outa the cold."

It's slightly warmer inside. Seamus directs me to a chair next to the stove and then takes his time to shove a log into it and adjust the vent.

"What's ya favour?"

I pause. I'm still not sure how I'm going to explain this. "Could I borrow your car?"

"What does ya want with me car?"

"I want to go to my grandparents'."

"Had enough of the South has ya?"

"No, it's not that." I'm going to have to tell him. "I remember some farming books at my Grandparents'. I think they might have some information on treating rust."

"Oh, ya gunna save us all, is ya?"

He's not smiling.

"It'll probably come to nothing. I just wanted to try."

"Ya want to take ya chances with me car?"

"I just thought I'd ask you about it. If you don't think it's a good idea, then I won't go."

He stands there looking me up and down. I don't know what he's looking at, but I'm sure he's not going to see anything to assure him. I'm just a scrawny 'Dreamer Boy'.

"Don't worry, me boy," he says. "You can use me car."

His smile is so big that I see his crooked teeth. He was playing with me! Still, I don't care. I'm relieved. Then I remember the other complication ...

"And, can you show me how to drive it?" I ask.

"Yer want to borrow me car and yer doesn't know how to drive?"

"We had a different type of car."

"Norden and them fancy dream cars. They're no good on dirt roads, ya know."

"No, I didn't know that. Why aren't they good on dirt roads?"

"I dunno. Somethin' about the way they work. I think they needs an even surface."

"Can you show me how to drive?"

"All right then. You make us a cup of tea while Spikey and me get yer car ready."

"Okay. Thanks, Seamus."

***

"This is yer accelerator. This is yer brake. There is yer clutch and ..."

"Clutch?"

"No clutches in Norden, is there? Ya need to put in yer clutch to change gear. They're yer gears there. Get in and I show ya how it works."

I shoo Spike from the passenger seat but as I sit he returns, sitting righteously on my lap. Seamus starts with slow laps around the farm house, showing me the sequence of the gears, and how to stop and start again, all the while balancing his tea in his lap.

"Now your turn."

I take the driver's seat and I start the car, just as Seamus showed me. The car suddenly lurches forward, stopping with a thud.

"Clutch," says Seamus.

"Clutch!" I say.

I try again, this time with the clutch in. The car idles okay, but as soon as I release the pedal, the car lurches forward, stopping with the same thud as before.

"What happened?" I ask.

"Slow," says Seamus. "Ya need to let yer clutch out slower."

"Sorry," I say.

I try again, releasing it very slowly and this time the car moves forward, slowly and steadily.

"Gear," says Seamus.

I change gear, taking extra care to release the clutch slowly.

"Look out!" says Seamus.

"What?" I say, looking up.

The vegetable garden! I brake as hard as I can and turn the steering wheel, but it's too late. I've run the car over the edge of the garden, and the car has stalled and stopped.

We both get out to check the damage. The car is okay, but the garden has deep wheel marks through one corner."

"Sorry, Seamus. I'll fix that," I say.

"Don't ya worry. Try again," he says.

I start the engine. This time I take more care.

"Gear," says Seamus.

I change the gear and continue directing the car around the house track.

"Now, stop," says Seamus.

I bring the car to a halt using the brake and clutch at the same time. The engine revs but the car stops.

"That's good enough. Yer can work out the rest on the way. I'll get the fuel for ya."

Before I know what to say, he's out of the car and he's gone to his shed, collected a large fuel drum, placed it in the back of the car, pointed to where the fuel goes, and is returning to his house.

"Come on, Spikey," he says.

"Thanks, Seamus," I say, but he waves me away, barely looking back.

I'm stopped in the driver's seat for a few moments. This trip is becoming real. I have a car and fuel and I'm going to Norden! I wonder what Kala will think about this. And Dana! I didn't even think of her. Will she be okay with it?

**

From Seamus' house, although stalling at each of the turns I manage to drive back to the main road and onto the road to our house. I seem to be getting better at the gear changes. Nearing the house, I'm now using the brake and changing to the lowest gear.

I see something move on the veranda. What is it? Oh, no! The car jolts suddenly and give seems to groan. I've stopped short of where I wanted to be. It's Kala.

"I didn't know you could drive," she says, laughing.

"I'm just learning," I reply, unnecessarily, as my driving would have clearly shown that.

"I can't believe Seamus let you take it."

Kala is still chuckling, although her hug is approving and reassuring.

"I wasn't sure he would."

"What's the plan?"

"The plan is to go to my grandparents'. If we leave now, we can get there sometime tonight and come back tomorrow. Will you come?"

"Of course, I'm coming," says Kala, kissing me. "You're becoming an action man, Tomas."

I suppose she's right. Seamus' veggie plot was my first action. This is my second. I feel good, except for some nervous twitches in my arms. I kiss Kala on the forehead and have my arm tightly around her waist as we walk to the house.

Dana isn't up yet. Kala and I exchange whispers about what we should take on our trip.

"Bread," suggests Kala.

"Do you think she'll mind?" I whisper.

"Mind what?" asks Dana, emerging from her room.

"Good morning," I say.

I pause. There's nothing else I can do now. I'm going to have to tell her the whole thing.

"What are you two up to?"

"My grandparents have some old books. A few of them are about farming. I think there's a chance that they will have something on treating the rust. I thought that Kala and I could go to my grandparents in Seamus' car."

"Do you think he'll let you use his car?"

"It's outside," says Kala, grinning.

"Seamus lent you his car! I don't believe it."

Dana opens the curtains to check outside and then pauses. "We have farming books here. There's nothing in them about treating rust. Why will your grandparents' books be any different?"

That's a good point. Why should my grandparents' books have more information?

"I remember one farming book in particular; a thick one, with lots of information. There could be something in that book."

The look on Dana's face is discouraging.

"You're probably right," I concede. "There isn't much chance of it having anything different."

"Shouldn't we try though?" says Kala. "If we don't go now, we'll just keep wondering about it. Seamus has lent us his car. He must have thought it was a good idea."

Dana is thinking. I watch her anxiously. I don't think she wants us to go. I really don't know why Seamus lent me his car.

"It's okay," I say.

"Just a minute," says Dana. "I'm not saying you can't go. You two are free to do as you please."

"But do you think we should try?" I ask.

"We'll," says Dana. "I doubt your grandparents' book is going to have anything new."

That sounds like it then. That's okay. I'll just have to return the car to Seamus.

"But," continues Dana. "As Kala said, you won't know unless you go. If you go, I want you to be careful. The Dream Patrol has no proper reason to detain you, but that doesn't mean they won't."

"So, we can go," says Kala, excitedly.

"It's your choice."

"Yes!" exclaims Kala.

"Thanks, Dana," I add.

We're going! I'm relieved although unsure of whether Dana actually supports it or if it's really a very good idea.

"When are you going?" asks Dana.

"After breakfast," says Kala.

"Is it okay with you if we take some extra food with us?" I ask.

"Absolutely! And you should take something for your grandparents."

"How about some spices?" I suggest.

"And some eggs?" adds Dana.

"Thanks!" I say and I'm relieved. Dana seems to be okay about us going.

***

I have the car in top gear. We're cruising along the road to Norden. There isn't much to do except steer and monitor the speed.

This trip is going to take a long while. It was more than nine hours with Kala's parents and I'm driving slower than them. It seems to be just us on this very long road.

135

"Are you okay?" asks Kala.

Hearing her question, I become aware that I have slowed the car. "Sorry. I'm just worried that this trip is likely to be for nothing. And we're taking a risk going to Norden. What if they decide to detain us?"

"We'll be okay," says Kala, confidently placing her hand on my leg.

Neither of us talks for a while. I'm thinking about what the Dream Council would want with us.

"Car!" says Kala.

I'm startled for a moment but then see the car in the distance, heading towards us.

"Should we turn off?" I ask.

"No, just leave room for it to pass."

"Room?"

I slow down and concentrate on steering the car to the left of the road, positioning the car as close as I dare go toward the dirt bank that slopes away from the road.

I feel myself tensing as the car nears. Am I giving it enough space?

Whoosh! The car passes. It didn't slow at all.

"Did you see who that was?" I ask.

"No, didn't recognise them. It was a wheeled car though. Someone else from the South, I guess. Hey, Tomas?"

"Yes?"

"Let me know when it's my turn to drive."

"How about now?" I say and I slow the car, this time working through the gears and bringing the car to a controlled stop.

"Nice," says Kala.

We change seats.

"What now?" asks Kala.

"Clutch in. That's the left pedal. Turn the engine on and accelerate a little."

"You'll have to show me."

"Okay," I say, realising that I should be showing Kala in the same way Seamus showed me. We swap seats again.

I show Kala and then she tries. We practice a few starts and stops and then, with little effort, she's driving.

"Are you sure you've never done this before?" I ask.

"I didn't say I hadn't done it before."

"You already knew how to drive?"

"Paros showed me. She wanted me to know how to drive these old wheeled cars in case of some kind of emergency. And here we are now. It's a good opportunity for me to practice."

***

It's now dark and I'm driving. It seems like so very long ago that we left the South. Kala drove for three hours and then it was my turn again. We're travelling downhill and I see lights in the distance. It's Norden!

We pass through an intersection. That's the third road I've seen in the last fifteen minutes. Kala says we need to continue along the main road for a while yet.

It's only been a few weeks, but everything looks so different.

"The lights; they're kind of beautiful," I say.

"Yeah!" says Kala. "It's Norden, drawing us in."

"Like moths around a light."

"Not me; I'm a butterfly."

"I'll be a bat then," I say.

Kala feigns a sullen look.

We're soon driving in one of the suburbs: row upon row of identical houses.

"Left here," says Kala, pointing.

"Are you sure?"

"No, not certain. There is something about that tree on the corner."

I see what she means. The tree is larger and older than anything else around. This road could be one of the older roads that links to the older suburbs. As we travel further I see a house with a different design.

"That's the orange tile roof house," I say.

"You recognise it?"

"Yes. It's an oldie. I'll turn left here."

"How much further?" asks Kala.

"I don't remember. Maybe five minutes."

We pass through another intersection at the edge of a suburb of old houses, each looking slightly familiar, although none of them stand out enough for me to be certain of where we are. I wish I'd taken more notice when I travelled with my parents.

A dream car is approaching! It slows as we pass; its three occupants glaring at us and our wheeled car. From what they've been told about the South, they'll be wary of us. They probably think we're here to steal something.

"Just a family," says Kala, confidently. "They'll be okay."

Further along, I notice a particular tree. "It's the big pine," I say.

"You know it?"

"It's not far now. I'll take the next left."

And there it is. I recognise the corner that leads to my grandparents' street. We're going to make it! I can't wait to see the surprise on Grandmata's face when we arrive in this car.

This car! I'm worried again. Surely they've reported us. The Dream Patrol could even be waiting for us. We've taken a big risk coming here.

Approaching the house, everything looks normal though.

"Which house?" asks Kala.

"This one," I say, turning into my grandparents' driveway.

The house is an old brown brick house with an orange roof—similar to the other old houses except for the circular flowerbed of roses and daffodils that surrounds an old apple tree in the front garden. With the flowers in bloom, I think it's the best-looking garden of the neighbourhood.

I continue along the driveway, past the house, and through to the back lawn.

"We made it," I say.

"Tomas!" says Kala, noticing the elderly man approaching.

"It's Grandpata." I open the car door. "Grandpata!"

"Tomas! It is you. Tomas!"

He's shaking with excitement. I'm quickly out of the car and my forehead greeting with Grandpata quickly becomes an embrace.

"And you must be Kala." He gives Kala a warm forehead touch and holds Kala as strongly as he held me. Kala lets out a playful squeal.

"Tomas," says Grandmata, arriving next to me. "Tomas!"

Her greeting is as enthusiastic as Grandpata's. She also hugs Kala and before I know it we're all hugging together. It was never like this before. They were always loving and good to me, but we never held each other this tight.

"Just a minute," says Grandmata.

We wait until she returns from the house, with a blanket. "For the car," she says.

We help her spread it over the car. I collect a few garden rocks and put them on top of the blanket to hold it in place, noting that it won't matter if they happen to scratch Seamus' well-worn car.

"Where'd you get this old thing?" asks Grandpata.

"It's from our neighbour. Is it like the one you had?"

"It's older than the one I had. You've got yourself a classic car there."

I don't have any idea what he means but guess from his smile that he likes it.

"Come on," says Grandmata.

Entering the house, I'm thinking again about the reason for our trip. The books! I walk ahead, directly to the living room that had the bookshelf with the books.

What? They're not there! The book place is now occupied by Grandmata's collection of teapots. Teapots! I remember her collecting them, but they were never on that bookshelf. I quickly scan the rest of the room, searching. No, not there! I try the kitchen, then the other room, opening each door and checking for books. Each room is exactly as I remember it. Nothing has changed except for the annoying teapots!

"Are you okay?" asks Grandmata.

"Where are the books?"

"The old books?" asks Grandmata.

"Yes, the old books that were over there," I say, pointing at the bookshelf.

"You were the only one who ever looked at them."

"But do you still have them?"

"Yes. We've still got them."

I'm so relieved that I hug my grandmother.

"What is it?" asks Grandpata.

"I'm so glad you've still got the books. I'm glad that we made it here and that you're okay. I was worried the Dream Patrol would be here."

"Well, they did come here one time," says Grandmata. We told them you were kidnapped. That's what your parents said to say."

"Did they believe you?" asks Kala.

"They seemed happy to believe it," replies Grandmata. "They said they were going to try to get you back."

"And now you're here," says Grandpata. "And you brought your kidnapper with you. Has she come for us?" he adds, laughing at his own joke.

I laugh with him. "That's my Grandpata."

"So, that's where Tomas gets his sense of humour," says Kala.

I chuckle. She's probably right.

"Are you hungry?" asks Grandmata.

"Starving," I say. Kala smiles.

"You two sit down. I'll get some supper." Grandmata goes to the kitchen. Grandpata sits Kala and me down like it's time to talk seriously.

"Did you come all this way for those old books?" he asks.

"Yes," I say. "I remember that you had one on farming. We came for that."

"The books are in boxes in the laundry. The patrol officers that came here seemed to take an interest in them so we packed them away."

"I don't get it," says Kala. "What would they want with the books?"

"I'm not sure. They just don't seem to like people that hang onto things from the old times."

"Mind if I look?" I say, eagerly moving towards the laundry.

"Go ahead," says Grandpata.

Kala joins me. There are three cardboard boxes on the shelf. I lift one of the boxes and set it down on the floor for Kala and take another one for myself.

Kneeling down to search through the box, I quickly see that they're the smaller books: story books, tales of myth and adventure—good books, but no use for treating rust. I move to the remaining box on the shelf.

"How about this one?" asks Kala, showing me a book with vegetables on the cover.

"That one might be okay but it's not the one I was thinking of. The one I want is more about farming."

I join Kala, taking the next book from her box.

"It's this one," I say, recognising the thick book and the four pictures arranged in quadrants on the cover. There's a cow, a sheep, a crop of some kind, and a tractor. It's called 'Modern Farming' which seems a strange title given the age of the book.

"Here we go," I say, nervously opening the old book. My hands are shaking.

The book has three content pages. I scan through the major chapter headings: 'Suitable land', 'What to Farm and When', 'Farming Methods', 'Harvesting', 'Stock Care' and 'Treating Disease'.

"Treating Disease—that's it!" I say. "Page 231." From the table of contents, I calculate fifteen pages dedicated to

143

treating disease—a good sign. My fingers take me quickly to page 231 and the heading 'Treating Disease'. There's a close-up picture of a green leaf with yellow spots.

The first five pages are dedicated to 'Disease Identification'. I move to the next section, 'Disease Treatment', on page 236.

I scan the pages, looking for a mention of 'wheat' and 'rust'. I find several mentions of wheat, touching each with my finger, but no mention of rust. Kala watches on, her eyes gleaming.

On page 240 there's a table, summarising disease treatments. Surely it will be there.

"There it is!" says Kala, excitedly, pointing further down the page.

And I see it too: 'Wheat Rust' on the left column and beside it, a treatment.

"Sulphur based fungicide," I say. "Do you know what that is?"

"No idea," replies Kala.

I scan the remaining pages of the treatment section. It's all about other diseases. All we have is three words: 'Sulphur based fungicide'.

"Let's ask Grandpata."

Kala nods and we soon re-join Grandpata.

"How'd you go?" he asks.

"Do you know anything about sulphur based fungicide?"

"Fungicide?" says Grandpata. "Why do you want to know about that?"

I'm suddenly aware of how rude I've been. I haven't explained anything.

"Sorry, Grandpata," I say. "I'll tell you the full story." I sit down on the couch, pausing briefly to think.

"As you know, we're now living in the South. It's beautiful down there. There are wide ..."

"Just a minute," interrupts Grandpata. "Grandmata, come and listen to this."

He's right, she should hear it. I've been rude again—just wanting to know about the fungicide. I'm going to have to wait a bit longer. Kala squeezes my hand.

Grandmata brings in fruit and tea. "You're in luck, Tomas," she says. "Today's dessert was strawberries. That was one of your favourites, wasn't it?"

"Yes," I say, although it wasn't my absolute favourite. That was lychees. I'm grateful for something to eat. I start with the tea, which is hot but bland. The strawberries are large and they look perfect, but when I bite into them, nothing. They're tasteless.

"Back to our story?" I say.

"Just a minute," says Kala, whispering, "The spices," in my ear. She returns with the small container of spices we bought from the farm. "See if you like this," she says as she sprinkles what I guess to be cinnamon on the strawberries and something else in the tea.

"What is it?" asks Grandmata, enthusiastically grabbing her cup.

"Nutmeg," says Kala.

"It's good," says Grandpata.

"Lively," says Grandmata.

"Just like old times," says Grandpata.

They're equally enthusiastic about the cinnamon on the strawberries.

"Back to the story," I say. "As you know, I was captured by Kala."

"Evil Kala," jokes Grandpata.

"Yes. I was captured by evil Kala and her parents and taken to the South. We're living there on a farm with a woman called Dana. The main crop we grow is wheat, but we've also got cows and chickens, and we grow vegetables.

"The problem is that some of the farms are getting rust in their wheat. They're having to burn entire fields to stop it spreading. We're worried the same will happen to all the wheat fields, including ours. We're after a way to treat the rust without burning. Do you know anything about sulphur based fungicide?"

Grandpata lifts his head and slowly reclines his chair.

"Sulphur based fungicide," he says thoughtfully. "I remember farmers using fungicides but I don't know exactly what they used. People would just say 'fungicide'."

"What about you, Grandmata?" I ask.

"No, people only said 'fungicide'. I remember using it on our tomato plants."

"Do you remember where it came from?"

"We just got it from the farming shop."

"Any chance the shop is still there?" asks Kala.

She's being extremely optimistic. There were shops in the old times, but they're virtually all gone now. They all went after the dream work started. No one needed shops when you could get everything you needed from dream work.

"Wasn't it down on Orchard Road?" says Grandmata.

"Yes, I think it was there," says Grandpata. "But those old shops went over ten years ago. It's all dream houses there now."

"That means no fungicide," I say. "I'm afraid that our trip has been wasted."

"At least I'm getting to meet your grandparents," says Kala.

She's right. I'm glad to see them too.

"How bad is the rust?" asks Grandmata.

"It's not too bad yet," I reply. "We don't have it in our wheat. It's just that it could get worse and the only thing we can do is to burn it."

"I see," says Grandpata.

"Do you like it there?" asks Grandmata.

I tighten my grip on Kala's hand, wondering how I should explain how good it is to be with Kala.

"Well, there's no dream work there, so there's different work to do ... but yes, I like it." I pause and look to Kala before continuing, "I have a lot to learn but I already feel like I belong there. It's like there's a purpose to us being there. Maybe we were destined for this life. I think we'll be there a long time. We might have children one day."

Who said that? I'm shocked at my own words. I'm only sixteen and talking about children.

"And the food is amazing," I add. "They have herbs and spices, and everything tastes better than anything I'd ever had before."

"What are the people like?" asks Grandpata.

"They don't live close to each other but they are a tight group. They help each other to get things done. It's just like here, I guess, except they all get to choose what they do every day. It's a community but everyone has the freedom to make their own choices."

"And they're treating you okay?" asks Grandmata.

"Yes," I say. "They even gave us our own farm. They've been good to us and that's why we're here. We want to try to repay that kindness. I hoped that we could get something to help with the rust."

"It was Tomas' idea," says Kala.

"You say this fungicide is sulphur based?" asks Grandpata.

"Yes," I say.

"The only place I know that has sulphur is the hot spring. You know the one out along Mountain Creek Road?"

"The place we went swimming?" checks Grandmata.

"The place we went skinny dipping," replies Grandpata cheekily.

Grandmata is smiling—it must be true.

"I was always told that the rotten smell you got around there was from the sulphur," continues Grandpata. "I guess you could collect the sulphur. Or the water there might already contain the sulphur. It could be a ready-made fungicide."

"That's fantastic!" I say. "Can you tell us where it is?"

"There's a map in one of those boxes," says Grandmata, walking to the laundry.

I'm tempted to go with her, but I stay seated, enthusiastically patting Kala's leg.

"Here you go," says Grandmata a few minutes later, handing me a map.

It's a folded paper titled 'Norden and Surrounds'—in good condition except for some deterioration along the fold lines. Looking at the map I notice that the layout of Norden is different. The urban centre is based on the northern side of a 'Haystack River'. There are five suburbs, spread out like arms from the centre. It must be Norden layout pre-dream work. Haystack River is now called the Zennuta River and there's very little left of the urban centre. All of it has been redeveloped with dream houses, planned schools and straight roads.

"There it is," says Kala, pointing. "Mountain Creek Road."

"Was it far along the road?" I ask.

"I don't remember exactly," says Grandpata. "Try about there," he adds, pointing to a track marked on the map.

"I remember a car park and walking along a track," adds Grandmata.

"I hope it's still there," I say.

"It should be there," says Grandpata. "It's just a matter of finding it."

"Shall we give it a try?" I suggest to Kala.

"Why are you even asking?"

"I guess we'll be going there tomorrow then," I say, happy that our rust treatment plan still has a chance.

"Hey," says Grandpata. "It would also be great if you came back in a few weeks to visit us again. You could stay a few days."

I'm not sure how to respond. Right now, all I can think about is the hot spring, the rust in the wheat and Norden moving further and further south.

"Maybe we can come back in three or four weeks. It will depend on whether Seamus will let us use his car again though."

"I hope you can make it," says Grandmata.

"Can we take these with us?" I ask, holding the map and the book.

"Take them," says Grandpata. "We've no use for them. Take some of the other books too if you like."

***

After supper, I'm yawning. Kala and I wish Grandmata and Grandpata good night. Grandmata says that we have the room that was once my father's bedroom. There's only a single bed but I look forward to being in it and close to Kala. Grandmata doesn't seem to mind that we'll be in the same bed. We're soon nestled tightly under the bedcovers.

"They're so sweet," says Kala.

"Yes, they are."

"And your Grandpata. He's an ideas man."

"And Grandmata's an action woman," I jest.

"You're just like them," says Kala.

"I'd like to be."

I hold Kala tightly. I feel affection and strength flowing through her arms. We touch and whisper for a while before giving each other our good night wishes.

11. The hot spring

I'm sad to be leaving my grandparents but excited about our planned trip to the hot spring and collecting a potential treatment for the wheat.

Grandmata found us four large containers for the spring water. Grandpata helped me fill the car with the fuel from Seamus' drum. We're now standing beside the car and ready to go.

"Do you want to drive?" I ask.

"No, you drive and I'll navigate."

"Something for your trip," says Grandmata, handing me a bag of food. It's practically the entire lunch that appeared in their cupboard this morning.

"Thank you," I say, giving her a loving forehead farewell and a huge hug. I squeeze her tightly and whisper another "Thank you."

"Sweet dreams, my boy," she says and she's crying.

Grandpata's embrace is just as tight and he also has tears.

"You're worthy of that pendant," he says.

I'd nearly forgotten it. I take it out from under my shirt. "It's yours Grandpata."

"No, it's yours," he says. "Wear it well."

"I'll try."

They embrace Kala as warmly as me, even wishing her the same sweet dreams.

"See you in a few weeks," says Grandpata.

"Yes, see you then," says Kala.

"Any message for your parents?" asks Grandmata.

Her question soothes my emotions. I do have a message. It should be that I love them, but there's also something else.

"Tell them that I love them. And tell them that I'm with Kala and we're both okay."

"Okay."

"And can you tell them something else?"

"Sure."

"Tell them there are a thousand people in the South."

"A thousand people? But we're told there are only a hundred."

"Well, that's not true. And there isn't any Island of Contemplation either."

"I've always been suspicious about that island prison," says Grandpata. "But, a thousand people in the South. Are there really that many? The Dream Council keep saying how few people there are down there and how they're so poor, they're always stealing."

"A thousand people," I confirm, not adding more. I'm keen to get going. I reverse tentatively, back along the driveway and past the old apple tree, but stop the car there.

"What is it?" asks Kala.

"It's that tree. I always liked it. Its apples were lumpy and sour, but I always took one. I liked that they weren't perfect."

I run out and twist two apples from the tree and dash back to hug my grandparents again, now in the front garden before returning to the car.

***

The first part of our route to the hot spring takes us through Norden, back the way we came. We pass three dream cars, all going the other way. Again, the people stare. Now, looking in the rear vision mirror, I'm seeing a black car about one hundred metres behind us.

"Right here," says Kala.

I turn right at the corner and soon after I see that the car behind has also turned.

"There's a car behind us," I say.

Kala turns. "I see it."

"It took the last turn as well. It might be following us."

"Try not to worry. Let's see what happens when we're out of Norden."

"I'd rather find out now," I say, taking the next left.

It follows us around the corner and then again at the next left. I'm getting nervous. I take the next left and again it follows.

"This will confirm it," I say, taking the left that will see us back on our original course. And there it is. It has followed us all the way around the block.

"What now?" I ask.

"Well, they know that we know that they're following us," says Kala.

She's right, but I can't see that it makes that much difference.

"We can't exactly outrun them," I say.

"If it's the Dream Patrol and they were going to arrest us they would have done it already. All we can do is keep going to the spring as we planned."

"How much further do you think?"

"Another two kilometres, then a right, then left onto Mountain Creek Road. It looks like forty kilometres from there to the track your Grandpata showed us. That's about half an hour I guess."

Kala is calmer than me. I can feel myself sweating.

"It'll be okay," she says, placing her hand on my leg.

"Sure," I say, straining a smile.

We take the right turn and it's not long before we see the next junction. Mountain Creek Road is a dirt road and I wonder if the dream car can follow us there. Seamus said they weren't good on dirt roads.

We take the turn and I watch to see if it follows us. Unfortunately, though, it makes the turn and continues behind us, easily maintaining the same distance. That's worrying. Kala sees it too, but we don't say anything. For a while I try to forget about it and try to look at the rear vision mirror less often. I decide that I should drive normally. The problem is that I'm not sure what normal is. Maybe it is normal to watch other cars in the rear vision mirror.

"I've got an idea," I say. "Let's just be normal at the spring."

"Okay?" says Kala quizzically.

"Maybe we can have a swim or something."

"Okay. Good idea, but we don't have bathers."

I raise my eyebrows. "Neither did my grandparents."

Kala laughs. "You are a chip off the old block," she says.

"What's that mean?"

"It's a saying from the old times. My grandfather says that it means that you are just like your Grandpata."

"I hope so," I say, feeling my pendant.

***

We arrive at what Kala has guessed to be the car park for the spring. Old logs seem to define a parking area, although some of the gravel has been invaded by grass and small shrubs.

We take the lunch bag and two containers each and take off along an overgrown path that we find at the edge of the car park. Looking back, I expect to see the black car, but it isn't there.

The track winds through patches of thick bush. It's undulating, but mostly downhill. In a few places the track isn't easy to follow but each time we're able to find the line of the path a little further along.

After around ten minutes and perhaps only 500 metres, we come to a grassy clearing with a marshy pond at the centre.

"This must be it!" I say confidently, noticing a rotten smell.

"Yippee!" says Kala.

The pond water is brown, a bit like the colour of brewed tea and a stark contrast to vivid green of the surrounding plants. One edge of the pond is thick with reeds. The other end, where a creek enters, has a grassy beach. It's very pretty. I'd say idyllic if it weren't for the foul smell.

"It must be the sulphur that Grandpata was talking about. It's terrible."

"This place is beautiful," notes Kala. "It's just like our dreams, only this is better."

She's right. We couldn't have dreamed of anything so pretty. If only it didn't have the awful smell. Kala drops her two containers and puts her hand in the water.

"Perfect," she announces and removes her shoes, socks and then her shirt.

I check back along the path. The view is obscured by trees. What I can see is clear, but that isn't great assurance. The people from the black car could be anywhere. Now Kala's taking off her pants. That's enough for me. I rush to catch up, stumbling as I pull off my pants.

Kala is naked. She's beautiful. She enters the spring ahead of me. I join her and we're both there, nude in the hot spring together, just as my grandparents were, years ago. I feel a slight breeze on my face.

"This is perfect," I say, holding Kala.

I look around. The track seems clear. I return my focus to Kala. She's smiling at me.

"Thank you," I say quietly, kissing her gently.

"For what?" she whispers.

"For being you and for rescuing me."

"That's okay. I actually think we rescued each other. I wouldn't have gone alone."

"You know what?" she says.

"What?"

"I think that this, right now, is our passage. I feel like I've grown up, and more today than any other day."

"I know what you mean. The spring water might work or it might fail, but, we've done something. I agree. Today can be our passage day."

I'm holding Kala, naked in the water. It's just Kala and me in the spring in this moment.

"I'm with you," I say.

"I'm with you," she says. But then she takes a mouthful of the tea-like water and blows it onto my face. "I declare us to be grown up," she says, before dunking herself in the brown water.

That's my Kala. I grab her and bring her to the surface. "You're fantastic," I say before kissing her with a mouth full of water.

We kiss again, this time, more passionately. I pull Kala into me, holding tightly. "I'm taking you ashore," I decide. Kala smiles, knowing exactly what I want.

I carry Kala out of the spring and gently place her on a soft patch of grass; hovering there for a moment, admiring the softness of her skin, the inviting curve of her hips, and the wanting look she has for me.

"Tomas," she whispers. "Make love to me."

We've touched each other many times by now but we haven't yet made love. "Are you sure?" I whisper.

"Yes," she says, pulling my hand between her thighs.

I need no further encouragement. I'm with Kala. This is amazing. We're moist and warm and we're wanting. The people from the black car could be watching us, but I don't care. I'm totally with Kala and I know she's with me. This really is our passage.

***

We've lain tightly on the grass for what I guess is half an hour, not saying a lot, just whispering and holding each other. I don't want to move, but I'm beginning to worry about the time.

"How about we warm up?" I suggest.

"I don't want to move," says Kala, sleepily. She has her hand on my hip and she pulls me slightly towards her and again I'm stirred.

I pause above her for just for a moment. "You're beautiful!"

"No, you are," she replies.

I feel so lucky. She's gorgeous and she wants me the way I want her.

***

Back in the hot spring, I'm soon overheating. The water must be warmer than our body temperature. I'm standing at the edge with most of my body out of the water. Kala is beside me, standing bare breasted and proud above the water.

The only distraction for me is time slipping away. Maybe we should go soon.

"Sulphur?" I ask. I haven't seen anything that I could identify as sulphur. We're just going to have to collect the water.

"Do you want to go?" asks Kala, moving from the water and sitting naked on the grass.

I reply by getting out and sitting beside her. "This is a wonderful place," I say, looking at the spring and the bush.

"This can be our place," declares Kala. "It could be from one of our dreams."

"Was it as you dreamt it would be?" I ask.

"It was better. You're better than any dream."

"I love you."

"I love you, too," replies Kala and we kiss again.

Being with Kala and being here at the spring is better than anything we could dream.

***

"Maybe we should eat," says Kala.

I'd forgotten all about the food! I walk over to the food bag that we left with the containers.

"Let's eat and get going," I say. "But I want to come back here again."

I'm sure that what I mean is that I want to be here, together like this, again. That goes without saying!

"This is our place. Of course we'll come back," says Kala, grinning.

We scoff the food Grandmata gave us. The fruit and vegetables look fantastic, but have little taste.

A Dream Passage

I hand two containers to Kala and take the other two for myself. We fill them by submerging them in the spring water and watching the air bubble out. The containers are now very heavy to lift. I'm tempted to let some of the water out to make them lighter. The trouble is that we don't know how much spring water we'll need. The more we have, the better.

I glance up the path as I dress. I'm still wet and the clothes stick to me. It feels icky but that isn't what is bothering me: it's that black car.

"Let's get some big sticks," says Kala, slipping on her shoes. "We can use them to carry the containers."

We search the bush until we find two suitable branches about five centimetres in diameter and two metres long. I feed them through the container handles, two containers on each stick. Lifting them is heavy and our walking is awkward.

We're only about 100 metres along the path when suddenly there's a *crack* from the bush ahead, to the right of where I guess the path goes.

"Did you hear that?" asks Kala.

"It's like someone threw a rock at a tree. Let's get out of here."

We try moving faster, but our load is heavy.

"Do you think we need all of it?" I ask. There must be 300 metres to go.

"We may as well take our time and take it all. If they're after us, they're going to get us."

We don't have to wonder for long. There's someone on the path, about sixty metres ahead.

"Tomas," says Kala.

"I know. Is it just one?" Patrol officers usually travel in pairs.

"I only see one."

"Let's keep going."

Getting closer, I see that it's a man of about my height wearing the grey uniform of the Dream Patrol. There's little we can do. He's between us and our car. We keep going until we're about ten metres short of him.

"What do you want?" asks Kala, dropping her end of the sticks.

The man stands there for a while, saying nothing.

"What do you want?" repeats Kala.

"What are you doing with that?" he replies.

"It's water for our plants," I say. "What do you want?"

"Are you Kala?" he asks.

"Yes," replies Kala.

"I've been asked to take you in for questioning."

"About what?" asks Kala.

"Kidnapping."

"Kidnapping me?" I question. "That's ridiculous. As you can see, I'm here by choice."

"It's nothing personal. She's on our list. I'm just doing my job."

"If it's nothing personal, then you can leave us alone."

"Too late for that. I've reported you and your car. You'll have to come with me."

A Dream Passage

I move in front of Kala. "She's not going anywhere," I say, although I've got no idea how I can stop him. He's looks stronger than me and I can see that he has the standard issue patrol officer stun gun. He'll be trained for this kind of thing. My chances against him in anything physical are poor. All I have are words and my less than intimidating stare.

Just a minute! Something in my head twigs. I have an image of this guy in my mind. It's an image of him in a photo.

"Wait a minute," I say. "I know you! You're Harrop!"

He's silent.

"Are you Harrop?" asks Kala.

"That's my name," he says. "But, I don't know you."

I weigh up what to say next. Maybe I shouldn't mention Dana at all. I don't want to get her in any more trouble. From what I recall Dana loved him but Harrop chose to stay in Norden. Still, what damage can it do now?

"Dana showed me a picture of you," I say.

"You know Dana?!" he asks, surprised.

"We live with her."

"Really?! How is she?"

"She is well. She still thinks about you."

"Really?"

"Yes. I think she still cares about you. Maybe there's still a chance for you."

"A chance for us? No, you're wrong. There was never a chance for us. They were never going to let Zennuta's daughter marry a man like me."

"Dana is Zennuta's daughter?!" I say, stunned.

163

"Yes, that's right; Zennuta's daughter. She didn't mention that?"

I can barely believe it. He's got no reason to lie about it though, and Dana is short for Danata, which is 'daughter' in the old language. It could very well be true.

"No, she didn't mention it," I say.

"I suppose they keep it quiet … same as they do in Norden. Anyway, none of that changes this situation. I'm here to take you in."

He's looking past me to Kala.

"Did they make you become a patrol officer?" I ask.

"This isn't about me," he says, avoiding the question.

"It's not too late," I say. "You can come with us … to Dana."

He pauses. His body seems tense.

"I can't. That decision was made long ago. Now, come on Kala, you need to come with me," he says, retrieving a pair of handcuffs from his pocket.

"No," I say. "You can't have her."

He moves forward towards Kala. He's going to walk straight past me like I don't exist.

"No!" I say and my grip tightens on the sticks we used to carry the containers. Before I know what's happening I've dropped the stick I held in my right hand and I've instinctively raised the other stick above my head.

Heave, drop, hit! I've used the stick just like the way I used the mattock. This time though, I've hit a man and he clearly didn't expect it. I've caught him on the temple with a solid blow and he's fallen to the ground in front of me. I think he's unconscious.

"Tomas," says Kala.

What have I done? It was all so sudden and instinctive. I'm horrified.

"Is he okay?" I ask.

We both kneel to check him. I move him onto his side, like I was shown in the first aid lesson at school. There's a red bump on his head.

"I can feel a pulse," says Kala. "And he's breathing. He should be okay."

I'm relieved. Kala and I look at each other.

"Should we take him with us?" I ask.

"Well, I don't think we can leave him here."

He's twitching. He'll be conscious very soon and he won't be happy.

"Let's go," I say.

"Hang on," says Kala, picking up the handcuffs from the ground beside him and searching for the key in his pocket.

"There you go," she says, cuffing him and placing the keys she found in her own pocket. She also takes his identification pass.

"We can't leave him here," I say.

"A minute ago you were hitting him and leaving," says Kala. "And now you're all worried about him?"

She's smiling.

"Let's take him back to his car," she adds. "But leave his pass here. He'll need his pass to start his car."

"Good idea."

Kala pours some of the spring water into her hand and splashes it on his face. Harrop stirs again and opens his eyes. He struggles with his arms but then stops.

"What happened?" he asks.

"I'm sorry," I say. "I hit you with a stick. Are you okay?"

"Get these cuffs off me."

"The cuffs are staying on," says Kala. "You're going to walk back to your car now. We're going to leave your pass here. When we go, we'll give you the key to the handcuffs and you can come back and get your pass."

"And if I don't come with you?"

"Suit yourself. We'll take the handcuffs' key and your pass with us."

I can see him thinking.

"I'll come," he says begrudgingly.

"Good," says Kala. "We'll leave your pass here beside this rock."

"Okay."

"Where's your partner?" I ask.

He hesitates to answer.

"What do you mean?"

"You have a patrol partner, don't you?" checks Kala.

"Yes, I've got one."

"So, where are they?"

Again, he's hesitating.

"Any other day and he'd be back at the car but he was sick today and so I'm on my own. You got lucky."

"One more question," says Kala. "Why the black car?"

"It's one of the plain patrol cars. We use them for surveillance."

"Surveillance?" I query.

"Watching out for people like you."

"Oh," I say. I had no idea the Dream Patrol had such cars.

He sits quietly as we reposition the sticks through the container handles, lift and recommence our awkward walk towards the car park.

"What are you doing with the water?" he asks.

"We told you what it was for," says Kala. "The hit must have affected your memory."

"You can tell me again."

"I'm sure you'll remember. Just give it some time."

I start to think about what he might say in his report. "You don't have to tell anyone about what happened here," I suggest. "You could just say that you lost track of us."

"Or you followed a car but it was just two old people going for a swim," offers Kala.

"I'm not in the habit of lying," he says.

"Well, the Dream Council isn't so principled," says Kala. "They lie all the time. And you know it, don't you?"

He doesn't reply. I appreciate his position. I wouldn't want to lie either. "You're right," I say. "It's best if you don't lie. I sometimes say nothing if I don't want to lie."

"Saying nothing isn't necessarily being honest," he says.

I agree with that too, although I don't say it.

Our walk with the water is slow but we don't have far to go. We're soon at the car park with Harrop's black car parked next to ours. It's a relief to set the heavy water down. Harrop silently watches us load the water into Seamus' car.

"You can change your mind," I say. "Come with us."

"Thanks, but no. I've made my choices."

"All right then," I say. Without thinking, I put my arm on his shoulder and I give him a forehead farewell.

"Dream well," he says.

"We are," says Kala. "We're living our dreams."

We get into the car and I start the engine.

"The key," yells Harrop.

"Here," says Kala and throws the handcuffs' key to the ground near him.

"Tell Dana I said hello."

"Sure," says Kala. "Better if you told her yourself, though."

And we're off, with four full containers of spring water.

***

"Where to now?" asks Kala.

"I don't know. I hadn't thought any further than getting the sulphur. To a farm with some rust?" I suggest.

"How about four farms? That way we can have four people prove or disprove the treatment."

"Good plan," I say, placing my hand on Kala's leg. "You're a chop off the block too."

"You mean a chip off the old block?"

"Oh, yeah. You're a chip off your old blocks," I say.

"Thanks, my action man," she says smiling.

I'm still shocked about what I did. I hit Harrop hard. He could have been badly injured.

"I'm sorry that I hit him. I don't know where it came from. I've never hurt anyone before."

"It's totally okay. If it wasn't for that, he'd have taken me."

"I know, but he could have been seriously hurt. I don't want to be a violent person."

"Don't worry; you're not a violent person. You only did what had to be done."

"I suppose so," I say, but I'm not convinced.

***

"Car," says Kala.

I see what she means. There's a car approaching us on the other side of the road. We're on the main road and we should expect other cars, but given what's happened, it could be a patrol car. If he ran, Harrop could have collected his card, returned to his car, and radioed someone to pick us up by now.

I'm holding my breath as it approaches. I hold the wheel as steady as I can.

"Act normal," I say, but we both gawk at the car as it passes. It's only an old couple though. They look about the same age as my grandparents.

Kala laughs. "We were very normal, weren't we?"

"Yes," I laugh. "We're just like all the other sixteen-year olds heading to the South."

***

It's now dark. Kala is slumped in the passenger seat, asleep. I was able to rest for a few hours while Kala drove but I didn't sleep. My brain is still buzzing from what happened with Harrop.

I looked at the farming book for a while. I kept on going back to the page with the rust treatment, each time expecting to find more information. Every time though, I found nothing other than 'sulphur based fungicide'.

I've been wondering what Harrop has reported, whether the spring water will work and what we can do to stop Norden moving south.

My mind has been cycling for hours now. Sometimes I feel my eyelids dropping. I should stop to rest, but even that thought is lazy. Something in my head is telling me that we need to be back at home in the South tonight, but I've forgotten why.

I see a star. It begins to move. It's almost dancing. Fancy that, a dancing star. I have to stop. I just need a suitable place to park. Or do I? I could just stop on the side of the road here. Hang on, there's a turn off. That's what I need. I take the turn, drive a further one hundred metres and pull over. I'm so tired.

12. Treatment

I wake to warmth and movement. Sunshine and Kala!

"Sweet dreams?" she asks and I feel her kiss on my forehead.

"Still tired," I mumble. "You okay?"

"Yes, good, but hungry. Do you know where we are?"

"Not really. On the plain somewhere. I'd guess around three hours from home."

"That's okay. We're in no rush," says Kala, stretching and grinning.

"What are you smiling about?" I ask, taking hold of her.

"Yesterday was a good day."

"Yes," I say, remembering. "It sure was."

***

Kala has been driving for around two hours now. We've passed the plains and now we're seeing the first of the cultivated farm land.

We've been reliving yesterday's events, from when we left my grandparents' house, our time at the spring, Harrop, and seeing the other car. It's been good but I'm also hungry now. The only thing we've had to eat in the car was the sour apples from my grandparents' tree.

"There," I say, pointing at some smoke in the distance. I guess that's about a kilometre on our left. "You see it?"

"Yes," says Kala. "Maybe they're burning wheat. Want to take a look?"

"Sure," I say, but I'm thinking more about the prospect of food than the wheat.

"Yeah!" says Kala enthusiastically.

We pass several dirt roads, each remarkably straight. Kala continues along the main road until we reach a point where we appear to be level with the smoke.

"This one," she says, turning the car left onto the single lane dirt road. The car vibrates from the corrugation in the road.

As we near the smoke, we confirm that it's a wheat field burning. And there are people on the road ahead—a man and a woman. Both are wearing blue shirts with their sleeves rolled. They're charred and untidy. The man is tall and solid and has a flaming torch in his hand. He's walking along the edge of the field and lighting the wheat at intervals. The woman is looking at us. As we near, I recognise her.

"It's Anita."

Kala stops the car beside her. The man walks over.

"Hello, Anita," says Kala.

"Hello ... Kala? Hello, Tomas. What are you two doing here?"

We get out and greet her with a forehead touch.

"This is my husband, Leroy. Leroy, this is Kala and Tomas. Kala is Paros and Neros' daughter."

We greet Leroy. His hands are blackened. He keeps looking back at the burning field.

"What brings you here?" repeats Anita.

"We've got a treatment to try on the wheat," replies Kala.

"Something for the rust?" asks Leroy.

"Yes," says Kala. "We hope it'll work as a fungicide. It's in the containers in the back."

"Did Dana send you?"

"No, it was Tomas' idea."

"We're not sure it will work," I say. "It's water from a hot spring."

"Where did you get it?"

"Just outside Norden," says Kala.

"You went to Norden?" asks Leroy, clearly surprised.

"Yes. I remembered that my grandparents had an old farming book. That's how we found out that rust could be treated using a sulphur based fungicide. Hopefully the spring water has enough sulphur in it to work."

"It's worth a try," says Anita.

"I'll try anything," adds Leroy. "We're burning this field today and that one tomorrow."

The wheat in the other field is tall, but looks dry and yellow in patches.

"Could we try it on that field?" I ask.

"Why don't you come up to the house? We'll have some tea and make a plan," says Anita. "And, you can meet our children."

"Sounds good," I say. "I'll get the book from the car."

The house is on a slight hill, only a short walk away from where we've parked. Anita directs us to a table on a wide veranda that extends around the entire house. The house itself is an impressive construction of large, earth coloured blocks. I've seen nothing like it before.

Two children, a boy and a girl, are seated at the table and staring at us. The boy is tall and thin. He could be my age. The girl looks similarly slender, but she's younger. Both have blonde hair, like Anita.

"This is our son, Teague, who's fifteen and our daughter, Rachus, thirteen," says Anita. "Meet Tomas and Kala."

"Are you the two from Norden?" asks Rachus.

"Yes, that's us," I say as we greet them in the usual way.

"These two aren't much older than you," continues Anita. "And they've chosen to live here in the South."

"Why would you live down here?" asks Teague.

"We wanted to follow our own dreams," says Kala.

"But, you could have had an easy life in Norden," says Teague. "You get your food from dreams. You don't even have to work. Why would you choose this?"

"It's not easy to explain unless you've lived there," says Kala. "Norden is good in some ways, but you don't have freedom."

"I'm going to Norden as soon as I'm sixteen."

I'm surprised by Teague's comments, and particularly the idea that someone from the South would prefer to be in Norden.

"That's your choice when you're sixteen," says Leroy.

"That's what I'm choosing," says Teague. "It's nothing but hard work around here."

"You're lucky to have a choice," I say. "If it weren't for Kala and her parents, I wouldn't have had that choice."

"Where will you live?" asks Kala.

"I don't know," says Teague.

"We'll work it out for him if he makes that choice," says Leroy.

I can't believe how open they are with each other. We've barely met and already they've told me so much about their family situation. Rachus is staring at me.

"I like your house," I say.

"What's it made of?" asks Kala.

"It's mud brick," says Anita. "We built it ourselves."

"Was it hard?" I ask.

"No, it's just dirt, grass and water to make the bricks," replies Leroy. "But, it took us a whole year just to make the walls."

"A bit longer than a Dream house," I say.

"Yes, but you won't find a house like this one anywhere," says Leroy. "Come inside and I'll show you the wooden floors. They're made from the pine we have in our plantation."

"Leroy is a carpenter," says Anita. "Have a look at what he did in the kitchen."

The wood flooring is made from timber of varying lengths, all mixed in together. It's smooth and polished though. The kitchen is also made of wood. The timber bench has two types of wood. The edge of the bench is a darker wood, an attractive contrast to the lighter wood at the centre.

Anita takes a pot from the stove and pours us tea. Leroy adds milk and sugar, stirs the tea and takes the cups. I hold the door for him as he returns outside to the veranda.

"The wood is beautiful," I say. "You wouldn't think the odd lengths in the flooring would work, but it looks fantastic."

"It's the variations in the length, colour and grain that make it work," says Leroy.

"Did you make the table, too?" I ask, referring to the long table with fat legs at the end of the room. "It's twice as long as the table we have."

"Anita and I made that. It's big enough to seat us and the people we get in to help with the harvest."

"Maybe we could help you sometime," I say as we return to the veranda.

"I think you're already helping."

"It might not work."

"Well, what's your plan?"

"Just a minute," says Anita, carrying a plate of biscuits to the table.

Kala quickly takes a biscuit and I follow.

"Oh!" I say. "They're good."

"You two look hungry," says Anita. "I'll make you a sandwich."

"Thanks," I say and then pause before adding, "You were asking about the plan for the fungicide ..."

"Yes," says Leroy.

"Well, it isn't much of a plan," I continue. "We have four containers of spring water and we'd like to try it at four different locations. I think sites that are infected but aren't too far gone would be best. The problem is that we're not sure of the concentration of sulphur so we won't know how much spring water to use or how often to use it. I'd like to try different approaches at each of the four sites and see if anything works."

"Do you know of any suitable places?" asks Kala.

"There are plenty of infected places," says Leroy. "We have a spot here and there are other sites on farms nearby. You won't have to go far."

"Why don't you leave it with us?" offers Anita. "We'll see that it gets tested and we'll give Dana the results over the radio."

"That would be great," says Kala.

"Could we see it used on your field?" I ask.

"Sure," says Leroy. "We'll do it this afternoon. I'd rather be spraying than burning," he adds, looking at his blackened arms.

"Do you have something to use as a spray?" I ask.

"We've got a backpack pump we use for putting out fires," says Leroy.

"Seems fitting, doesn't it," notes Anita. "Hopefully your spring water will put out all the fires."

"Yes," I say with a slight smile. "I just hope it works."

"I'm glad to be trying something," says Leroy, warmly.

"What was the spring like?" asks Anita.

"Well," says Kala. "It's about 500 metres from a car park. It's in a grassy clearing, surrounded by forest. The water is dark like tea but it's the right temperature for a swim and there's a leaf litter base that tickles your toes."

"It sounds beautiful," says Anita.

"Oh, it was," says Kala. "We'd love to go back," she adds, squeezing my hand.

"Is it far from Norden?" asks Leroy.

"It's about an hour away," I say. "My grandparents used to go there to swim."

"Nude," adds Kala.

"Really?" says Anita.

"We might have to take a look at these springs," says Leroy, giving Anita a wink.

"We'll have to see if it works first," says Anita, overstating her return wink.

"Any trouble with the Dream Patrol?" asks Leroy.

"We were followed ... but we managed to get away," replies Kala without explaining further.

"You were lucky," says Anita. "I heard they were looking for you."

"I'm wanted for kidnapping this one," says Kala.

"Can I ask you a question?" says Teague.

"Sure," says Kala.

"What is the passage ceremony like?"

"The passage?" says Kala. "It's all symbolic. You wear a fancy costume and you travel on canoes, with other boys and girls on your way to the Passage Hall.

A Dream Passage

"At the hall, you hold hands, sing songs and make a pledge to dream well, commit your allegiance to the Dream Council, and say that you will follow the dream rules. From there, you start your dream work."

"It sounds fantastic," says Teague with glowing eyes.

"It's really just a show," says Kala. "And after you take the passage you lose your freedom."

"You're no longer able to dream your own dreams or make your own decisions," I add. "Here, you can choose to go to Norden, but once you're there, you'll lose all your choice. They might not let you come back."

"That's what worries me," says Leroy.

13. Back at the farm

Kala and I are on the road again. I'm driving. We've been talking about Anita and Leroy.

"Teague's comments were interesting," I say.

"Yeah, that surprised me, too."

"We'll have to ask Dana about it. And Rachus was bit odd. She kept staring at us."

"I think I can explain that one," offers Kala. "She wasn't staring at us. She was staring at you. I think she likes you."

"Really?"

"What thirteen-year-old girl wouldn't like you? You're a good-looking man. And you've raided Norden, escaped from the Dream Patrol, and you might just save the entire wheat crop. You look like a hero!"

"That's ridiculous. Besides, it was as much you as it was me."

"It's not ridiculous to a thirteen-year-old girl."

"Or me," adds Kala, putting her hand on my leg, smiling and fluttering her eyelids.

"Well, thanks for that!" I say.

I'm not sure what to make of all that. Kala seems serious. I shake my head. "Hopefully Rachus will meet someone her own age."

***

We're welcomed at Seamus' house by Spike barking and wagging his tail. I park just outside the shed.

"Yer drivin' better than ya did when ya left," says a rough-looking Seamus, sidling up to the car.

"Thanks for loaning us your car, Seamus," I say. "My grandfather says it's a classic."

"That it is," replies Seamus, slowly, admiring the old car. "Well, how'd ya go, then? Did you get the book you were after?"

"Yes, here it is," I say, showing him the book.

"And we brought back a treatment to try on the rust," adds Kala.

"We're not sure it will work, though," I say.

"What's ya treatment?"

"The book says sulphur based fungicide," I answer. "But we couldn't get any of that, so we're trying water from the hot spring. We're guessing it has sulphur in it."

"From that spring near Norden?"

"Yes, you know it?"

"I had meself a few dalliances there back in the old times."

I'm not sure what a dalliance is, but I am amazed that he's been to the hot spring. It's hard to imagine Seamus being far away from his farm ... although he does have his car. I suppose he could have gone anywhere he wanted.

"What's a dalliance?" I ask.

"It's just a bit of a swim, a drink and what not."

"Oh, well, we had a dalliance down at the spring then," says Kala earnestly.

"Well good luck to ya," says Seamus, giving us a wink in the same way Grandpata did.

181

"Seems like there was a lot of dalliancing in the old times," I say, returning his wink.

"That there was. They was good times," says Seamus, giving us a slight grin.

"Anyway," I say. "Thanks again for the loan of the car."

"Any time ya want it, ya can 'ave it."

"Thanks. We might need to go back for more spring water in a week or two."

"Sure," he says. "I might come with ya."

"Sure," I say as we start walking towards our house, although I'm wondering what it would be like to be on a long journey with Seamus. Maybe it would be okay, I decide. He seems to have warmed to us.

***

And, we're home! I'm tired and relieved to be home. Looking at Kala, I'm pretty sure she feels the same. We share a touch of hands and a warm look before opening the door.

Dana is sitting at the table.

"Hello, you two. It's great to see you!" she says. "Would you like some tea?"

She has two cups ready for us.

"Oh, yes, please," says Kala, laying down her bag and easing into a chair. I soon follow.

"You two did well," says Dana.

"You've been speaking with Anita?" I say.

"Yes, we talked on the radio. It won't be long before everyone knows about your trip and the treatment."

"We don't know it will work."

"It doesn't matter," says Dana, pouring our tea. "You've given us hope and that should stabilise things around here for a while."

"For a few weeks anyway," I say. "We still have the problem with Norden."

"Tell me about your trip," says Dana, passing us our tea. "And how were your grandparents?"

I look at Kala. "They were well," I say and then pause.

"We've got something to tell you," says Kala.

"Sounds serious," says Dana.

"Harrop followed us to the hot springs," continues Kala. "He wanted to take me in for questioning. And he would have if Tomas hadn't stopped him."

"Tomas stopped Harrop?" queries Dana, wide-eyed.

I can understand her questioning it.

"Yes, Tomas stopped Harrop. He stopped him with a stick."

"And we handcuffed him," I add.

"You hit him with a stick?"

"Yes. He's okay though," I reply.

"Yes, Harrop is fine," continues Kala. "He would have taken me in if it weren't for Tomas."

"So, you hit Harrop him and handcuffed him?"

"Yes," answers Kala, "But then we let him go. He said to say hello to you."

"What else did he say?"

"We asked him to come with us," I say.

"What did he say to that?"

"He said those decisions were made long ago."

"The way he said it though," adds Kala. "I could tell that he cares for you."

"Did he say anything else?"

"Well, yes ..." I say, hesitantly.

"What?"

"He told us about you. You're not just Dana. You're actually *the Danata*; daughter of Zennuta."

"He told you that?"

"Is it true?" I ask.

"Well, yes, it is true," admits Dana, speaking slowly. "It isn't really a secret. It just isn't something that I talk about. There aren't many people who know about it. The Dream Council keep it quiet too—they don't want anyone to know that the Southern leader is Zennuta's daughter."

"Why don't you tell people?" I ask.

"It won't help us. Telling everyone would anger the Dream Council and that would put us all in danger; Harrop too."

"What happened with Harrop?" asks Kala.

"That was long ago now. Harrop and I were a bit like you—we were young and in love. We spent every minute we could together. Our favourite thing was to walk in the bush near Harrop's parents' farm. It was just outside Norden. It was through his parents that I learnt about the South.

"I was sixteen and Harrop was seventeen. Things were good for a while. But then my dad died and everything fell apart. My parent's tenets of openness and honesty were soon set aside in the name of progress. It was then that the Dream Council became more controlling and vastly increased the numbers in their Dream Patrol. They told us we could not marry."

"Why?" I ask.

"I was the daughter of Zennuta and he was the son of farmers who didn't support the dream system. They were never going to let us be together. I decided to leave Norden. I asked Harrop to go with me ... In the end, he chose to stay."

"Why?" I ask.

"He was pressured. The Dream Council seemed happy for me to go, but Harrop was harassed. They told him I would be prosecuted for kidnapping if he went with me. In the end, he chose to stay. I think it was because they would not have given him or me any peace."

"But, what about now?" I continue. "Could he join you now?"

"I don't know. Maybe he could come here now." Dana pauses as if pondering that possibility. "But, it wouldn't help us," she adds. "It would just bring us more attention."

"You and Harrop should be together," says Kala. "And we could make it happen."

That's Kala, always positive about the possibilities. I nod in agreement.

"You two are insatiable."

"We'll find a way," I say.

"Thanks," says Dana. "Right now, though, drink your tea and tell me about these hot springs."

185

"Have you been there?" I ask.

"The ones just outside Norden?"

"I bet she's been there too," says Kala. "Did you go skinny-dipping with Harrop?"

"Actually, the first time I went there was with my parents. I was only small, but I can remember it. And yes, we were all naked."

Dana is smiling.

"And the other times you went to the spring," I ask.

"Yes, I did go there another time and it was with Harrop."

I smile. "I wondered why Harrop didn't confront us at the springs."

"Did you swim there?" asks Dana.

"Yes," I say, taking Kala's hand quietly. "It's a beautiful place."

"It's a shame that it isn't used now," follows Kala.

"I agree. It's nice to have a special spot like that."

"You know, even Seamus knows the hot springs," I say.

"It seems to be a special spot for him too," adds Kala.

"Seamus is always full of surprises."

"He says he might come with us when we go back to Norden," I say.

"You're going back to Norden?"

"We hope to go back for more spring water. But that's if the treatment works. We made a bit of a plan to meet up with my grandparents in a few weeks."

"You'll have to be careful."

A Dream Passage

"Yes," I say. "We've been wondering what Harrop would have reported."

"What did you tell him about the spring water?"

"We said it was water for our plants," I say.

"Did he believe that?"

"Probably not, but we didn't tell him anything else."

"And that was before you hit him on the head," adds Kala "He might not remember."

"Do you think he'll report what happened?" I ask.

"I think he would have reported the facts," answers Dana. "He's an honest man. You'll have to be very careful when you go back."

I nod in agreement. I'm relieved to have Dana's support for our return trip. I know we have freedom, but it helps to know that she's behind us.

"Don't forget your tea," says Dana.

"Thanks," I say, gulping it.

14. Big ideas

We sleep in late. I notice how heavy I felt in bed. I must have needed the sleep—perhaps, this time, I even earned the extra rest.

I awake to Kala's gentle touch and quickly have my hands on her. In fact, I hold Kala like never before. I am proud, confident and controlled. I feel different. Maybe it's because I've finally done something towards paying back her confidence in me.

And I help myself to Kala—all of her. It's as if I am finally worthy of her. And it isn't just me. Kala is different. It's not that she yields to me. She shows me her want for me as her man and she lets herself go with her desire. We are tangled, sweaty and even noisy at times.

We don't discuss things but, if I had to use words, I would say that we had our passage at the springs. But that morning, our consumption and enjoyment of each other shows something further. It's lust, but with love and security. I think that it's my self-belief that is changing things for me. Kala was already confident. I'm just catching up.

We stay in bed late into the morning, holding each other and talking. The only thing that gets us up is the thought of Dana doing all the farm chores for us again. Kala and I agree that we should focus on learning all the farming work we need to know before Dana leaves.

***

A Dream Passage

We begin the following days with farm chores: cleaning out the shed, changing the water for the cows and chickens, feeding them, milking the cows, churning butter, collecting eggs, baking bread, picking vegetables and planting new vegetables, collecting vegetable seeds, cooking meals, and making cups of tea.

On one of the days we weed the vegetable garden and thin out the growing seedlings. Another day we go to Seamus' farm to grind some wheat. The day after that, Dana shows us how to use the radio to contact Jessup and arrange the trade of flour for chickens.

***

It's now Friday and we're up early to milk the cows. As we walk outside, Kala and I notice a rabbit in our new vegetable plot. It's eating our seedlings!

I'm annoyed. For a moment, I even wish Hollis was here to shoot the rodent. I remember him saying 'Shootin' rabbits is as easy as making tea'. He'd have killed it by now and he'd be drinking his tea.

"That cheeky bunny is eating our veggies," says Kala.

She's not at all angry. I suppose it's because she likes all living things, even if they are eating our food.

It looks happy and healthy. It's obviously doing well, eating our food. That gives me an idea.

"You mean, the delicious, plump, juicy, rabbit is fattening up on our vegetables," I say.

189

"Yes, it is," laughs Kala. "Have an idea, do you, ideas man?"

"We're going to trap it," I say confidently, although I haven't any idea of how to do it.

"What kind of trap?"

She's smiling. She knows that I haven't got a clue.

"I'm not really sure," I say. "Maybe an enclosure with an entrance that becomes blocked once the rabbit enters."

"They seem to like the carrot leaves," says Kala. "How about we use that wire netting in the shed? We can make a kind of maze that ends with carrots. We'll wait until it goes in and then close off the entrance before it can get out."

"Sounds good. But why will the rabbit go for the carrots in the trap when it's got fresh carrots in the vegetable plot?"

"Because they're curious," answers Kala.

"Curious? This sounds curious to me. Are you playing a trick on me?"

"No, of course not. Let's try it."

I'm not convinced, and I start wondering what we're going to do if we catch it. "Any ideas on how to kill it once it's trapped?"

Hollis would shoot it, but we don't have a gun. Killing it with a knife seems gory and I'm not sure I'm strong enough to kill a wriggling rabbit with my bare hands.

"I'll leave that to you. You're the violent one," jokes Kala.

"Maybe I'll use my stick," I say in jest, realising just after I've said it that it actually could be a good idea. In the end, I decide that a rock will do the job as humanely as I can make it without the use of a gun.

I feel sorry for the rabbit. I know we've been joking around, but I'll have to become comfortable with this cruelty in order to prosper and provide for Kala and one day, for our family.

The thought of having a family sends a shudder through my body. Am I growing up too fast? I'm barely sixteen years old. I love Kala and I love how we are now, but am I really ready for a family?

"You okay, Tomas?" asks Kala seriously.

"Sorry. I was just thinking about how quickly our lives have changed."

"Are you sure you're okay here in the South? Are you missing Norden?"

"No. Not at all. I love our new life. It's just the fact that we kill things. I'm going to have to get used to it."

"Oh. The killing. Well, we don't have to do that," says Kala in a matter of fact way. "We could leave it."

"And watch it eat our carrots?" I say. "No, let's dispatch the varmint. I'll be cured through eating it."

"Rabbit stew?"

"I was thinking of roasted rabbit with potatoes, peas and pumpkin."

"Done," says Kala, ending the discussion, although I am still left wondering if I am really ready for this role as a rabbit killer.

***

The trap is set. Kala and I are waiting comfortably on the veranda. The rabbit appeared an hour ago and has been happily eating the grass beside the trap. We quietly watched it for a while but it didn't move. Now we're drinking tea and talking.

"Have you thought any more about Teague?"

"Teague wanting to go to Norden?" checks Kala.

"Yes. I was shocked to hear it."

"I guess the problem is that he hasn't experienced life in Norden. He thinks it's all easy there—a life of leisure and luxury."

"I just wish he could try it. I think he'd be back before too long."

"Yeah," says Kala. "He'd just need one bad experience: an unsupported idea, forbidden love, a breach of custom or a bland tasting apple. That would sort him out."

I laugh at the suggestion of the apple being enough to change his mind.

"But, what if he likes bland tasting apples?"

"If he likes apples with no flavour, then he belongs in Norden," insists Kala.

"We should make that the test."

"Yes, let's get some dream apples from Norden."

She's serious.

"We'll give them to all Southern children," continues Kala.

"What are you two talking about?" asks Dana, emerging from the house.

"Hello, Dana," we answer, simultaneously.

"We were talking about Teague wanting to live in Norden," I say.

"There's a few like him," says Dana. "For some of them, I put it down to laziness."

"And the others?" I ask.

"Some people are suited to dream life," says Dana. "They are happy to live their life through other people's experiences and dreams."

"But they don't get to make their own choices," notes Kala. "They don't get to express themselves. They can't be who they want to be or with the person they choose."

"And they will never know the taste of a Southern apple," adds Dana.

"You heard us!" says Kala.

"Just the bit about the apples. I know it sounds bad to you but not everyone has a need to follow their own path. I meant what I said at the Origins' meeting. We need to find a way that gives everyone a choice. People can choose to live here or in Norden. They can be part of the Dream Council if they want. What's important is that people are free."

"I agree with you," I say. "But how can we make it happen?"

"I don't know, Tomas. Years ago, I was angry. I wanted to destroy the Dream Council for what they did to Harrop and me. But now, I've changed."

"What do you want now?" asks Kala.

"I want peace and happiness. I want people to have a choice. I want respect, cooperation and consideration."

"Can you really see that happening?" I ask.

"Yes. Why not? We already have it here in the South."

"What about Norden moving south?" I ask.

"That is a problem. But, we've got to find a way to make things change."

"How?" I ask.

"People," says Dana. "People make things change. Just one person doing one thing can make a difference. Take you two for instance. You two came here and now we might have a treatment for the rust."

"Look," whispers Kala, pointing.

The rabbit is in the trap and is moving cautiously towards the carrot leaves.

"It's working," I say.

"Shhh!" says Kala. "Just a bit longer."

We wait and sure enough, the bunny has moved through to the carrot leaves. It's time to act. I quietly grab the rock I have on the floor and slowly move towards the trap. The rabbit stops still and looks right at me.

"Go," says Kala, bolting for the trap.

I reach it just after her. The rabbit tries to escape but is blocked by the wire. It's stuck! Kala pushes the wire in, closing the exit.

It's now my time to act. I put my hand under the wire, taking hold of the fur on the back of its neck but just as I grab it, it kicks its back legs. I end up with a hand on its left leg. Then I feel a piercing pain in my hand. The desperate animal has given me a solid bite.

"Ouch!" I screech, releasing my grip. Somehow, it finds a gap below the wire and it's gone.

I failed!

"Damn! I'll be ready next time," I say, but then wonder if there will be another opportunity. "Do you think it will fall for our trap again?"

"Not that rabbit," says Dana. "But don't worry. There are plenty of others around."

"Sorry," I say to Kala.

"That's okay," she says, kissing my forehead gently. "You'll know what to expect next time."

And she's right about that. I will know what to expect. The rabbit will fight for its life. I need to be prepared to take it.

15. Crops

It's been two weeks since our return from Norden. We're now in a good routine of farm work, trading flour, cooking and eating.

I love my new life with Kala. We're so close and physically, we're together just about every morning and evening. We're being careful that we don't start our family just yet. That's been tricky at times as we sometimes get carried away. I'm literally absorbed by Kala's body and it is so very good.

At other times, I find it hard not to be touching her. I'm even beginning to wonder if I will become a pest to her with my insatiable need. Although, Kala is as bad as I am. At times, it must be hard for Dana to be around us.

At breakfast, Dana says that we should check our wheat crop for rust. The wheat near the house appears healthy, so we don't have great concern, but we'll need to check the rest to be sure.

At first, I think Dana is wanting us out of the house to have some time to herself, but then she says that Anita requested that everyone check their crops and stock today, and report back to her on the radio between six and eight p.m. Anita will give her local report at tomorrow's Origins' meeting.

I'm nervously excited about the update on the treatments although, realistically, I estimate less than fifty percent chance of success. I just don't think the spring water will contain enough sulphur to effectively treat the rust.

A Dream Passage

Kala and I began our crop inspection after breakfast. So far, we've checked three of the ten checkpoints we marked out on the rough farm map. We're now walking, hand in hand, on our way to the fourth.

"Do you think Dana minds us touching each other so much?" I ask.

"I don't know. I guess we should ask her."

"Let's do that. I don't want her to feel uncomfortable around us."

"Okay, but, Tomas ..."

"Yes."

"Dana and Harrop should be together. I want to make it happen."

That's my Kala.

"I'd like that too," I say. "But shouldn't we be leaving that to the two of them?" I'm not sure we should interfere. "Besides, what can we do?" I add, although I know Kala. She won't stop until Dana and Harrop are united.

"We've got to help her. After all, it was Dana who supported the plan to liberate you and that's how we got to be together."

"Yes, but it was you and your parents who acted."

"You've seen how it is at Origins' meetings. It was Dana's standing up for our freedom that convinced the others."

She's right.

**

We're now at the most southerly point on our farm. The wheat here is less mature but clear of rust. I place a tick against the checkpoint on the map and point in the direction of our next check, located on the eastern edge of our farm.

"We need to find a way," says Kala. "I think if we could get them to meet, they'd sort it out from there."

"Wouldn't they have met up when Dana was captured?"

"I don't know. We'll have to ask about that."

"I don't want to push for a meeting. It could be dangerous for Dana."

"Yes, but I know it will work out," says Kala.

I believe her. My experience is that she's right about these things. She was right about us.

As we near the eastern edge of our field I notice the wheat is slightly yellow at the edges and I think I see a few spots. It could be early stages of rust. Walking further east, my fears are realised. There's a spot where the wheat is fully browned and in poor condition. It's on the edge of our road. Looking across, we can see our eastern neighbours', Kyle and Hannah's wheat is also affected.

"We're infected," says Kala, stating what we both can already see. "It seems to have crossed the road."

"Yes, either from our side or theirs."

"It doesn't stop at boundaries."

"I wonder if they know?" I say.

"Poor Hannah," says Kala.

Hannah and Kyle are nearly as old as Seamus. Hannah seemed frail when we met her. It doesn't seem fair that they should have to battle this.

"Hopefully, this is the only spot," I say. "Our next point is further north," I add, pointing in the direction of the next survey spot.

***

We return home around noon. Dana is in the kitchen and there is a delicious smell of baking bread in the air. I'm instantly hungry although the rust in our wheat has dampened my mood.

"How'd you go?"

"Mostly good," says Kala.

"Mostly?" queries Dana.

"There's a bad patch of rust on our eastern boundary," says Kala. "We're clear apart from that."

"So, we're infected?" says Dana.

"Yes," I say.

"Oh. That's terrible," responds Dana. She drops her head into her hands.

"It's in Kyle and Hannah's field too," I add.

"Poor Hannah," says Dana, the same way that Kala said it.

"Is Hannah sick?" I ask.

"No, she's not really sick. She has a bad reaction to eating wheat."

"You mean she can't eat their main crop?" I ask.

"Yes, it's a cruel thing," says Dana. "But there are worse things."

Her comment makes me think of Dana's situation. I glance at Kala and she's already looking at me. Now doesn't seem the time to ask about Harrop.

"What is it?" asks Dana.

It's Kala who breaks first. "I hope you don't mind, but we were talking about Harrop."

"Harrop? What about him?"

"We were wondering if he went to visit you when you were held in Norden."

"No, he didn't visit me. Harrop works at a suburban patrol station so he wouldn't have been near to where I was held. I guess he would have seen me on the broadcast but there would have been nothing he could do to help me. He did the right thing, staying away."

"So, you haven't seen Harrop?" checks Kala.

"Well, actually, I had seen him once before. I waited near his station one day. I wore a hat and glasses so I wouldn't be recognised. He looked well, but different. He's so very quiet now. He used to have a kind of sparkle about him. He was cheeky and always joking around—a bit like you, Tomas. He seems to be missing that now."

"It's because he's not with you," says Kala.

"Kala!" I say. I think she's pushing Dana a bit too far.

Kala gives me a loving but disapproving look before looking again to Dana.

"It's okay," says Dana. "I'll admit something … Seeing you two together has made me remember what it was like with Harrop. I've heard you two talking. It was like that for us."

"So, you still love him?" I ask.

"Yes. I still love him. I just don't know what to do."

"That's easy. You just need to see him," says Kala, adamantly.

"Maybe. But how can I persuade him to be with me?"

"Just be yourself. Let him see you again and see who you are. He just needs a reminder of how great it was to be with you."

"We'll see," says Dana.

"There's no 'we'll see' about it," says Kala. "You have to do it."

"Okay, okay. Let's work it out after our meeting tomorrow. You two sit down while I make the salad."

"Could we have some of your bread?" I ask.

"Oh! The bread!" says Dana.

It's obvious that her mind is on Harrop.

"Yes, of course. We'll have sandwiches."

***

It's now evening and I'm in bed, checking through the farming books page by page. I want to make sure I haven't overlooked anything.

It would be useful to know how often to apply the treatment and how long before the treatment works. Unfortunately, though, there's no information on it. There's only one treatment that gives specific instructions and that's the one for tiny insects called aphids. You have to apply that treatment every day for a week.

Kala enters our room and hands me a cup of mint tea, then strips down to just her thin, plain cotton underpants that she fills so wonderfully.

She looks to see if I'm watching. She knows I am! Then she smiles, like she's had an idea. She walks, no, parades, in a kind of slow dance. She raises her arms and turns a full turn, gracefully showing herself to me. She then lifts one leg onto the bed and slides it, foot pointed towards me. She lifts herself, then turns and slides, twists, and ends up lying next to me, looking away with her head held from her hand raised above her elbow.

This woman is amazing. I cast my books aside, turn off the light and go to her. My hands move easily where I like them— neatly holding her hips.

"You did well," I say, proudly holding my beautiful, capable, confident woman. "You turned a bad day for us into something good."

"Yes, I did," she says, placing her hands over mine.

***

Later, I'm lying in bed, warm and relaxed even though my thoughts have returned to our problems: Norden moving south, the rust in our wheat, Harrop and Dana, and even that rabbit. I'm thinking, but I'm not stressed. Maybe we will find a way.

A Dream Passage

The security that we have with each other seems to be energising us both. Kala has brought out things that I didn't know I could do. I don't dance well, but I know that I can dance with Kala. I don't sing well, but I could sing with her.

"Sweet dreams, my love," I whisper.

***

I awaken to the sound of birds chirping. It's already eight a.m. The meeting is at ten, at Hammond and Roget's farm. Seamus offered to drive us. He's picking us up at nine. That doesn't leave us much time for breakfast and chores.

Kala is lying peacefully on her side, her head facing away from me. I imagine her dreams. She'll be righting wrongs, bringing people together, and enjoying every moment. That's Kala—caring and beautiful in body and spirit.

I move my arms around her, careful not to wake her, but wanting to hold her for a few minutes. When I wake her, we share a few peaceful minutes, quietly holding each other. We need to get moving, though. Dana is up.

We shower, dress, release the animals from the shed, fill the water troughs, and gather the eggs.

At breakfast, Dana is quiet.

"Are you okay?" I ask.

"Yes. I'm just thinking about the meeting."

I hear Seamus' car outside and gulp down my tea. We rush to be ready, Dana grabbing some notes, Kala and I brushing our teeth hurriedly.

"Hello, Spike," says Kala, patting the little dog. It's not long before we're on our way. Seamus seems happy enough, although he isn't talking much. We tell him about the rust in our wheat.

"That rust is a terrible thing," he says. "Nothin' seems ter stop it."

Kala grips my hand. I don't mind his comment. I just hope that he's wrong.

**

We arrive at a house similar in size to ours except it's brightly painted and meticulously maintained. The grass is low cut and the vegetable gardens precisely measured, lush and weedless.

"It's immaculate," I marvel.

"Yes," agrees Dana. "That's Hammond and Roget. Not a blade of grass out of place."

"They waste their time makin' things look good," says Seamus.

"Seamus is just jealous," says Dana. "They're hard workers. Roget is often a prize-winner at the festival. He grows the largest and tastiest vegetables you could ever imagine."

Looking at the vegetable plots, I believe her. Their shed is bright red with glossy white window frames. It looks freshly painted. There's a group of people in front of the shed.

"You could live in that shed," says Kala.

I agree. It would make a nice home.

"All that colour. Waste of effort," says Seamus.

I can see Anita and Leroy are there, looking scruffy in their matching blue shirts. I hope they have good news.

Seamus parks the car. It's not long before we're entering the shed. I make a line for Anita, but we're intercepted by others. We meet Hammond and Roget which is nice, but then we meet their parents and their neighbours. They all greet us with the forehead touch, which is fine, but many of them are holding on to us beyond the custom. They're saying how good it is to meet me and they're asking about our trip to Norden. All the questions and repeating the same information is annoying, but I'm as polite as I can be. All I want to do is get through to Anita and find out about the treatment. I look at Kala. She looks as frustrated as I am.

Hollis is there on the left. I move with Kala towards him. Surely he won't over-greet us.

"Tomas," he says. "Good to see ya," and he pulls me in for the greeting and follows with Kala.

"Nice to see you," I say.

"I heard about ya run in with the Dream Patrol. We need people like you down 'ere. People that will take a stand and fight."

"It wasn't really like that," I explain. "We were lucky to get away."

"You clubbed 'im, didn't ya?"

I feel terrible. I don't want to be known as a violent hero. I hope Dana isn't hearing this. "I was just protecting Kala. I was lucky. He probably just slipped and fell."

Kala nods in support.

"It's okay. Yer can tell me. I reckon you must 'ave got him good … They'll show ya more respect next time. That's what we needs from them—some respect."

I'm not sure what to say. I can't really explain how lucky I was. If it had been anyone other than Harrop, they would have stunned me from a distance. It would have been as easy as Hollis says it is to shoot a rabbit startled by a light. I really have to change the subject.

"We hoped we'd see you today," I say. "We wanted to ask you about catching rabbits." I know he's going to say we should shoot them, but I'm interested to know what else he might suggest.

"Catching rabbits takes too much time. It's much better to shoot 'em."

"But we don't have a gun," says Kala.

"Why don't ya get one?"

I don't want a gun and I'm sure Kala feels the same.

"It's just one rabbit," I say.

"I spose yer could trap it then. 'Ere's what you do …"

The bell rings. Dana is starting the meeting.

"There's a trick to it," continues Hollis. "Tell ya later."

We sit next to Hollis, but then I see Anita waving at us. "Over here," she mouths, pointing to two vacant chairs to the left side of the leadership table. I look at Hollis.

"Go on," he says.

"Okay, talk later," I say.

As we move to the front, I keep thinking about the greeting we're getting. I know that I should be happy, but I can't help wondering if it's because of the 'clubbing incident'. Are these Southern leaders impressed by violence? I guess many of them are like Hollis. I just wish they were appreciating the potential of the wheat treatment.

"Thanks for coming," says Dana. "Please pass on my best wishes to the people in your areas."

She pauses, looking at Kala and me.

"This is an important meeting for us. We have some decisions to make today. We'll start with the local report. Anita."

"Thank you, Dana," says Anita, standing. "First of all, I'd like us to welcome Tomas and Kala."

Suddenly, there is clapping. I turn to see absolutely every person at the meeting standing and clapping. What is going on?! I was looking forward to the report on the rust. Kala takes my hand. All we can do is stand here. I don't feel comfortable.

"What is this?" I whisper to Kala.

"I don't know," she says.

"I feel like a trapped rabbit."

"I know. Just smile and nod, Tomas."

I do as Kala suggests. Eventually, the ruckus subsides.

"I'll start with the crop report," continues Anita. "Our vegetable production is good. So are the oats. I'll talk about wheat in a minute. I'm sorry to report that we have a new problem. For the first time, we have rust in a barley crop. It's only one patch right now and that will be burnt, so we might be okay, but I'd like you to ask everyone to check their barley as soon as they can and report any issues at the radio hook-up next week."

"What about the wheat?" asks Seamus impatiently.

"Now to the wheat. As you know, I asked everyone to check their crops. The bad news is that the rust infection is spreading. Last time we met it was a hundred farms. Now it's one hundred and thirty-six. That's half of our farms!"

There's a murmur. The rust is bad, but what about the treatment? I watch Anita, wishing she'd hurry up.

"It's bad, but I have some good news. As many of you will have heard, our newcomers, Tomas and Kala, went to Norden and brought back water from the hot springs to try as a rust treatment. The idea was that the sulphur in the spring water would act as a fungicide."

This is it.

"We tried the spring water in four locations, using varying quantities of spring water. I'm happy to report that the rust improved in two of the test sites and it completely disappeared where we used the water every day. It seems that the spring water will work where we get to the infections early and use the water daily. It takes a week to cure the rust."

There's a hush. The news is fantastic. It works! I can't believe it. I look at Kala. Then there's a cheer and clapping but I don't care this time. I'm hugging Kala. I know that getting the book was my idea, but Kala is the one who had the confidence to follow her dreams. She believed in me and brought me here. Without her, there would be no treatment.

"Thank you, everyone," says Anita, raising her hands to ask for quiet. I'm still holding Kala.

Anita continues when the noise eases. "I propose that we honour Tomas and Kala today. They are only recently of age but are already thinking and acting with courage. They're a fine example for my children ... and for us all. With your permission, I'd like you to honour them with a seat at our leaders table and I'd like us all to thank them properly."

Anita ushers us to move. We stand and another man takes our chairs, moving them to the table.

"You now have a permanent seat at this table," says Anita.

Kala bows her forehead as she takes her seat and I follow.

"Now for our thanks," says Anita.

There is silence and then everyone bows their forehead to us. I can feel the respect from all, and thankfully, it's not for my violence. It's for our thoughts and actions. I'm sorry to have doubted these good people. Their bow lasts for what seems like ages.

"Thank you, Tomas," says Anita. "Thank you, Kala."

"Thank you," I say.

"And now we need to work out a treatment plan," says Anita. "We're going need a lot more spring water. That's going to mean trips to Norden. What we need to agree on is how to manage it. I'm wondering if it might be better to coordinate one big water gathering trip—getting all the spring water we need in one go. Or would a series of smaller trips be better?"

"A big trip might draw attention to us," says Dana. "If they see us, they'll know we need that water."

"If they sees a lot of smaller groups they're gunna know too," says Hollis. "I say we gets it done in one go. Besides, it will be safer with more of us there."

I think Hollis is right. But, I don't want to miss out on my meeting with my grandparents or miss the chance for Dana to hook up with Harrop.

"How about a reconnaissance trip?" suggests Kala.

She's thinking faster than me.

"A few of us could go there, take notes, and make a detailed plan so that we could get all the spring water we need in one go the next time."

"I'll go," says Seamus. "I know how to get there."

"Who else has been there?" asks Dana.

"I went there once," says a grey-haired man with a walking stick. "It's a beautiful little pool. I'll go if you need me."

"Thanks, Dino," says Dana, "It's good of you to offer, but the walking might be a bit much for your leg. Has anyone else been to the spring?"

"I'll go," says Hollis. "I haven't been to the springs, but I'm the best person for the water carrying."

It's an offer that's going to be hard for Dana to refuse. Hollis is one of the largest, and probably the strongest, people in the shed.

"Okay, then," says Dana. "Seamus, Hollis, Tomas, Kala and I will do the reconnaissance trip. We'll meet back here in one week to plan for the bulk water gathering."

"Will it be safe for you and Kala?" asks Anita. "It might be better if I went."

Anita's right. The Dream Patrol want both of them. It would be best if someone else went. On the other hand, I'm aware of Kala's plans for Dana and Harrop.

"We'll be okay," replies Kala. "We'll have Tomas and Hollis with us."

"It's settled then," says Dana. "The five of us will work out the details. I'll now give the update from Norden."

It's going to be an interesting trip, stuck in a car with Hollis and Seamus. On the positive side, we'll learn everything there is to know about rabbit trapping. The negative thing is that I can't see any way that I can wrangle the meeting with my grandparents. I'll have to try and see what I can do … I said I would try to visit them again.

16. Spring water

It's very early in the morning, two days after the meeting, and we're in Seamus' car on our way to the hot spring. Seamus is driving, Hollis is in the passenger seat, and Dana, Kala, and I are squashed together in the back. I hope it isn't too bad for Dana.

We have a trailer with eight large containers behind us. One of them will be ours and that could be enough to treat the rust in our wheat. That alone makes this trip worthwhile for us.

We tried, but Kala and I weren't able to talk Dana into the visit to my grandparents. She said there was no purpose to it. I could see her point, but I explained that I had given my word that we would be back. She said she understood that but that I could keep that promise on another trip. She said we needn't go on the reconnaissance trip if we didn't want to but there was no way we wanted to miss it. In the end, I had to give up on visiting my grandparents.

I'm excited by our journey. All this has been mostly my idea and I want to see it through. We also have Kala's idea about Dana and Harrop seeing each other.

"What's our plan? How are we going to get them together?" I asked Kala yesterday.

"We don't need a plan," she replied, smugly. "They will make it happen."

She could be right. I can imagine Harrop carefully patrolling the spring area each day, wondering what use we had for the water and if we'll return.

I didn't highlight it, but there was really no particular purpose to Kala and me being on this trip. I suppose it had to be someone though, and it may as well be us. Plus, we do know the way to the hot spring.

***

Hollis is talking about our rabbit problem. "Yer should just shoot 'em," he says. "Other ways is just muckin' around."

"But we don't have a gun," says Kala. "You said you had a trick."

"Yep, there's another way yer can use, but yer need a dog."

"A dog?" I say. "How do you use a dog?"

"Yer need a small one."

"Like Spike," notes Seamus, patting the sleeping dog on his lap.

"Yep. A small dog like that and four or five nets."

"What sort of nets?" I ask.

"Rabbitin' nets. They're about so big," he says, extending his arms to their full length. "And they're made of a tight string. Yer put the nets on all the rabbit 'oles in one place. Then yer send the dog down one of the holes to chase out them rabbits. The little varmints run straight out into the nets. All yer have to do is stand close by and knock 'em off when they comes out. Scratcher and me once got five rabbits from just one burrow."

"Sounds good," I say, although I'm still squeamish about the idea of 'knocking them off'. "Could you lend us your dog?"

"It's not my dog. It's me neighbour, Scratcher's dog. But, I reckon he'll lend it to ya. People will lend ya anything yer want once yer fixed their crops."

"His name is Scratcher?" I ask.

"That's not 'is real name. Everyone just calls him Scratcher 'cause he's always scratching. You'll see when yer meet him."

"It's true," says Dana. "He is always scratching. His skin is red from it. I don't know his real name."

"Does he need some sort of treatment?" asks Kala.

"I'm sure he does," replies Dana. "Some people though, don't want any help. They put up with things like that even when it can be treated. Often it's because they're too proud to accept any help."

"Not Scratcher," corrects Hollis. "He's not too proud. He just don't want to be helped. He wants to be left alone."

"Yes, some people prefer to be left alone," agrees Dana.

"I still think we should help him," says Kala.

"Be careful with Scratcher," suggests Seamus. "Some people gets annoyed if ya try to help 'em."

From the look on Kala's face, I can tell that we'll be helping.

"I think we'll give Scratcher's dog a try when we get back," I say. "It'll be roasted rabbit for us," I add, rubbing my stomach.

"Slow cooked rabbit stew," says Seamus, patting Spike.

"Rabbit pie," says Hollis.

"Okay," says Dana. "Enough talk of rabbit killing. Let's go over the plan for the spring."

"We're just gunna get the water, aren't we?" queries Hollis, looking back at us. "Does we really need a plan?"

"Maybe not so much a plan, but we need to take notes on how to get there, make a map, and work out a way of getting a lot of water out quickly on our next trip."

***

"That's the turn," says Kala, pointing to a right turn, about a hundred metres ahead of us.

"Mountain Creek Road," says Dana.

"It's about thirty minutes from here," notes Kala.

"Thirty minutes, Spikey," repeats Seamus.

It's funny that Seamus talks to his dog like that. He seems to talk to Spike more than he talks to people. It was the way that Dana said 'Mountain Creek Road' that was telling, though. How did she remember the name? I guess she just takes in that kind of information. She's observant and clever, probably just like her father. I should ask her about him.

I think about it some more but decide not to ask now—not in front of Hollis and Seamus. Perhaps though, I could ask about her mother. Dana hasn't spoken about her. I guess if I ask about her, Dana can decide what she wants to discuss.

"Dana, what happened to your mother?" I ask.

"My mother … She passed a long time ago."

"I'm sorry to hear that."

"It's okay. I have wonderful memories of her. She was beautiful. And she loved my father and me very much. She got sick when I was ten. She must have been sick for a couple of years—didn't say a word. One day we found her fallen in the shed. She finally told us she was unwell. She died a few weeks later."

"That's terrible," says Kala.

"Yes. My father was inconsolable. He was also mad at himself. He realised that he'd spent so much time working when he could have spent time with mother and me."

"What was his work?" I ask, carefully.

"He was a farmer. Our life was simple and we were happy until my mother passed. That affected my father deeply and he never went back to farming. He became so quiet. He was always thinking.

"I remember him saying that there had to be a better way than working so hard for everything we needed. He desperately wanted to free us from our everyday work. He said that once people were free from work we could then concentrate on things that mattered."

"Your father was a great man," says Seamus.

"Yes, he was. I can still remember the day he worked it all out. I saw a spark in his eyes. It was as if he'd come back to life. Then he worked to convince people in Norden to try it. There were so many doubters. It took two years, but he did it. He set up the broadcast network with Paros and Neros. Did you know that Kala?"

"They said they helped."

"They more than helped. My father said that he would never have done it without their help and the wristbands that your mother designed. Do you know what the first thing they dreamed up was?"

"No," I say, intrigued.

"It was just one apple. The whole thing started with the dream of an apple to appear in Norden Square. My father placed a triangle in the very centre of the square and at precisely six a.m. the apple appeared. People were amazed!"

"I remember it," says Seamus. "It was a miracle. Your father was a genius."

"That was the beginning of the dream work," continues Dana. "And it was a good idea for a time. It was a time of hope and dreams."

"And for a while those apples tasted good," adds Seamus.

"For a while, the dream work produced wonderful, tasty food. But then, some people wanted more. They saw the opportunity to dream of roads and housing and schools. They wanted more and more, and that was going to require greater organisation and discipline to get consensus. My father was against it. 'Let people be free,' he would say. 'They'll get consensus on important things. The rest doesn't matter.'

"Then Krakus got involved. He took over the council. My father tried to talk with him, but Krakus would not stop. He was greedy and wanted more powers to control people. It all started as a good idea, but it went bad. And here we are now, worried that we might meet up with his Dream Patrol. My father would never have told lies or threatened anyone to keep them compliant. He would have insisted on freedom and he would be helped the people in the South."

"I believes that too," agrees Seamus earnestly.

"We never needed any help," says Hollis. "All we want is to be left alone."

"Like Scratcher," says Kala.

"Yes, just like Scratcher."

"What happened to your father?" I ask.

"I'm sure you heard the story," replies Dana.

"He passed in his sleep?"

"Yes, he passed in his sleep. It was just before I turned sixteen. He really missed my mother and became so disillusioned with what Krakus was doing to his dream system, that he stopped his work and went back to dreaming his own dreams. I think he found my mother in a dream and decided not to return."

To me the idea of moving from life to death in a dream is incredible. I look at Kala, wondering if she believes it. I don't believe that he would have left Dana. Surely, it was a heart attack or another health issue.

"He must have been an amazing man," I say.

"He was. He was an undisciplined dreamer, just like you two. To him, there was nothing wrong with that. I think that in the end, he left me to follow his own dreams."

She really does believe it! I suppose that if anyone could leave this life in their dreams, Zennuta could.

***

It's mid-afternoon when we get to the hot spring car park. It's as decrepit as it was when we last saw it.

"No sign of them dreamers," notes Hollis.

"No," says Dana. "Let's hope it stays that way."

Dana looks across to Kala and me. I tighten my grip on Kala's leg and we share a glance.

Seamus skilfully backs the trailer and turns the car so that we're facing the way out. "All right, off you go," he says.

Seamus is going to stay at the car.

"Just over 500 metres along that track?" checks Dana, pointing.

"Yes, it's not far," I reply.

"Too narrow for a car," notes Dana.

"What about horses?" suggests Hollis. "We could use them to move the water containers."

"Quicker than us moving them," I agree.

"Still slow though," says Dana. "I'd prefer something faster."

Hollis, Dana, Kala and I take two containers each. It's going to take two trips to bring the water laden containers back to the car—at least an hour.

Dana stops a short way into the bush. "You hear this, Seamus?" she says, talking into her radio.

"I hear ya," returns Seamus. "Off ya go."

Further along the track I try to identify the exact place that we were stopped by Harrop, but all the bushes around the overgrown track look the same. I decide against mentioning the incident.

"What about a water pipe?" suggests Hollis.

"Would it work on this hill?" questions Dana.

"Sure, we just needs a pump. A hand pump would do it."

"All right, good idea. Glad you came along, Hollis."

I can see Hollis is walking tall, proud of his idea. I'm glad to see him getting recognition for a non-violent suggestion.

"It's just down here," says Kala.

And there it is, the steaming, tannin stained, pond—as beautiful as when we left it.

"This is a beautiful place," I say, looking at Kala. She smiles back at me and I think about what it would be like if it were just the two of us here again. We sneak a quick hug after setting down our containers.

"What's that bad smell?" asks Hollis.

"That's the sulphur," I say.

"Stinks," says Hollis.

"You okay, Seamus?" asks Dana, into the radio.

"All good here," says the radio.

"Let's get and go," says Dana, economically, but unnecessarily, as Kala, with her shoes off, is already filling the first container.

"Can you help find some carrying sticks?" I say to Hollis.

"Carrying sticks?"

"Over here," I say and Hollis follows me to where Kala and I found suitable branches last time.

After a minute of searching, I find a suitable stick about two metres long and five centimetres in diameter. I throw it to Hollis and search for another.

"That what you used on that dreamer?" asks Hollis.

"Yes. I was lucky to catch him unaware."

"It's not the stick. It's what ya do with it that counts," he says, aggressively poking the stick forwards in a mock attack.

That wasn't my move, but I'm not going to correct him. "Here's another stick," I say.

"How 'bout this one?" says Hollis, holding up a thicker branch.

"Yep, that'll do." Three is one more than we need. "Let's get back to the spring."

Kala and Dana have filled all eight containers. Hollis and I line up two containers, hurry the sticks through the handles and repeat with another two. Kala puts her shoes on and we're ready to go. Kala and I walk with two containers held by one of the carrying sticks and Hollis and Dana follow with the other two containers. We leave the surplus carrying stick behind with the remaining four filled containers.

It's as heavy and awkward as it was last time. I notice a drop of sweat fall from my forehead. So far, all is clear. No sign of the Dream Patrol. I try telling myself not to worry. Dana has been quiet ever since we arrived. I think she's nervous.

Arriving at the car park, we see a casual-looking Seamus sitting in the driver's seat of the car with the door open. Spike is on the ground in front of Seamus, lying lazily and enjoying the last sunshine of the day.

We load the water on the trailer and quickly return down the path for the remaining containers. We should be out of here before dark.

"Seamus looked relaxed," I say, making conversation.

"He's a good man," says Dana.

"He used to 'ave one of the best farms," adds Hollis.

"What happened?" I ask.

"His wife died. After that, he went all quiet and he stopped his farmin'. Now 'e does as little as 'e can."

"You know," says Dana, "Seamus was the Origins' leader back then. But, when his wife passed, he stopped talking. He wouldn't go on the radio or meet with anyone."

"We 'ad to tell him to step down," adds Hollis. "Then we made Dana leader."

"The last few weeks are the best we've seen him for a while," notes Dana. "I'm glad he came with us."

We're approaching the spring again. The filled water containers are just where we left them so it's just a matter of feeding through the carrying sticks and we'll be on our way.

"Dana," says the radio. "They're here."

We hear Spike growling in the background.

"The Dream Patrol?" queries Dana.

No reply.

We drop the containers. Hollis has grabbed his stick and I have mine. We run along the track towards the car park as fast as we can. In my head, though, I'm wondering what we can do when we get there. The only thing we have is numbers.

"Shoulda brought me gun," mutters Hollis, running ahead of us.

I'm just behind him with Kala just behind me, and Dana ten metres back. Dana wouldn't let him bring his gun. She held her line about violence not being the answer. Right now, as we race towards the unknown, I find myself almost wishing that he did have it.

Rushing through the bush is tiring. It's mostly uphill. We're nearly there though.

"Wait!" yells Dana from behind. Hollis keeps going. "Hollis, wait!"

He takes a few more steps and then stops. "What ya waiting for?"

"Let's not rush in. Let's have a look at what we're dealing with."

"Tomas and I will go ahead," says Hollis. "You and Kala stay here."

Dana pauses, before conceding. "Be careful," she implores.

Kala asks the same and kisses me. I kiss her back, and Hollis and I move forward towards the car park clearing.

At the clearing, it's evident that we're too late. Seamus and Spike are lying on the ground. Both are motionless. Standing beside them is a man in a patrol officer uniform, holding a stun gun, and his black car is parked directly in front of our car, blocking our exit.

It's Harrop! I can't believe it. I thought he was a good man. "What have you done?" I yell.

Hollis starts moving towards Harrop, pointing his stick aggressively. This is all happening so fast. Harrop won't take any chances now. I'm certain Hollis is going to be stunned.

"Stop," I call, but Hollis doesn't listen. He lurches forward and thrusts his stick.

Harrop though, is ready, and steps back one step and fires his stun gun. Hollis is caught off balance. The stun turns Hollis around and he drops heavily towards the ground. There's a terrible thud as he hits the car park gravel.

Remarkably, Hollis remains conscious. He groans in pain.

"I'll get you," he says, trying to sit up.

Harrop takes another step back. He's adjusting his stun gun setting. No doubt he's increasing the power.

"Stop, Hollis," I say. "Let's talk to him."

"Nothin' to talk about. Look what he's done to Seamus."

I move to Seamus and crouch down. I can see his chest moving.

"He's alive," I say before moving him as best I can to a recovery position. I then shuffle over to check on Spike. His tongue is out and his eyes are white.

"Spike's gone."

"You are scum," says Hollis, his eyes murderous.

"It was an accident," says Harrop. "Our guns are set to stun people. The dog attacked us. Your man will be okay. Give him a few minutes."

He said 'our' and 'us'. I look around for his partner. Sure enough, there is another one. He's found Kala and Dana and he's walking them towards us.

"Nice work," says the other officer.

I can see the alarm in Kala's face. "Seamus is okay," I say.

"Spike?" asks Kala.

"Dead," says the other patrol officer. "The old man wouldn't call him off."

"Why'd you shoot Seamus?" asks Dana.

"The old man went crazy after we got the dog," says the officer.

"You have no right to do this," says Dana. "I'm holding you responsible."

"Take it easy," says Harrop.

"We know who you are," says the other officer. "You're Dana, daughter of Zennuta, and you're Kala, daughter of Paros and Neros. You're both coming with us."

"For what?" asks Dana.

"You were convicted of stealing. You will lose your hand. And we're arresting Kala for kidnapping."

"But I told you I went willingly," I say, appealing to Harrop.

"It's not up to us," says the officer. "Our instructions are to take you in."

"I'll be reporting you for this violence," says Dana.

"You can say whatever you want. We're still taking you in."

This is terrible. I wish that Dana and Kala had never come. I should have stopped them. I have my stick in my hand, but it's useless. I drop it to make a point to Hollis. Our only chance is to work on Harrop.

"You both know Dana didn't steal that printing press," I say. "It was a set up and you know it."

"We're just doing our job," says Harrop.

"You two are shameful," I say. "You're doing terrible things. Take another look at the dog you just killed and the old man lying there."

"It isn't up to us," says the officer.

"It is up to you," says Dana, looking directly at Harrop. "You have to decide to do the right thing and act now."

"Sorry, Dana," says Harrop. "We can't help you. You're going to have come with us."

I detect something in his tone and the way he said 'we'. The only thing we can do is go along with him. We've got to give Harrop some space and give him a chance to come good.

"Go, then," I say. "You do what you think is right."

"You're going to let them take them?" asks Hollis, anxiously.

"Take it easy, Hollis," says Dana.

"We'll be okay," says Kala.

I can tell, by the way Kala is standing back, that she's nervous. I slowly edge over. When close enough, I hug her tightly and whisper, "Keep trying. Your plan will work. I love you."

"I know. I love you too."

Harrop handcuffs Dana. The other patrol officer removes his set and moves to Kala.

"I'll do it," says Harrop. "This was my catch."

"Here you go," he says, handing Harrop the cuffs and keys.

Dana and Kala are ushered into the back seat of the black patrol car.

"Where are you taking them?" I ask.

"The Dream Council lock up," says Harrop. "You're welcome to follow."

I'm not sure what to say. I don't want to leave Kala. I could go, except I have Seamus on the ground and Hollis is barely controllable.

"You take care of them," I say.

And they're gone in the black car. It's just Hollis, me, and Seamus, who's still unconscious.

I felt some hope with Harrop but now that he's gone I wonder if he will ever change his mind. Kala should be okay. They can't make a sixteen-year-old responsible for my kidnapping. They're going to blame it all on Dana. Dana will lose her hand and that's barbaric! I wish we had never come on this trip. All of this is my fault.

17. Action

Hollis and I are crouched next to Seamus. I still can't believe they stunned him. The Dream Council doesn't like people using 'unapproved' violence. Could this have been approved? Would they have done that, just to catch Dana and Kala?

"I'll get those dreamin' bastards," says Hollis.

"Right now, we've got to help Seamus," I say. "Get some water," I add without thinking.

I can't believe that I said that. I can virtually see Hollis thinking: 'Who is this boy to tell me what to do?' I just hope that he can think beyond that. I'm relieved when I see him move towards the water containers. Without Dana, I'm going to have to be firm with him. Things could get out of hand, and that won't help Dana or Kala.

When Hollis returns with the water, I empty a little onto my hand and splash it on Seamus' face. There's no reaction so I try again, using a little more water. It doesn't work.

"Give me that," says Hollis, taking the container and crudely pouring it directly onto Seamus' head, drenching him.

"Careful!" I say, but, it has worked.

Seamus shakes his head and coughs. "What happened?" he grumbles. "Where are ..."

His memory is returning. He turns his head to look around, but can't see Spike. The motionless dog is three metres directly behind him.

"I'm sorry," I say. "Spike's gone."

"Where is he?" he groans, using all his effort to sit up.

"I'll get him," I say. "You stay there."

I go to Spike, slowly lift him from the dust, and gently place him next to Seamus.

"I'm sorry," I say.

"Spikey," says Seamus sadly, placing his hand on the dog.

Hollis and I back away to give Seamus space and leave him with his beloved dog for a while.

"Dana and Kala?" asks Seamus. "Where are they?"

"Gone with the Dream Patrol," I reply.

"Bloody dreamers. Curse them all."

"Should we get the other containers?" asks Hollis.

I don't answer. Seamus is getting up.

"You okay?" I ask.

"I'll be okay."

Then I notice Seamus' leg. "You've got a bad cut there."

"It's nothing," says Seamus, reaching down for Spike.

I look again at the cut. It's not that bad. It will need a clean and a bandage, but he'll be okay. I could clean it now, but I don't have any supplies. I could use my shirt or something. Maybe we can go to my grandparents and tend to the cut there. That way Seamus can get some rest. I wonder if I should suggest that now. No, I'll wait. There'll be time to bring it up later. Right now, it's time for Spike.

Seamus slowly lifts his dog, cradling him in his arms and starts walking towards the track.

"What ya doing?" asks Hollis.

"I'm gunna bury 'im near the spring."

"But it'll be dark soon," says Hollis.

Hollis is right, but I'm not going to push the point.

"We'll help you," I say. "And we can get the other containers on the way back. Okay, Hollis?"

"Okay."

Our walk to the spring is slow and quiet. Seamus is limping. It would be faster if Hollis or I carried Spike, but I don't dare suggest it. I start thinking about Harrop and whether he will help Dana. Surely, he won't let her lose her hand. Another concern is the water. They'll be asking questions about that. We're in trouble if they block our access to the hot spring.

The light is well faded by the time we reach the spring. Hollis and I search for something to use for digging. I find a rock that might be suitable. Hollis collects a fallen tree branch and uses a large knife to shape the end. A knife! I didn't know he had a knife. If he'd gotten closer to Harrop, he might have used it. I'm suddenly glad that Harrop got him. Hollis could have made things even worse.

Seamus chooses a place on the hill above the spring. The digging takes a while, even with Hollis and me sharing the work.

"That'll do it," says Seamus when we've made a hole about half a metre deep. He gives Spike a forehead touch and a kiss, whispering his farewell, and then lowers him into the hole.

Seamus stands silently facing the grave for a while. Hollis and I stand beside him. I guess that Seamus is thanking Spike for his life. Poor Seamus lost his wife. Now he's lost his faithful little dog.

"Dream well," says Seamus.

That surprises me a little, but I'm composed enough to repeat it. "Dream well," I say, and Hollis says it too.

Standing there solemnly, I know I should be thinking about Spike, but again I'm thinking how stupid it was to bring Dana and Kala here.

Seamus sprinkles the grave with a handful of the dirt we removed. Hollis and I follow with a handful each, and then the rest of the dirt, after Seamus has walked away.

The light from the two quarter moons is reflecting off the spring water, giving us just enough visibility to see where to feed the stick through the container handles. Kala loves this phase of the moon cycle. She calls them 'winking moons'.

We walk slowly back along the trail. Seamus is limping, but able to carry one container. Hollis and I have three full containers on a carrying stick that is bending from the weight.

Hollis is taller than me and the angle of the carrying stick adds more weight to my end. It's extremely heavy. I struggle to hide the strain. I'm sure Hollis is seeing me as less of a hero now. If I show weakness, Hollis is sure to take control of what we do, and the idea of that is worrying me.

Seamus drops his container as we approach the car park. I'm glad for the rest.

"What now?" asks Hollis.

This is my chance. "We'll go to my grandparents'. My Grandpata can fix up Seamus' cut. We can stay the night there and leave first thing tomorrow."

"Yer can wash it with water," notes Hollis, but he's not adamant.

"It's just a scratch," adds Seamus.

"It's only an hour away," I insist. "We can tend the cut and Seamus will get a proper rest."

"I don't need tending."

"We might as well get some sleep though," says Hollis.

I'm glad that Seamus leaves it there. We're soon loading the containers into the trailer. Seamus accepts the backseat door I've opened for him. I quickly take the driver's seat, which feels strange as I'm the youngest and undoubtedly the least experienced driver, but I am the only one who knows the way.

***

I park in the driveway beside the old apple tree. We're soon met by my grandparents.

"Tomas," says Grandmata, walking towards our car.

"We weren't sure you'd be back," says Grandpata.

"We need your help," I say, exiting the car.

"What's happened?" asks Grandmata.

"Where's Kala?" asks Grandpata.

"The Dream Patrol got her and Dana."

"That's terrible," says Grandmata. "But why? They've got no reason to take her."

"It's that stupid kidnapping thing." I pause to greet them properly, starting with Grandmata, who smells of lavender.

Our forehead touch is quick, but our embrace lingers. Grandpata holds my head into his.

"This is our neighbour, Seamus, and this is Hollis," I say. "They're both from the South," I add unnecessarily.

Both greet my grandparents respectfully with a gentle touch of forehead.

"You've hurt your leg," says Grandmata, noticing the blood on Seamus leg.

"It's not too bad," says Seamus.

"What happened?" asks Grandpata.

"Seamus was hit by one of the patrol officer's stun guns." I say.

"I must have fallen on a rock or something," adds Seamus.

"They killed his dog," I say.

"They killed his dog!" exclaims Grandmata.

"Yes ..."

"Was that at the spring?" asks Grandpata, looking into the trailer.

"Yes, it was at the spring. We were going back for more water."

"Why don't you come in and have some tea?" says Grandmata. "And I'll clean up that cut."

"Do you mind if we stay the night?" I ask, knowing it won't be a problem.

"Stay as long as you want," says Grandmata.

Inside, Grandmata leads Seamus away to tend to his cut. Hollis and I sit at the table and Grandpata joins us, placing two oranges on the table.

"Sorry, but that that's all we have to offer you now. We'll have something else for you in the morning."

"It's okay. We brought food," says Hollis, getting up to go to the car.

"I can't believe they took Kala," says Grandpata.

"Kala and Dana shouldn't have come."

"Could you have stopped them?"

"I should have tried."

"So, the spring water worked?" asks Grandpata.

"Yes, it works," I reply, without enthusiasm.

I'm being ungrateful. It was Grandpata's book that had the information.

"It works," I add quietly. "It works and we've got you two to thank for it."

"Not us. Getting the book was your idea," says Grandpata.

Hollis returns with two bags, sits, and places sandwiches and a biscuit container at the middle of the table.

"Do ya have cups?" he asks, adding a bottle.

"Sure," says Grandpata.

He quickly returns with five cups and Hollis pours out an amber liquid.

"Is that beer?" asks Grandmata, arriving at the table with Seamus.

"Yeah, it's a Southern brew."

"I haven't had a beer in years," says Grandpata, tasting the foamy liquid. His eyes light up and he looks at Hollis. "Oh, this is good. It's so good! You've got to try this, Becca."

Becca is Grandmata's real name. I sometimes forget that.

"It aint that good," says Hollis. "It's too sweet. Scratcher didn't let it brew long enough. I paid 'im four rabbits for a batch of this brew and it's no good. I'll catch up with 'im."

I've never drunk beer before. In Norden, you're only allowed to drink once you've taken the passage. I don't hesitate to try it now. I've taken my passage, I think, as I raise the glass.

It tastes different. I'd actually call it sour and bitter. I don't really like it.

"Oh, yes! It is good," says Grandmata. "And thanks for the sandwiches. They're tasty."

"You haven't forgotten what real food tastes like?" queries Hollis, speaking as well as I've ever heard him.

"Problem is," says Grandpata. "This whole place is relying on dream work now. We've got no way of feeding ourselves or doing anything else the way we used to do."

"Yer right," adds Seamus quietly. "There's nothin' of use in Norden anymore. I remember the days when it was different. People worked hard. We 'ad shops full of just about everythin' you could want. Back then, people knew how to farm. They could grow just about anythin' and they knew how to fix things when something was broke. I remember there was a farmin' shop near here."

"You mean The Fancy Farmer on Orchard Road?" asks Grandpata.

"Yeah, that's the one. It wasn't that fancy. We called it The Fumy Farmer because of the stink from their fertiliser."

"That's the way I remember it too. It's all gone now though. It's all dream houses down there."

"Things have changed too much."

"It would take time to change things back," I note. "We'd have to phase out the dream work."

"We just need to sort out that Krakus," says Hollis, pouring the remaining beer into our cups.

"We'd just have another dreamer take his place," says Grandmata. "There are so many like him—all full of plans to make things bigger and better."

"Right now, I'd just settle for having Dana and Kala back," I say.

I'm now feeling a dull pain in my head. It could be the beer, but it's probably the situation I'm in. I hardly feel like talking, let alone working to keep Hollis in check.

"You look tired," says Grandmata.

"It's been a big day. Would you mind if I got some rest?"

"Not at all," says Grandpata. "You get some sleep. We'll take care of your friends."

"Sweet dreams, Tomas," says Grandmata.

"You too," I say, wandering towards the bedroom.

***

I'm tired, but the other reason to go to bed is to dream. There's a chance I could meet up with Kala in my dream. We haven't discussed the time or place, so it will be hard, but it's worth a try. I'll try for our forest. That's where Kala would want to meet me.

A Dream Passage

I struggle to dream. Thinking of Kala is easy, but I'm thinking about being with her and holding her. They're nice thoughts, but I'm also thinking about what's happened and I'm annoyed with myself over the danger for Dana and Kala.

I'm not getting anywhere near our deep green forest with fragrant flowers and that chirpy pair of parrots. I see the rust in our wheat, Spike dead on the ground, Kala and Dana locked in a room somewhere. I've got to find a way to fix all of this.

I fall asleep with an image of my mother, Beth, in my mind. She's here at my grandparents' house. "Be careful, Tomas," she says.

Before, my response would have been to be annoyed with her. I would have said, 'I am being careful.' Now though, things are different. She's not talking about my dreams, she's talking about my actions. I agree with her. I need to sort out this mess and I need to be careful.

18. Beth

I feel a touch on my shoulder. Kala?

No. This is not a dream. Now it's a hand on my shoulder and a whiff of a perfume that I know but can't quite place. I open my right eye and there she is in my periphery. It's my mother, Beth, beside me! It's as if I'm back at home with my parents and the last weeks have been a long dream.

"It's you," I say, moving my hand to hers.

"Yes, it's me." She bends down to gently touch my forehead. Her eyes are glistening with the beginnings of tears. "It's so good to see you," she says as she hugs me through the sheets.

Now she's crying. She's more emotional than I've ever seen her before. I have an inner sensation of warmth. It's a feeling I had at home with Beth and Davis when I was a young boy. Everything was simple back then, when all I knew was the love of my parents.

My body shivers though, as I'm struck the other memory of being at home, this time waiting for my passage and the angst I felt when I was destined for a path I didn't choose. Back then I couldn't do anything. It is so very different now.

I sit up and take a hold of Beth, hugging her tightly. I want to tell her everything. I want her to know about the South, and about Kala and me, and how different I am.

I want to be strong. I am responsible. My actions will affect her life. I could tell her that we have a plan and that everything will be okay, but that might be a lie. I hope that things will be okay. Maybe though, I've just made trouble for her, Dana and Kala, and for Seamus.

Her sobbing slows.

"I dreamt that you came here," I say.

"It was the broadcast," she says. "They said that they'd captured Kala and the woman called Dana. I came here on the off chance you were here."

It makes sense. I didn't think of the broadcast. Maybe there was logic in my dream that my conscious didn't fully appreciate.

I'm holding Beth, but now I'm looking ahead, wondering if it's the right time to ask her for help. With Paros and Neros and with Beth's help we could bring down the entire dream system. I'm playing events out in my head. I hesitate. I see risks. I see Kala captured. I imagine Dana with no hand. I see the South unable to support Norden. I see starving people and they're angry. They trusted me.

"Are you okay?" asks Beth.

"Yes, I'm fine. What did they say on the broadcast?"

"They said they caught Dana and Kala according to a plan they had."

We fell straight into their trap!

"They didn't mention the killing?" I ask, knowing that Beth will react. This is my plan and I feel bad about it, but what else can I do? It's as if everything is running on autopilot. The next steps are set. I feel like all I can do is fill in the details.

"Killing?" asks Beth.

"The old man staying here, Seamus. They stunned him and his dog."

"The dog died?"

"Yes, it was a small dog. The stun gun was too much for it."

"I believe you, Tomas. I've thought about everything that has happened. I was living in a dream before. Now my eyes have been opened. I got your message about the lying. You are right. There is no Island of Contemplation and they lie about the numbers in the South. They also lied about Kala being a kidnapper and they hide their violence. There are so many lies. I'm so sorry about Kala."

"Kala should be okay. It's the other woman, Dana, who I'm worried about. She could lose her hand."

"Yes, I remember that. I want you to know that Davis and I are with you. We are here for you and Kala, and we'll help you any way we can."

She's with Kala and me! I feel tension release from the back of my neck through to my shoulders. She is with us!

"Thank you," I say. But then my back tightens. The course ahead isn't easy. If Hollis has his way, there will be a fight. I know that isn't the answer but I'm not sure how I can stop it. I must try to find a way.

"We'll join you in the South," says Beth. "If that's what you want."

"Thank you," I repeat. "But, I'm worried. We've got problems in the South. There's rust in our crops and there are people who want to fight Norden. We can sort it out, but we need time. I don't think we can support Norden right now. Things will have to stay as they are for a bit longer."

"You've grown up so quickly," says Beth.

"I guess I have," I say. "Now I see that things are complicated. Before, I thought it was just a matter of right and wrong. Now, it's a matter of different perspectives. I am sure about one thing though. I'm still your son. I will always be that."

"And Kala. Is there a way we can get her back?"

"We have a plan. Kala and Dana will try to get a man called Harrop to release them. Harrop and Dana were once a couple. It might work, but only if Harrop decides to help."

"Is there time for that? Dana has already been sentenced."

"How long do you think she has?" I ask.

"I don't know. We've never seen a situation like this before. It could be days or it could be a week. Are you sure about Harrop?"

"He won't let Dana lose her hand." I say, adding, "I'm sure of it," as if I am certain.

I really do think he'll do something. I just hope that it works.

"It's a big risk," says Beth.

"I know. There's little else we can do though. That's why I think Harrop will act. He knows we can't rescue them."

"Why did you come back?" asks Beth.

"We came for the spring water. We need it to treat the rust in our crops."

"Yes, your Grandpata told me about that. Did it work?"

"Yes! We're going to need a lot of that spring water though. We'll have to come back for more."

"When will you leave?"

"We'll go this morning. Hollis and Seamus will want to get back."

"I hoped we'd have more time ... Can you stay?"

"No, I need to go too. I need to help plan what we're going to do next. It's going to be tricky. People like Hollis ... They'll want to fight, but that will put Dana and Kala in more danger. I've got to stop it."

"Will they listen to you?" asks Beth.

"Probably not. But I've got to try."

"You stand up for what you think is right," says Beth.

This really is a new Beth.

"Thank you," I say, again taking her hand and feeling the strength in her hold.

"How is Davis?" I ask.

"He's fine. He wanted to come but we agreed that it was better if just one of us came. Sometimes they follow us."

"They follow you?"

"Yes, we're sure of it. They don't trust us. They think we're working for the South."

"But what about your work? Do they let you broadcast?"

"Yes, they let me work. They just watch us closely. If Krakus had the slightest thing on us, we'd be prosecuted."

"It's not safe for you here. You should leave."

"I don't care. Let them prosecute us," says Beth defiantly.

The thing is that I need Beth to have her job. We might need the access she has.

"You really need to go home now," I say. "There will be a time for change, but it isn't yet. Can you do something for us?"

"Of course. What is it?"

"You need to go now and act as if everything is normal. You need to work for those schools as you did before. You might be able to help us, but not now. Can you and Davis wait for me?"

"Yes, we can do that."

I'm again thinking of the risks. Beth could be seen here. What if she was arrested? Apart from being bad for her and Davis, it would mean she couldn't help us. It's only a small risk, but from now on, I'm going to be more careful with the people I care about.

"I'll get a message to you through Kala's parents. Now though, we all need to be more careful. Can I ask you to go now?"

"If you need me to go, I'll go."

"Thank you," I say, kissing her on the forehead.

"I need to tell you one more thing."

"What is it?" I ask.

"Just that I'm sorry. I'm so sorry about the passage. I should never have made you go."

"It's okay. It's all okay. Everything will work out," I say, feeling my pendant. "Tell Davis I said hello. Tell him that I love him and I miss him, and I said to dream well. You really have to go now. Dream well."

I hug her one last time and then release her towards the door.

"Be careful, Tomas," she says, exactly as she said it in my dream.

"I will," I say and usher Beth past Grandmata, Grandpata, Hollis, and Seamus, who are seated at the kitchen table.

"Your mother brought us breakfast," yells Grandpata.

"She's got to go," I say. "It's not safe for her now. Dream well," I repeat, farewelling her at the door.

"Dream well," she says in return and she's gone.

***

Beth left us a colourful spread of fruits, cereal and yogurt. Grandpata has made a pot of our Southern tea.

"Lychees," I note enthusiastically.

Hollis and Seamus eat a little and gulp their tea. They obviously want to go and I have no reason to stop them. We delay a moment to farewell Grandmata and Grandpata, and for me to grab one of the spotted and lumpy apples from the old apple tree. I'll eat it later.

19. Leadership

We're halfway home. Seamus is driving and it's quiet in the car. I tried to sleep but kept thinking about what might happen. There'll be an Origins' meeting tomorrow and Hollis will propose that we rescue Dana and Kala. He'll want to use guns. Perhaps he's right about doing that. Most people in Norden are against violence—we could even win that kind of fight.

On the other hand, Krakus will be expecting something. Kala will be there and if something happens, she won't stand back. She could be hurt. So could Dana and other people too. The whole thing could go bad. Krakus will do whatever it takes to stay in control. He's using Dana and Kala to show his power and to convince people to support him. He'll accuse them of more crimes and have them punished, just like he did the last time with Dana.

I consider talking to Hollis now. I could say that the risks are too high. The trouble is that I'm not sure that Seamus will support me, having lost Spike yesterday.

I also doubt Hollis will listen to me. Who am I to convince him? I'm just a boy who was lucky with a stick and some water. I'm no threat. He doesn't need to discuss it with me. He'll be figuring out what he's going to say tomorrow. I decide to stay quiet now and save it for tomorrow. Anita is the one to take on Hollis.

***

The quiet in the car is beginning to get to me. I decide to bring up rabbit catching.

"Do you think Scratcher will let us borrow his dog?" I ask.

"Dunno," says Hollis. "You'll have to ask him."

Okay. That didn't go so well.

Later, I'm thinking about what happened at the spring. I really can't believe that it was Harrop who shot Spike and Seamus.

"Seamus, can I ask you something?"

"What?"

"Which officer shot Spike? Was it the skinny one or the larger one with the shorter hair?"

"The larger one. He got 'im from behind."

"And which one shot you?"

"Same one. Got me when I went for 'im."

"What does it matter?" asks Hollis.

"The skinny one was Harrop. He didn't want to shoot anyone."

"He shot me, didn't he?"

"Yes," I reply, remembering the way that Hollis gave Harrop little choice but to stun him. "But I don't think he wanted to. And I think there's a chance he will try to help Dana and Kala."

"You're dreamin'," says Hollis.

I decide to leave it there.

***

It's late afternoon when we reach my place. Seamus to my surprise, helps me unload a water container.

"Don't worry," he says. "We'll get Kala back."

"I'm sorry about Spike," I say as we touch foreheads. Seamus holds my arm and we look at each other.

"Dream well," he says.

"Dream well," I reply, and he returns to his car.

***

The house is awfully quiet. I sit down to a drink of milk and one of Dana's oat biscuits. I have little else to think of but Kala and Dana. While I assume they're okay, I don't really know anything for certain. Where are they and how are they being treated? And will Harrop help them?

I'll try dreaming with Kala again tonight. Cowsy's mooing interrupts me as I'm thinking about the best time to catch Kala. I should milk Cowsy. I'll also have to put the chickens away before the seven-thirty p.m. radio hook up.

I should really eat something more than a biscuit. I make myself a cheese and lettuce sandwich. It's probably the most tasteless thing I've eaten in the South. I think about making myself a cup of tea but starting the wood fire seems like a waste of effort when it's just for me.

Cowsy looks happy to see me. She would have been worrying that she wouldn't be milked today. I soon have her milked and the chickens safely in the shed. I freshen their drinking water, bring the milk inside, and skim the cream from the top of the milk to make butter.

That's enough work for now. I've only a few minutes before the radio hook up. Paros and Neros will be as worried as I am.

At a little before seven-thirty p.m., I go to Dana's room and for a while I stand there looking at the radio, wishing I had been more attentive when Dana showed it to Kala and me. I try a few buttons. The one that turns the light green is promising. When I move the volume dial, I hear someone talking. It's Anita talking about the meeting tomorrow.

"Hello," I say. No response. I try again with the handset button pushed in.

"Is that you, Tomas?" says a voice.

The voice said my name and no code words.

"Yes, it's Tomas. Is that ... you?"

"Yes, it's Paros. I'm here with Neros."

"You sound tired," says Anita. "Are you okay?"

"Yes, I'm okay. Any word on Kala?"

"No," says Paros, "Nothing since yesterday's broadcast. We're going to try to get a meeting with Krakus tomorrow."

It's a good idea. Maybe Krakus will release Kala to their care. They'll have to be careful not to give away that they know Dana, though. On the other hand, Krakus is not foolish. He might have worked out what happened when Paros rescued Dana.

"It's worth a try," I say. "Though I should tell you that Kala had a bit of a plan. Is it safe to talk on this radio?"

"It should be safe," says Paros, "But ask yourself if we need to know. Do we need to know about it now?"

"Ummm ..." I say, thinking. "No, I don't think so."

"Okay then, we'll just see what we can do tomorrow."

"Be careful," I say.

"It might be an idea for just one of you to meet up with Krakus," notes Anita.

"We were just talking about that," says Paros.

"Let us know what you decide," says Anita.

"Shall we talk about the meeting tomorrow?" asks Paros.

"Okay," says Anita. "We need a plan."

"To take on Hollis?" asks Neros.

"We can hardly discuss it on the radio," notes Anita. "You'll have to leave it to Tomas and me."

"All right, Anita," says Paros. "We'll leave it to you. Is there anything else you want to discuss?"

"No," replies Anita. "Let's talk again tomorrow night. Good luck for tomorrow."

"You too. Dream well," says Paros. "Dream well, Tomas."

"Dream well," I say. "See you tomorrow, Anita."

"See you, Tomas. Dream well," says Anita.

I turn off the radio.

I think about making the butter but decide that I'm too tired to do it. I go and lie on Kala's and my bed and think about what might happen tomorrow.

Paros and Neros are going to see Krakus. I doubt that they'll be able to convince him to release Kala, but it is worth a try. Maybe I should try to sleep now. I want to dream with Kala. I'm tired though, and that makes it difficult. I focus on trying to reach the state of both relaxation and concentration I need to dream well.

I imagine Rexus talking to me, telling me that it's the details that will make it come true. I'll need those details now; the specifics of the clearing in the forest, the flowers that smell like Kala, the chirpy little parrots and Kala there with me.

And … I am with her! We're there in the forest and holding each other tightly. I can smell her perfume and I even feel her touch.

"Tomas," she says, smiling.

"Are you okay?" I ask.

"Yes, I'm fine. We're being held under guard at a house."

"Is your plan working?"

"I think it will work. Harrop will be here tomorrow. He won't let Dana—"

Then I don't see her. "Dream well, my love," I hear, fading away.

"Kala!" I say, but there's no answer. "Dream well, my love," I whisper.

I try dreaming twice more, but I don't make contact. I'm left dreaming in the forest, without Kala.

***

It's morning and I've used my dream training to focus and remember the specifics of my dream with Kala. She's okay!

I also recall another dream where I saw Hollis and he was threatening to shoot something. It must have been a rabbit. I saw it stopped still and startled by the glimmer of sunlight reflected from a truck. The strange thing was that the rabbit had a human face. It was all very odd.

The clock is saying seven forty-five. I don't have much time. Seamus will be here at nine to take me to Hammond and Roget's. I rush to light the fire, milk Cowsy, feed and release the chickens, and boil an egg for my breakfast.

I hear the sound of Seamus' car arriving as I'm making the bed. Just as I'm about to leave the room, I notice that on the ground beside the bed is that lumpy old apple I took from my grandparents' tree. The funny thing is that I don't remember leaving it there. I pick it up and put it in my pocket and move quickly to meet Seamus.

"You okay?" I ask.

"It's quiet without Spike."

I know what he means.

"What do you think will happen today?" I ask.

"We'll vote yer a new leader and work it out from there. They's picked Anita the last time Dana got caught. It could be her again or Hollis, if 'e stands."

"Do you think he'll stand?"

"Dunno. Being hit by that stun gun made 'im mad as ever. He might."

"And if he becomes leader?"

"He'll want action—to go to Norden or something like that. It's gunna be hard to stop him. He'll want to take his guns to rescue Dana and Kala and get that water."

"I'm worried about Krakus," I say. "He would have been embarrassed by Dana getting away last time. This time the Dream Council will be more careful. They'll have more patrol officers and stun guns and Hollis and his buddies will have their guns. I'm worried that someone will be killed and afraid that it could be Kala or Dana."

"Yer has to speak up at the meeting then. Tell 'em what you just said."

"You think they'll listen to me?"

"Yeah. Don't forget, you're the guy that's savin' our crops."

"Okay," I say.

"Just talk as if ya mean what yer saying. People will listen."

It will be Anita and me speaking against Hollis. Even with the two of us, it's going to be difficult. I'll need to see Anita before the meeting.

***

It was only days ago that Kala and I were at Hammond and Roget's. Entering their shed alone this time feels very different. I'm greeted warmly, but I can tell that people are anxious.

"Don't worry, we'll get them back," says Roget's mother.

"We'll get her," agrees his father.

Their keenness for action makes me nervous. I should be talking with them and asking for their support to stop Hollis, but I don't. Instead, I pass through the rest of the greetings as quickly as I can. I just want to get to Anita.

I find her sitting quietly at the leadership table.

"Hi," I say, and we share the traditional forehead greeting.

"I'm glad you're here," she says. "Are you all right?"

"Yes, I'm okay. I'm worried about this, though. I'm afraid that trying a rescue with guns is going to put Kala and Dana at risk. Do you think we can stop Hollis from taking guns?"

"That's what I wanted to see you about. If Hollis stands, I think he'll win this time. I don't think I can beat him."

"You've got to try."

"I'll stand if he doesn't nominate. But if he does stand, I'm going to need your help."

"Sure," I say. "What do you want me to say?"

In my head, I've been working out what I can say about Krakus, the danger for Dana and Kala, and the risks of using guns.

"If Hollis stands, I need you to stand against him."

"What? You want me to stand for leader?"

"Yes. If Hollis stands, we're going to need you to stand against him," she says. "And we'll need you to win," she adds, smiling.

"But I'm the youngest here. I'm only sixteen. I've only just arrived."

"I know that, but you are the only one who will have a chance against him. The people from the far South will support me, but the farmers from our Northern areas are sure to support Hollis. The Northerners will only support someone willing to confront the Norden dreamers and act. That is you."

"But, that's not me. I don't want action. I want to negotiate."

"I agree with that. The problem is that I'm not seen as a person who acts. I won't be able to convince the Northern farmers. If you stand, you'll get some of them. You'll split Hollis' support and that will be enough. All you need to do is say that you agree that we should act, but only after trying one last time to negotiate. If the negotiation fails, we will take strong action."

"What action?"

"I don't know. We'll have to think of something."

"But we don't have long," I say.

"Yes, I know. I've got to get this meeting started. If Hollis nominates, then you have to stand against him. Talk strongly and you'll get support."

Anita rings the bell before I can say anything more. I have little choice but to go to my chair at the leadership table. As I sit, I feel the apple in my pocket press against my leg. I take it out and place it on the table. Great, I think. Hollis will be asking for violence and I'll be sitting here behind my apple.

When everyone is seated, Anita stands and thanks everyone for coming. As she's explaining events, I'm assessing what I should do. Hollis is almost certain to stand. I look at the vacant seat next to mine. It's Kala's. I know what she'd say if she was here. She'd be telling me I should do it. She'd talk as if it was obvious and I was certain to win.

"And now I'm calling for nominations to become temporary leader in place of Dana."

"I will stand," says Hollis, standing.

"Hollis is standing," says Anita. "Any other nominations?" Anita is looking directly at me.

I will my legs, forcing myself to stand up. It's such an effort, it's as if someone else is controlling me and I'm stuck, watching this other Tomas rising from his chair.

"I will stand," says my voice in a tone that's so high and young that it won't convince anyone.

There's chatter and I think I hear someone laughing. Anita rings the bell. I return to my seat.

"So far, we have Hollis and Tomas standing. Are there any other nominations?"

Again, there is more talking. But no other nominations.

"As there are no further nominations, let's hear from the candidates. Would you like to say something, Hollis?"

"Yeah, I'll say something," he says, standing. "Ya all know me. Yer know that I prefers action instead of words. I reckon we've talked for long enough. We need to fight these dreamers. Now is the time for that. I say that we act now to take our people back. We get Dana and Kala back, and we go and get that spring water and we stop them dreamers moving south. That's all I has to say and I think that's all that needs to be said. It's time for action."

Hollis isn't a sophisticated speaker but he made his point well. The people standing around Hollis are clapping and some others join their applause. I don't like my chances.

"Thank you, Hollis," says Anita. "Your turn, Tomas."

I slowly rise from my chair. I can feel my hands shaking and I'm unable to remain straight. I seem to be rocking back and forth and I have the apple on the table in front of me.

I wonder if I should even try. Even if I speak loud enough to be heard, my words won't be strong enough to get support.

I look down to avoid all their expectant faces. The thing I see again though, is Kala's vacant chair. I have to try for her. I focus on the thing I need most right now, which is a strong voice.

"I also stand for action," I say, slowly and louder than I've ever spoken before.

"But I stand for a different kind of action. It's my Kala that's being held with Dana, and I'm worried about the kind of action that Hollis is proposing.

"Krakus and the Dream Council were embarrassed by the way Dana escaped last time. They won't make the same mistake again. We have to act carefully or we're going risk the lives of Dana and Kala. We've seen that they are prepared to be violent. If we act aggressively, we will risk our people.

"The other concern I have is that if we threaten them, the Dream Council will act strongly against us. They will make the move south their number one priority. I say that we do what Dana wanted. We negotiate to release Dana and Kala and to keep them away from our farmland."

"Why would they negotiate with us?" asks Hollis.

Is he allowed to ask me questions? I hesitate, but Anita is silent. It must be allowed. I stand silent for a few moments.

Hollis is right. I've got to tell them how we can get them to negotiate.

"What we have is knowledge," I say. "We know that they lie to their people. If we need to, we can bring down the entire Dream Council."

"How you gunna do that?" asks the skinny man standing next to Hollis.

"We make a plan," I say.

"It seems that we are debating the action rather than leadership," notes Anita.

"What's your plan?" asks the skinny man.

I pause for a moment. If I don't say more, I'm going to lose this. Anita gives me a nod. I feel my diamond pendant. Everyone is looking at me standing behind an apple with shaking hands.

Just a minute! Their dream work started with an apple and it could end with an apple. That's it!

"You all see this apple," I say, picking up my apple and holding it out with my shaking hand. "I don't know if you know this, but the entire dream movement began with one apple. The first thing they dreamed up was one apple that appeared in a small triangle which Zennuta placed at the centre of Norden Square. That first apple would have been juicy, crisp and tasty.

"But over time, they've lost all their experience of different-tasting apples. They rely on their dreams to get everything they want and they don't experience anything new.

If you tasted one of their dream apples, you'd find it tasteless. It's juicy and nutritious, but flavourless.

"All of their dream foods have lost their flavour. When I came here, I was amazed by the taste of Southern food. The people in Norden have no idea what they gave up. We can bring down the entire movement by showing them what they've lost. We can convince them by delivering an apple to each house in Norden."

"Who's gunna give away their apples for that?" asks the skinny man, scratching his arm. He must be Hollis' neighbour, Scratcher.

"I will," says a bearded man to my left.

"What's your name?" I ask.

"Tallis," he says.

"Thanks, Tallis. How many apples do you have?"

"About 2,000 ripe and ready to go."

"That might not be enough," says Anita. "There are around three thousand homes in Norden."

"You can have our oranges," says the woman next to Tallis.

"You can have our nectarines," says someone else.

"Thank you," I say. "We can send a piece of fruit for every person in Norden. And we can use their broadcast to tell them why the fruit tastes so good. We can explain what they've lost and tell them how the Dream Council lies."

"How are ya gonna get on the broadcast?" asks Hollis.

"My mother is one of the broadcasters. She wants to help us. We also have Paros and Neros. With their help, we can intercept the broadcast."

"Is that true?" asks Hollis, directing his question to Anita.

"Yes," replies Anita. "Paros and Neros have the capability to interrupt or even take over the broadcast."

"There you have it," I say. "We have a plan that we can use if Krakus will not negotiate with us."

"Hang on," says Hollis. "How are the dreamers gunna eat if they stop dreamin'? They'll starve."

"That's a good point," I say. "We'll ask them to continue their dream work. I'm not saying that we stop all the dream work. The idea is that each person is free to choose his or her own path. They can stay in Norden and be part of the dream movement or move to the South. We need an arrangement where every person has a choice. I was given that choice and that's what I want for every person."

"You can have my chickens," says Jessup. Some people laugh at this, but I thank him.

"Any more questions, Hollis?" asks Anita.

"No," he replies.

"Well, we have a clear choice here. We have Hollis' plan for action and we have Tomas' plan for action. I'll give you a few minutes to consider your vote."

I watch people gather and talk. I bet they're wishing that someone else had been nominated. Maybe it's not too late for that. I look to Anita, who mouths something I don't understand. I shrug my shoulders. She tries again and I hear her say, "Well done." I don't think it will be enough though.

Anita rings the bell. "It's time for the vote," she says. "People voting for Hollis and his plan move to my left," she says and points clearly to her left. "People voting for Tomas and his plan move to my right," she says and points right.

People seem to be moving in all directions. I wonder if I should move. I watch Anita move to the right and I follow. I'm glad to see Seamus with me. He pats me on the back. Other people are moving towards me too. I am getting a few votes.

More people are joining me. Hollis has support, but it is only around eight or nine people. I think I have more than that.

Hollis looks at me, knowing that he's lost. Two of his supporters cross the short distance to my side. Now another three from his side are moving. And two more. It's only Hollis and Scratcher on the other side.

I'm really surprised when Scratcher also moves to my side. Hollis is standing alone and now, I even feel a little sorry for him.

Am I really worthy of this support? With Hollis, they knew exactly what they would get. My plan might fail.

Now Hollis is moving towards me. He greets me warmly. "Ya won," he says and our foreheads meet.

Anita follows. "What now?" I whisper in her ear.

"You take the leader's seat," she says as she turns me towards the table and points to the chair she had occupied.

More people move to congratulate me. I accept their wishes, doing what I can to move towards the table.

At the table, I'm not sure what to do. I sit there looking at people looking back at me. Many of them are talking.

Anita points to the bell. I stand and ring it and then sit again, aware now that I've only a short time to work out what I should say. I'm not even sure of the correct procedure. Anita takes her seat next to me.

"What now?" I whisper.

"All you've got to do is to restate your plan. We can sort out the details afterwards. Ring the bell when you're ready to start."

Here goes. I ring the bell once more and stand.

"Thanks for your support," I say. "And thanks, Hollis, for standing. You're a man of action and we all respect that.

"You all heard my plan. Tomorrow, Anita and I will go to Norden. We will meet with Krakus and demand that Dana and Kala are released. We will ask for a peaceful truce, where they respect our right to our lands, stop their move south, and allow us free access to the spring water. In return, we will respect their right to live as they wish."

Picking up the apple, I continue, "And if Anita and I aren't back the day after tomorrow, we will go ahead with the plan to intercept the broadcast and distribute the apples and oranges the following evening. Hollis will be in charge of the fruit distribution. Is that okay with you, Hollis?"

"Sure," he says.

"Are there any questions? Does anyone want to say anything?" I ask.

No one speaks. They're all staring at me.

"That's it, then. Good luck," I say. "And dream well." I bow my head.

"Dream well," they say.

20. Krakus

It's early morning and I'm on my way to Norden again; this time with Anita and Leroy. We're in their car and Leroy is driving. They both look different—clean with brushed hair and ironed clothes. I barely recognised them when they came to collect me.

"You two look good. And is that perfume I smell?"

"Anita wanted to dress up," offers Leroy.

"It's a strategy," adds Anita. "I want to try and break the unruly farmer stereotype Krakus is pushing."

"Good idea. You really should be the leader."

"You did really well yesterday," says Leroy.

"Thanks, but I'm worried about today."

"You'll be fine," adds Anita.

***

It's now afternoon. We've travelled most of the way towards Norden. I'm looking for the turn-off for Mountain Creek Road even though this time we'll be driving straight past it.

Earlier, Anita asked if I had any more news of Kala. I told her about Kala and I meeting in our dreams, and how Kala said they were being held in a farm house.

Leroy seemed a bit sceptical about us meeting in our dreams. Anita wanted to know exactly how we did it without the wristbands. I told her how it didn't need anything special, just a little training. I said she and Leroy could do it too. Leroy laughed and said that they saw enough of each other during the day and he didn't want Anita getting into his dreams. Anita said that was fine with her; she didn't want to know all his secrets.

We also talked about whether Teague really will choose to live in Norden. Leroy thinks he will. Anita isn't so sure. She said I was a role model for Rachus and Teague. Leroy gave Anita a funny look when she mentioned Rachus.

***

"There it is. That's the turn off for Mountain Creek Road," I say, pointing.

"How far is the spring?" asks Leroy.

"It's about forty kilometres. It's a winding road though. Takes about half an hour."

"I'd like to see it," says Anita.

"I think you'd like it. It's in a grassy clearing surrounded by forest. My grandparents used to swim there."

"All going well, we can stop there on the way back," notes Leroy.

I hope he's right. If our negotiation with Krakus works, we could return tomorrow with Kala and Dana, and be able to go to the spring whenever we want. That would be fantastic!

I check myself there. It's too much of a dream for now. Kala and Dana are being held and we're on our way to meet with Krakus. I'm not even sure that he'll meet with us.

***

Anita is directing Leroy to the Dream Council office.

"It's just around the corner," she says. "Do you really want to park right out the front?" she asks.

"Yes," I say. "We need them to take notice of us."

And they do. As soon as we've parked, we're met by two patrol officers, both with their hands close to their stun guns.

"What do ya think ya doing here?" says the shorter one with a very square haircut as we get out of the car. He talks in a Southern style, like he didn't go to school—not many people speak that way in Norden.

"We're here to meet with Krakus," I say.

"Ya names?"

"This is Anita and this is Leroy. I'm Tomas. We're from the South."

"What time's yer meetin'?" asks the square-haired officer.

"Four p.m." I say, conscious that what I say will only be true if it happens.

"I don't believe them," says the standard haired officer. "Krakus left at two p.m. and won't be back until just before six."

We start walking, Leroy first with Anita and me behind. Standard Hair steps quickly ahead, blocking Leroy.

"You heard us," says Leroy, gently raising his palm. "We have a meeting at four. This isn't a matter for you two."

We keep walking. Square Hair moves ahead of us, toward the office entrance. Standard Hair stands back, watching me closely until we pass him, then takes a position behind us.

The door to the Dream Council office opens automatically. Through the door, I see a curly haired patrol officer seated behind a tall reception desk.

"Southerners," says Square Hair. "Say they has a four o'clock meetin' with Krakus."

The patrol officer looks down. She must be checking Krakus' diary. "There's no record of a meeting at four."

"There must be some mistake," I say. "Tell Krakus that the delegation from the South is here for their meeting."

"But Krakus isn't here," she says. "Who are you?"

"I'm Tomas and this is Anita and her husband, Leroy."

"What do you want?"

"We're here for our meeting with Krakus."

"Which one of you is the leader?"

"I am," I say.

The curly haired patrol officer stares at me. "How old are you?"

"I'm sixteen years old."

"This is a joke," says Square Hair.

"It's no joke," says Anita. "You people just need to do your jobs properly. Tell Krakus that we're here to see him."

There's no response. All three patrol officers seem to be looking at each other without any idea of what to do.

"We'll wait over here," says Leroy, moving towards a wooden bench chair beside the window. Anita and I follow and sit. Square Hair and Standard Hair exchange further glances before moving to guarding positions on either side of the entrance.

A Dream Passage

Curly Hair makes a call on her radio. I guess that she's checking in with Krakus. At least, I hope that she is. My plan relies on him deciding to see us. If he doesn't then this could be the first of many things to go wrong. All we can do is wait.

***

Twenty minutes later, Leroy gives Anita a funny look.

"What is it?" I whisper.

"His bum is going numb," says Anita.

"Why don't they dream up cushions?" says Leroy.

I laugh.

"Stand up and walk around," says Anita.

Leroy follows her advice, strolling in a circle, then stops and stretches forward, bending his front knee and leans over with his bottom aligned to the patrol officers guarding the door. I have to cover my mouth to hide my smile.

A few minutes later I start to feel uncomfortable too. I try a few of Leroy's stretches, although I am more considerate with my positioning.

Curly Hair receives a radio call and then looks to us. This is it. I'm guessing that in the next few moments we'll be either imprisoned, sent away, or meeting with Krakus.

"Come this way," she says, beginning down a corridor to our left. I quickly follow with Anita and Leroy just behind me. We walk for about twenty metres then take a right turn, and a further right turn, twenty metres along.

She knocks on the door. We're greeted by another patrol officer, a tall man.

267

"Come in," he says.

The room is large with high ceilings and decorated walls. I've never seen anything like it. The walls are adorned with purple paper patterned with a series of gold lines at each edge. There are two plush, purple couches and a mini table on the left. On the right is an oversized table made from thick timber. At the end is a solid looking wooden door with an ornately carved square border. My guess is that it's the door to Krakus' chambers.

"You'll soon meet with Krakus," says the tall officer.

I nod in agreement.

"But before the meeting, we'll need to search you. I assume that is okay?"

"Yes," I say, stepping forward.

We each submit to the officer's check. He gets each of us to raise our arms, bend, turn around, and spread our legs. It's an effective method. He barely touches us.

"Please take a seat. I'll let Krakus know you are ready."

"Thank you," I say.

Leroy runs his hand along the oversized table. "Not bad," he declares.

"Sure isn't dream work," I note.

"Shhh," says Anita.

I hear the door opening. I feel my heart throbbing. Calm down, I tell myself.

And there he is! It's the man I've seen on so many broadcasts. He's really tall. As he enters, his head is just below the top of the door jamb.

A Dream Passage

He reaches out towards Leroy. Leroy looks to me and Krakus understands. He turns to me.

"You must be Tomas," he says.

Krakus said my name! He's standing there, bald and tall, and looking at me with his milky white eyes which are unique but not as creepy as I imagined. Within them I see a jade iris. It's a sign of life that I didn't expect. You don't see that on the broadcast. He's still a strange man though.

He speaks as if it were a broadcast. It makes me wonder if we're being watched or recorded. I get an idea that I need to perform here.

"Yes, I'm Tomas," I say. "And this is Anita and her husband, Leroy. Thank you for meeting with us."

He points his open palm towards the oversized table and waits for us to take our seats. We watch him slowly, quietly, and confidently, take his seat. I can see what I'm up against. This man is a skilled performer. I'm going to have to be careful.

"It was good of you to come," he says, pausing to look at each of us. "How can I help you?"

"Thank you for meeting with us," I say again. "We would like your help." I pause before adding, "And also, we'd like to help you. In fact, we have an offer for you."

"We'd be delighted to help our friends in the South. How can we help?"

He ignored my offer to help him. I decide to leave that, for now.

"You're holding two of our people," I say.

"Dana and Kala?"

"Yes."

"Yes, we have them," he says directly. "Dana, as you know, is guilty of a crime. Dana will lose her hand. And Kala is being held for kidnapping. As I understand it, she kidnapped you when you were on your way to your passage ceremony. Kala's trial is tomorrow."

His voice is steady and constant. He talks and he watches us. I'm certain he's assessing our strengths and weakness. I've got to be strong here.

"You are holding Dana and Kala without cause," I say. "You know that Dana did not steal and you know that Kala is no kidnapper. You know the truth."

"Tomas, you know as I do, that justice is a matter for our community. We have a process for determining guilt or innocence. Dana was found guilty and will be punished according to the will of the community. Kala will have her trial tomorrow. That is the process and—"

"You know it is a lie," interrupts Leroy.

Krakus glances at Leroy dismissively before returning his gaze to me. "I know no such thing."

"What about Kala?" says Anita. "There was no kidnapping. You can see for yourself that Tomas is here and freely part of the South."

"Kala kidnapped Tomas and stopped him from taking his passage. I must apologise to you, Tomas. We should have stopped Kala. You would now be an adult member of our community. I am sorry that we failed you."

270

I pause. Krakus is calmly and deliberately twisting things. He's treating me like a child. He doesn't know anything of me or my passage. My actual passage was more than a group of children chanting about dreams. My passage was real.

"Is there anything else we can help you with?" asks Krakus.

I've got to take the lead, somehow. I stood and became leader of the South yesterday. I've got to be the leader now and make another stand.

I decide to do it literally. Slowly and deliberately, I move my chair back, stand up, and look directly at Krakus, staring into the jade iris' within his milky white eyes.

"I stand here as a man and as leader of the South," I say. "I have taken a passage that you did not offer. My passage was no ceremony. My passage was for me to live my dreams. I am here doing that now."

"Sit down," he says.

I ignore him. "We came here to make peace," I continue. "We want our people released and to make a truce with you. We were going to offer you a deal where you respect our land and we respect yours. But what you have said has changed my mind. You have no respect for us. What's worse is that you do not respect your own people."

I pause briefly and then go on. "Everyone deserves the right to choose their own passage. We're going to change things. You can join us now and be part of this change or you can do nothing and the change will be made without you. That is the choice that we offer you."

Krakus stares at me. "The way I see it," he says. "You're not in a position to offer us anything. You really should sit down."

I remain standing.

"That will change very soon. We will offer the people of Norden freedom. They will be shown the truth and we will offer them a choice of Norden dreaming or living in the South."

"What truth?" queries Krakus.

"The truth about the Island of Contemplation. The truth about the number of people in the South and the truth about your bland food."

"These things are minor. Do you really think people would choose a life of farming?"

"The truth is that you lie. There is no dream justice. You will cut off Dana's hand just to maintain your power and control. That's not justice. That is the truth of it."

Krakus turns to Anita. "This boy is an undisciplined dreamer. Are you sure he is your leader?"

He's calling me a child again. I try not to let it get to me, but my heart is beating so strongly that I feel myself start to sweat.

"Tomas is our elected leader," replies Anita. "And he speaks the truth."

"You should listen to him," adds Leroy. "There is no dream justice. You cut off people's hands for no justifiable reason."

"The people of Norden are different to you Southerners. They don't always dream of all the things that need to be done to maintain law and order in Norden. The Council intervenes from time to time to help them."

"You're a liar," says Leroy. "The people will be shown that."

"I tell the people what they need to hear."

I can see Leroy getting angry and I'm also stirring. This is getting out of hand. Hang on … that is what Krakus wants! He's recording this. We've got to stay calm and in control.

"Krakus," I say. "You have good intentions. I believe that you could be a great man, perhaps even as great as Zennuta. You need to act now to change things and to be that great man. We're asking for your help. Release Dana and Kala and join us now. You can lead this change for the good of all. All you need to do is to join us now."

Krakus looks at me for a few seconds but then his iris' seems to fade. His mind is on something else.

"Join us," I repeat.

"Thank you for your offer," he says coldly. "I will pass it on to the Council. Is there anything else you'd like to discuss?"

"You don't have much time," says Leroy. "If you don't act now, our people will rise against you."

"With guns? Are you planning violence?" says Krakus, reengaging.

"No, we will peacefully inform the people and bring down your council," I reply.

"You can't win this," he says. "The people will see you as gun shooting farmers who just want more farm land."

"The people will have a choice," I say.

"The people already have a choice," he says, standing up from the table. "We'll leave this discussion here. As you know, I have a broadcast. Thank you for this meeting. It was illuminating."

He walks away and leaves through the heavy wooden door without looking back. I can't help but admire his control.

"That's it, then," says Leroy. "Hollis was right. Krakus won't do a thing."

"Shhh!" I whisper. "We're being watched." As soon as I've said it, I remember the time I thought there was an extra person at the Origins' meeting. I could be wrong here too.

"Let's go," says Anita and we all get up.

We're met by the same tall patrol officer who searched us.

"This way," he says, leading us down the corridor in the opposite direction to the way we came. We pass through one heavy wooden door and then through another. We walk a little further and then we see the officer with the square haircut waiting beside an open wooden door.

"In ya go," says Square Hair.

"What's going on?" asks Leroy.

"We've been told to hold ya here."

"For what?" asks Leroy.

"Dunno. Ya has to wait and see," he says, his right hand hovering beside his stun gun.

"No, we'd like to go now," I say assertively.

"You heard him. In you go," says Standard Hair, who was already in the room.

"Why are you holding us?"

"In you go!" repeats Square Hair, hotly.

We've little choice but to do as he says.

Inside, the room is as big as our kitchen at home but it has no windows. It's empty except for a couch on one side and two plain looking chairs. I recognise them as a standard model dream couch and chairs.

Standard Hair leaves the room and Square Hair closes the door from the outside.

"What now?" asks Leroy.

"We wait," says Anita.

She's right. We've no choice. Great, I think. First Kala and Dana, and now I've gotten the three of us captured. Some leader I am! I wish I hadn't suggested trying to negotiate with Krakus. The only thing that moved Krakus' iris' was the idea of violence. Maybe I should have left the leadership to Hollis.

21. Harrop

It's been an hour or so since we entered the room. Although we're captive, I don't feel in danger. Krakus is hardly going to see the three of us as a threat. I think he's working on a way to use us.

My real concern is for Dana. She's the one who's sentenced to have her hand cut off. I shudder at the thought of how they will do that. Will they use an axe?

Anita and Leroy are settled on the couch, talking about Rachus and whether she'll take to farming. They seem to have given up on Teague.

Leroy begins to talk about their wheat but Anita's elbow and my glare halts him. I really do think they're listening.

The broadcast will be starting any moment now. Krakus will say that we threatened him or something like that. Or perhaps he won't even bother to mention us. He really doesn't need to. The only chance we have for change is to deliver those apples. I wonder how Krakus will react to that. Will he change his attitude and cooperate?

I feel a slight tingle in my groin. I need to pee! I mention this to Anita and Leroy and walk to the door. Leroy joins me there.

"You too?" I ask.

"No," he whispers. "But I thought I might go with you."

"Open up," I say, knocking on the door. I try opening the door but it is locked.

"What is it?" says a voice.

"We need the toilet," I say.

"Just a minute," says the voice.

And it is a full minute before the door unlocks and we're met by Square Hair.

"You don't need to go," he says firmly to Leroy.

They *are* listening!

Square Hair takes me back along the corridor where we came from. I hoped he'd take me the other way so I'd get to see other parts of the building. He points to a door on the left with the letters 'MT' on it—Men's Toilet.

Walking inside, I notice that it's a standard dream-work design public toilet with three stalls. I take the first stall and relax on the seat. I might as well take my time.

Then, to my surprise, I hear a noise. It's a hissing sound that seems to come from the stall next to mine.

"Pssst."

There it is again.

"Who is it?" I ask.

"Who's that?" says the voice, in an insisting tone.

I figure I've nothing to lose. "It's Tomas. I'm from the South."

"Tomas?"

"Yes, Tomas. Who are you?" I ask.

"It's Harrop."

"Harrop?"

"Yes. I'm going to try and get Dana."

That's fantastic, although he's in the wrong place to rescue Dana. "Dana isn't here."

"I know that. I'm here for you."

"Can we get Kala too?"

"Yes."

I feel the blood moving again in my veins. "How do we get out of here?"

"Listen carefully. When you leave the toilet, turn left and walk. Ignore the patrol officer. Just turn left and keep walking. I'll do the rest."

Briefly, I think about Anita and Leroy. It doesn't seem fair to leave them here, but what can I do? My thoughts for them are easily trumped by my concern for Dana and Kala.

Another thought I have is that this might be some kind of trap. But would Harrop be part of it? And why would Krakus bother? I take hold of my necklace with both hands and move my fingers along the edge of the leather to the diamond pendant.

"Okay. When?"

"Now! Go now!"

I move to the door but stop there for a moment, thinking again of Anita and Leroy. Again though, I reason that they should be fine. They've committed no crime. I open the door.

Square Hair is standing a few metres back from the door. He barely looks at me. This is my chance. I move left, walking as normally as I can.

"It's this way," says Square Hair.

I ignore him, continuing to walk with my head down.

"This way," he repeats, loudly.

I hear him moving after me. It's not long before he's upon me and takes a firm hold of my right arm.

"Where do you think ya goin'?" he insists.

I consider resisting, but hesitate. I'm no match for him. He turns me around and begins to walk me back towards the holding room. Ahead of us is Harrop, wearing his patrol officer uniform.

"What's going on?" asks Harrop.

"Nothing," says Square Hair. "He just went the wrong way."

"I meant, why wasn't he with the others? I have orders to take the young one to the prison farm."

"I didn't get that message."

"That's okay. I'll take him from here."

"All right. Take him," says Square Hair, releasing his hold. "This young one is the leader. Seems to have a mind of his own."

"Okay, I'll take no chances with him," says Harrop, drawing his stun gun. "This way," he says, pointing his gun along the corridor. I follow his instruction, walking in front of him again, as normally as I can.

We pass through the first door and take the first left turn. Walking quickly, we reach the second door and turn left again.

We're now close to the reception desk. Harrop slows his walk. Curly Hair is at her post, but she's looking down. I sense her movement as we pass, but I hear nothing. Harrop continues, shepherding me through the entry door.

Out front, I see Anita and Leroy's car where we left it, although two patrol cars have parked closely on either side of it, making it impossible to drive away.

"Car," says Harrop.

"Which one?"

"Left," says Harrop, followed by "Back seat."

We're nearly at the car when someone yells "Stop!" followed by, "You two, stop there!"

I tense, expecting to be stunned. I'm surprised to make it to the car door. I quickly get in. Harrop sits in the driver's seat. His gaze is fixed, ignoring the yelling from the officers approaching the car.

The acceleration forces me back in the seat. I feel a strain as I turn my head to see a very confused Square Hair, standing halfway between the front door and the road with his stun gun drawn.

I say nothing for a while and it's not out of choice. The speed of the patrol car is holding me back in the seat. On the corners, I have to push against the roof and the seat to hold myself steady.

After a few minutes Harrop slows. We don't appear to have been followed.

"You okay?" asks Harrop.

"Yes, fine. Are we going to the prison farm?"

"Yes, it's about ten minutes from here."

"What's your plan?"

"Put these on," he says, throwing me his handcuffs. "You'll act as my prisoner. Once we're in the farmhouse, I'll take you to the holding rooms, give you the door keys and pretend to lock you in. Once I'm gone, you get out of your room and release Dana."

"And Kala?"

"Yes, Kala too. They'll be in the same room."

"How long should I wait?"

Harrop doesn't answer straight away. I'm sure he's thinking about his options. He could leave and it will appear that it was me, acting alone.

"How many patrol officers?" I ask.

"Two."

"And how do I get past them?"

Again, he pauses. "I'll take care of them."

"What do you mean?"

"You wait one minute, then you release Dana and Kala. Just before you enter the main room, knock on the door three times and I'll stun the officers."

I'm a little shocked, but on the other hand, pleased that he's with us and also happy for Dana.

"Sounds like a plan. But won't they know we're coming?"

"They might. It depends on Officer Brivis back there at the office. Do you think he was onto us?"

"The one who asked us to stop?"

"Yes. Do you think he worked it out?"

"I don't know," I say, surprised by the question. "He yelled at us to stop. Why wouldn't he radio in and check?"

"He might. But most of us aren't that proactive. We tend to follow orders and we don't ask questions. I told him I was taking you to the prison farm and that's how it will appear to him."

I'm finding it hard to believe that Square Hair would be so passive and unassuming.

"What about your partner firing his stun gun at the hot spring? He was proactive."

"That was different. We were under orders to capture Dana using whatever force was necessary."

I accept what he says. Anyway, we're going to find out very soon. We must be only five minutes from the farm.

"What made you change your mind?"

"It was the broadcast. Krakus said that you walked into the Dream Council today as the Southern Parts' leader and threatened violence. He said you told him you would bring down the Dream Council and the Dream movement by using guns and violence."

"What else did he say?"

"He said that you were a child who had been captured, deprived of your rightful passage, and brainwashed by the Southerners."

"Lies," I say.

"And he told us that we must act now against you. He told us about Dana's escape from punishment last time and said that we must dream for her punishment again. He asked us to dream that Dana was at the middle of Norden Square tonight. He said to imagine her right hand severed from the wrist at midnight."

"You know what they really do, don't you?"

A Dream Passage

"I won't let them cut off her hand."
"We knew you would help us."
"I didn't think I would."

22. A different kind of farm

We're moving along a long, tree-lined driveway. There's a painted white fence along the edge of the road. The pastures beyond the fence are lush and green. On the left, out further, is a different kind of field. It could even be a small wheat field. What would they want with that?

We're nearing a long, rectangular building at the end of the drive. "Is this a farm?" I ask.

"Yes. It's a prison farm. This is your Island of Contemplation. There are crops here, vegetables over there, and a timber plantation on the other side of the farmhouse. That's how Krakus gets the things he wants."

I'm shocked. The Island of Contemplation is a prison farm producing things specifically for Krakus!

We're now only metres from the farmhouse. Metres away from Kala! I'm sweating and I notice my hands shaking.

"The cuffs," says Harrop.

"Yes," I say, embarrassed by my carelessness, and I quickly cuff myself.

Harrop stops the car next to another patrol car parked beside the farmhouse. He opens the car door and helps me out of the car. "Walk in front," he whispers.

I can't help but admire the pristine condition of the house. The brickwork and window frames are perfectly square. The tin roof is thickly coated in grey paint. Unlike a Southern house, there is no veranda.

Harrop places me beside the door before ascending the single step and knocking on the glossy white door. This is it.

"Who is it?" says a voice.

"It's Harrop. I have a prisoner for you."

The door opens and a male patrol officer's head appears. "We weren't expecting a delivery. Whose orders?"

"It's a Krakus special."

"They're all Krakus specials here," says the officer, seemingly satisfied. He opens the door. Harrop motions me in.

The officer is tall and skinny. His eyes seem to avoid directly looking at us.

"Who is it?" asks another officer who's seated at a table with radio unit, a cup and some papers.

"His name is Tomas. Says he's the Southern leader."

"He's the one Krakus was talking about," notes the sitting officer.

"Yeah, that's the one," says Harrop.

"Only a boy," says the seated officer. "Doesn't seem like much of a threat to me. We'll take him from here."

"My orders are to see him through to his cell," says Harrop.

"No problem. You can watch us lock him up," says the seated officer. The skinny one walks towards me.

"Stand back," says Harrop, raising his palm. "Krakus was specific with his orders. He said I was to lock him in the cell and take him the key."

"That isn't procedure," says the seated officer. "What's going on?"

"Just give me the keys," says Harrop. "I'll put him in the cell and be on my way."

"Hang on. We'll radio this in," says the seated officer. His hand moves towards his stun gun.

My heart is thumping. We're probably only metres away from Kala and Dana, and I don't think we're going to get to them. I feel helpless, standing here in cuffs. All I can do is wait to see if Harrop can pull this off.

"Don't you remember?" says Harrop. "I brought you the two women you're holding. That was on the orders of Krakus and I'm here again on the same instructions. Give me the keys now and let me do my job."

Harrop pauses while the two officers look at each other.

"Or I can report this to Krakus," threatens Harrop in a serious voice. "I'll use your radio," he adds, taking a step towards the radio unit and then pausing for their decision.

The seated officer looks concerned, but then gives a nod. He must be senior. The standing officer shrugs his shoulders, and then walks to the wall cabinet, where he retrieves a set of keys and throws them to Harrop. "It's the key marked with a two," he says.

"Thank you," says Harrop, maintaining his composure.

Harrop was right about the officers being unwilling to act on their own.

"Take that door," says Harrop, pointing.

A Dream Passage

I move through the door and into the corridor beyond it. Along the left-hand side of the corridor are five equal spaced doors, numbered one through five. They're obviously the holding rooms. Each door has a rectangular opening that I guess is for checking on the prisoners. Harrop follows me, closing the door after he's through.

Kala is probably just there behind one of those doors. I taste the air for her perfume, but it's absent. I just know she's there. My head says cell three.

"Cell two," says Harrop, walking ahead of me.

He opens the door and I walk through. It's a plain white room with two bunk beds and an open toilet in one corner. Harrop closes the door.

"Cuffs," I say.

He quickly unlocks the cuffs and returns them to the clip on his belt, then hands me the cell keys and gives me a nod. I nod back, thinking "Here we go."

I start counting the one minute I need to wait. My counting seems too fast, then too slow. I can't decide. At thirty seconds, I hear a dull thud from outside. It could be one of the officers or it could be Harrop. At sixty seconds I'm out the door and at cell three. I decide not to knock. I'll just open it with the key numbered '3'.

And there she is! Kala is sitting on the lower bunk bed, looking at me. And Dana is next to her. Kala looks exactly as she did when I last saw her at the hot spring.

"Tomas!" she exclaims, with her beautiful, excited eyes.

I move urgently to hold her. Our embrace feels strangely foreign. Her perfume is faint but familiar. I instinctively kiss her forehead. She nestles into my shoulder.

"What's the plan?" asks Dana.

"We need to go now," I whisper.

"Is Harrop with you?" asks Dana quietly.

"Yes, he is!" I release my hold on Kala and move out of the cell. "Let's go."

I stop at the main door and pause. Kala and Dana are just behind me. I give three knocks, wait, and then open the door.

Harrop is standing still with his stun gun in his hand. Both officers are down—one slumped at the desk and the other under the key cabinet.

"I'm thinking about whether to lock them up," he says.

I look at Dana for advice, but she's looking back at me.

"No, leave them," I say. As soon as I've said it, I wonder if I'm being careless. Our getaway would be much safer with them locked up. On the other hand, it could be days before these officers are found.

"Let's leave a note," I say. "Say that this was all under the orders of Krakus and he wanted to frame me for releasing criminals or something like that."

"Good idea," says Dana. "But don't bother with the details. Just say it was on the orders of Krakus. These two will believe anything if you tell them it is an order."

"Okay," says Harrop. "I'll say they should have put up a better fight and I'm still thinking of reporting them."

"Perfect," says Dana.

Harrop leaves the note on the desk, beside the resting head of the senior officer, and all four of us move outside.

Out the door, I quickly take hold of Kala, lifting her in the air.

"Eee," she squeals with a knowing smile. "I knew you'd come."

I'm as relieved as she is, but we're not in the clear yet. "We need to get going," I say, still holding on.

"What now?" asks Kala.

Kala and I watch as Dana and Harrop tenderly greet each other with their foreheads. "You came," says Dana.

"I couldn't let them take your hand," says Harrop and he takes hold of Dana, kissing her desperately.

I'd be happy to stand there and watch them, but we have little time. Every second will increase the risk of re-capture.

"We take the patrol cars," I say, to Kala, loud enough for Dana and Harrop to hear. "Dana and Harrop will take one car and return south. You and I will go to my parents."

"What did you say?" asks Dana.

"We don't have much time. You two need to go south as soon as possible. When you get there, go and see Seamus. He'll explain everything. Tell him that we're okay, and that Anita and Leroy are okay, but they're being held at the Dream Council offices. Tell him that I said to go ahead with the Apple Plan as scheduled. That message is critical."

"Apple Plan?" questions Dana.

"Yes. I don't have time to explain it now. We need go before those officers recover. Tell Hollis to go ahead, as planned."

"Okay," accepts Dana, still looking slightly puzzled. She moves to me and I realise that she wants to say goodbye. We share a short embrace and gently touch foreheads. "Thank you," she says.

I move to farewell Harrop. Hugging him seems surprising, given that I clubbed him and he captured Kala, but that's all in the past now. I actually find it easy. I like him. He's just stunned two officers for us. He's now with us and I trust him. "Thanks for helping us," I say.

"Thank you," he says. "I couldn't have done it alone."

We move to the patrol cars. Harrop gives us an access card and shows us how to start the car. He then pushes some additional buttons that he says will disable the tracking.

Kala and I leave first. I concentrate on driving, trying not to go too fast, just in case the officers see us. We've got to make it appear as normal as possible. The other reason I have to concentrate is because I have the distracting Kala beside me.

"Tell me everything," she says, grinning.

"Well, obviously, your plan worked!"

"Yes, it did!" she says. "Although, I was starting to get worried. There was nothing Dana and I could do. We were just sitting in that room, knowing that at any moment they could come for her."

It's the first time I've ever heard Kala doubt anything.

"But Dana was amazing," continues Kala. "She was prepared to lose her hand. It almost seemed like she was going to welcome it. She said that it did not matter. Things would change one way or another. If she lost her hand, it would be further proof of Krakus' brutality."

"Well, I'm glad she didn't lose it," I say. "I want her to have both hands and Harrop."

"I'm so happy for her."

"Me too. He's a good man."

"Of course he is! Dana would not be with anyone else."

There it is. She's back to her confident self. She takes my hand.

"Nor would I," she says. "Now tell me about this Apple Plan."

"Remember your plan to give bland apples to the Southern children?"

"I remember, but how will that help us now?"

"I'll start at the beginning."

I give her a brief rundown of everything that has happened, including seeing my mother and her offering to help, the idea to deliver fruit to Norden, being voted in as leader, and meeting Krakus.

"So much has happened! And all that time, Dana and I were here doing nothing."

"It wasn't nothing," I say. "It was your capture that made Harrop take action. It made me leader and gave me the plan for the apples. It even changed, my mother. Your capture changed everything."

I look at Kala, admiring her hair and her cheeky beauty. Despite being captured, she stayed positive and optimistic.

"Thanks for your dreams," I say. "It was your message that told me you were okay and the plan was working. If it wasn't for that, I would never have stood against Hollis. You are amazing." I gently squeeze her hand.

"No, you are amazing," she says, clasping my hand with both her hands. "And you're our leader," she says, grinning. "What are your orders for me?"

"That's an easy one. You are to be your lovely, smart, positive, dreamy, beautiful, self. And, if you want me, then I am yours."

"I get to be the leader's girl?" jests Kala.

"My second order is that I'm no longer the leader."

"But you'll have to see your Apple Plan through."

"I'll do that. But then it's back to Dana."

"As you wish, leader," says Kala, winking at me.

I can't help but smile at the idea of being Kala's boss. No one could ever be her superior. I move my hand to the leg that Kala has bent towards me and I touch her, noting her welcoming muscles. It occurs to me that every part of her body is an extension of her giving, trusting, and positive personality. I look at her gratefully and I'm reassured, knowing that we have so many things to look forward to.

***

It's now dark outside except for the standard, dream issue street lights. We're in the patrol car, nearing my parents' house and there's a dream car headed towards us. We pass it in our 'normal mode', looking ahead. The occupants don't seem to notice that we're in Southern clothes rather than patrol officer uniforms.

Driving this patrol car now seems a problem. I wonder where we should leave it. Perhaps the park in the next street or, to be extra safe, we could leave it on that dirt road where Paros and Neros took us on our passage day. That road would certainly be the best option, but it's a long walk back from there.

"I'm thinking about the car. Where do you think we should leave it?"

"How about out front of your parents' house?" suggests Kala.

That seems a bit risky. "Are you serious?"

"Yes. Does it matter if we're caught? The great thing about your plan is that it can go ahead without us. Dana will be in touch with my parents. They'll sort it out."

"You're confident!"

"Yes. It's a good plan."

I still think it's risky to park out the front of my parents'. In addition to Kala and me, my parents could be arrested. Maybe we should go to Paros and Neros' place. We could make sure they've been properly briefed.

One look at Kala though, and it's all resolved. She's calm and confident that everything will be okay. I feel my pendant.

23. Apples

"Tomas!" says Davis, opening the front door.

And there he is, my father. I'm so happy to see him, I hug him before our traditional forehead greeting.

He looks the same, except I notice some grey hairs. Did he have them before and I'm only noticing them now? His hold on me is long and tight—no changes there. After our greeting, I see tears in his eyes and he reaches for me again. He's never done that before.

"I missed you," he says.

"I missed you too."

"Hello, Kala," he says and he takes hold of her, giving her a proper greeting. He looks at me again.

"Now, what's going on?" he asks. "How did you get away? And what's with that patrol car?"

"We're just borrowing it," I say.

"Want to move it around the back?"

"No, it's okay," I say, looking at Kala. "We're done hiding."

"Having it there might worry our neighbours," he says.

"You'd prefer that we moved it?" I ask.

"Yes, just around the back should do it."

I'm happy to move it. I'm with Kala about not running, but on the other hand, if the Dream Patrol find the car here, they're certain to take us in. The Apple Plan will go ahead with us or without us, but I would prefer to be a part of it.

"I'll move it," volunteers Kala, and skips down the steps towards the car.

"Where's Beth?" I ask.

"At your Grandparents'. She'll be back soon. Come in."

I move through the entry to the kitchen and eating area I know so well. It looks just the same—blue walls and white table. I sit in my old chair. Davis pours three glasses of water and hands me one.

"So, what's going on? And how did you manage to get Kala?" he says but then adds, "Actually, wait for your mother. You can tell us both. Tell me what it's like in the South."

"Well, it's different. It's all so real down there. There are so many new things to learn and so many choices to make. There's work to do, but I'm happy to do it because it's important. And the food is amazing. You'll have to try it! And the people are great. They're different. And there's more of them than they said."

"Grandmata said over a thousand."

"Yes, and they can all do as they please. But, they also work together. Some grow wheat, some fruit, some raise cattle, and others sheep. One guy catches rabbits. The thing is that they help each other and trade so that everyone can live well."

I'm about to continue, but Kala enters the room, has a brief look around, and then sits next to me.

"We live on a farm with Dana. Do you remember the woman they said stole the printing press?"

"The one from the broadcast."

"Yes, that's her. Her name is Dana and she's not just any Danata. She's the daughter of Zennuta. She's our leader."

"That woman is Zennuta's daughter?"

"Yes. She moved to the South after Zennuta died."

"They didn't tell us that."

I hear a noise out the back. It could be Beth or the Dream Patrol. Kala and I sit silently, looking at each other.

"It's probably Beth," says Davis.

I'm relieved to see a smiling Beth enter the room.

"Tomas!" she says. "What are you doing here? When I saw the car out back, I thought it was the Dream Patrol."

I greet my mother warmly.

"Hello Kala," says Beth and she moves to her. Kala stares at me as Beth squeezes her with a huge hug and greeting.

"I'm so glad to see you," says Beth. "What's happened? How did you get away?"

"Tomas and another guy, Harrop, came and got us."

"It was mostly the other guy," I add.

"Did you use that patrol car?"

"Yes. Harrop is a patrol officer," I reply.

"So, what's going on? What are you doing here? How can we help?"

Wow! She has really changed. Kala sips on her water, watching us and smiling. "We'd like your help with tomorrow's broadcast," I say.

"Just tell us what you need."

"Just a minute. I'll need to explain a few things. Firstly, you know the woman, Dana, who was captured with Kala?"

"Yes," says Beth.

"She's Zennuta's daughter."

"Zennuta's daughter?" says Beth, shocked.

"Yes. Dana is a member of Origins. In fact, she's the leader. She didn't steal that printing press."

I pause to let Beth catch up.

"As you know, Kala and Dana were captured when we went to get the spring water to treat the rust in the wheat. When I went back to the South after that there was an Origins' group meeting. Some of the group wanted to go to Norden with guns."

"Hollis!" guesses Kala.

"Yes, Hollis wanted to take action, but others, including Anita and I, were worried that threats and guns would escalate to violence. We had to stop him. I came up with a plan to seek a truce with Norden and if that failed, to bring down Krakus peacefully. It was Anita's idea that I stand against Hollis for the leadership."

"You stood to become leader?" asks a shocked Beth.

"Temporary leader. Yes! And I won. The Southern people are good people. Most of them just want to be left in peace. They elected me as the temporary leader. My plan was that Anita, her husband, Leroy, and I would try to negotiate a truce with Krakus. We came back to Norden and tried to convince Krakus to let Dana and Kala go free. We were also going to ask for access to the spring water."

"I'm guessing it didn't go well with Krakus," notes Davis.

"No, Krakus only cares about his own interests."

"Does that mean people from the South are going to come here with guns now?" asks Beth, concerned.

"No, we have another plan. That's what we'd like your help with. Tomorrow, we're going to take over the broadcast. We're going to tell people what's been going on. We're going to tell them about the numbers in the South, that the Island of Contemplation is a prison farm, about the way Norden administers dream justice, that they actually cut off hands, and how it really is in the South."

"Wow! What do you want us to do?" asks Beth.

"Tomorrow, when they come to you to talk about the school, I want you to tell them how they falsely accused Kala of kidnapping me, your son. After that, I will tell them the truth about the South and about Krakus."

"Surely they'll block the transmission," says Davis.

"They will try, but we've got that covered."

"But why will they believe what we're telling them?" asks Davis.

"They will believe us because it will be you telling them, and I will be telling them, and Dana will tell them. And were also going to demonstrate one of the flaws of the dream system."

"What do you mean? A demonstration?" queries Davis.

"Tomorrow evening we will deliver Southern fruit to every house in Norden. One taste of the Southern fruit and they will believe us when we tell them that by dreaming of the same things each time, they are losing the experience of new things. That is why dream fruit is so tasteless, compared to Southern fruit."

"It's Tomas' Apple Plan," says Kala.

"It's our Apple Plan."

"They'll need to be good apples," notes Davis.

"They are."

"Not like the sour old ones from your grandparents'," adds Beth.

"It was those apples that gave us the idea," I say.

"The fruit in the South is amazing," says Kala. "You'll see. It will work."

"I think that in some ways, it does not matter," I reply. "All that we want to show is that there is an alternative and that everyone should have a choice in the way that they live. If we can show that, I think that the Dream Council will lose support."

"If they lose support, they won't get consensus," notes Beth. "The entire dream system will fall apart."

"That's part of the plan," I say.

"So, the dream movement that started with an apple will end with an apple," says Davis.

"It might," I say. "But we don't want to stop the dreaming though. We just want people to have a choice."

I see the expression on Beth's face change. I hope she isn't thinking that I'm having a go at her for not giving me a choice.

"I just realised that we haven't given you anything to eat," says Beth. "Are you hungry?"

With all that's happened I hadn't thought about food. Beth and Davis must be due to eat.

"Yes, if you have enough," I say.

"We'll see what we have in that cupboard. I'm afraid it is only dream food."

"It will do," I say.

Beth goes to the cupboard. Davis seems about to follow, but then he pauses and looks at me.

"So, Tomas," he says, "You're the leader of the South?"

Beth turns to stare at me, wide eyed. I can understand why. How could their son, at age sixteen, having left Norden a matter of weeks ago, now be the Southern leader?

"I'm the temporary leader," I reply. "Just until the end of the Apple Plan."

"And what happens after that?" asks Beth.

"We'll have to work that out," I reply. "I don't see why we couldn't have an arrangement where people who wished to could stay in Norden and carry on with dream work. Others who want to can move to the South."

"And Krakus?" asks Davis.

"He'll have the same choice."

"I don't think he's going to let things go that easily," says Beth.

"I expect that he'll try anything he can to stop us. In the end, though, the people of Norden can decide what they want. They will know the truth and that the Southern people are prepared to take action."

"Action like stealing patrol cars?" jokes Davis.

"I guess so."

Beth hands each of us a plate with a sandwich. "Chicken, cheese and lettuce," she says.

"Thanks," I say. "I'm hungry."

The sandwich looks fantastic. I poke the bread with my finger and it springs back nicely. The bread is thick and grainy looking, and the lettuce looks crisp and green. The chicken and cheese are both white and clean.

I bite into it and there it is. Nothing! Blandness pervades my palate. At least it will cure my hunger. I'm grateful for that.

"Your plan will work," whispers Kala.

"Thanks," I whisper, kissing her gently. I really hope she's right.

After the sandwich, Davis shares the strawberries and blueberries they have in the cupboard. I'm hungry and probably eat more than my share.

We talk about the South. Davis has many questions that Kala and I are happy to answer. At one point, I'm wondering if he'll want to live with us.

Now, I'm nicely nestling into Kala. I put my hand on her leg. She responds with her hand and we share a knowing look. From that moment, my ability to answer further questions is diminished. All I can think about is being with her. It's not just wanting her body. The thing I most desperately want is the feeling of peace I'll have when our bodies are satisfied and I'm holding her, silent and content.

"Do you mind if we get some rest?" I ask.

"No, of course not," answers Beth. "You've had a big day."

I get up to leave. Beth and Davis both look at me warmly. I'd say they are proud.

"Sweet dreams, my love," says Beth, followed by Davis. And they say the same to Kala.

Just walking to my room is like a dream. Inwardly, I'm cheering. We've been accepted as a couple and we're going to sleep together at my parents' house!

I close my bedroom door and turn off the light. I slowly undress, knowing that Kala is already in bed. My eyes adjust to the moonlight coming through the window. I see Kala's head above the sheet and the line of her body filling my bed. I think she might be smiling at me.

I stand naked for a few moments. I'm now more confident about my body. I stand admiring Kala's silhouette, amazed that she's in my bed and we're at my parents' house— together!

My muscles are small. I'm not standing in a strong or provocative way, but I know that Kala wants me. Perhaps now I'm beginning to be worthy of that confidence she has in me. I move to the bed, lift the sheet and move to Kala. She's already naked. She's warm and she wants me.

"I missed you," I whisper unnecessarily. Kala responds by smoothing her hand along the top of my arm and over my shoulder, gently motioning me to move over her.

24. Norden

I wake to the sound of voices. Is that Davis? I can't quite hear enough to tell. Kala is sleeping, beautifully. I'll leave her to that. Hopefully the voices are unimportant and I can cuddle her, and sleep some more.

Just a minute! That could be the Dream Patrol. And we've left that stupid patrol car out the back. I quickly dress in my jeans and t-shirt which, I now notice, smell of sweat. The voices continue as I walk along the corridor.

"I told you, you can't take her," says Davis. "She's done nothing wrong."

"We've been told to bring her in," says the other voice.

It *is* the Dream Patrol!

I freeze, not sure whether to show myself or wait and see what happens. I remember though, what Kala said. We're done hiding. I join Davis at the door.

"Are you Tomas?" asks the patrol officer, her hand conspicuously beside the stun gun in her holster.

"Yes," I say.

"My instructions are to take you and Kala to the Dream Council office."

I see the patrol officer's partner in their car outside and another patrol car parked on the other side of the road. They'll be intent on following their orders. This isn't good.

"What if we won't go with you?" I ask.

"We've been told to use force if we need to."

"You can't have them," says Davis.

We're cornered here. There are four of them. We won't get far if we run. They might even take Beth and Davis, and I don't want that. I just need a few more minutes to go over the plan with Beth. With that, it might be okay.

"It's okay," I say to Davis. "We'll go with them." Then I look at the patrol officer. She's not that much older than me. She doesn't care about whether Kala and I are being fairly treated. She's just doing her job.

"Your instructions are to take us in," I say. "And you're only to use force if necessary."

She looks back at me, disapprovingly, as if to say that what I said is true, but what is my point?

"We'll go with you," I tell her. "We'll return the patrol car. You can escort us."

Again, no response from the patrol officer.

"You'll just need to give us a little time," I add, talking as authoritatively as I can. "We need to eat something and take a shower. We'll leave in two hours."

"That's not possible. We've been told to take you in."

"You were just told to bring us in. They didn't say when."

She's thinking. Maybe I've pushed it too far.

"Wait there," she says and moves away. She's going back to her patrol car.

"What are you doing?" whispers Davis to me.

"Just stalling."

"You could run. Use the back door and go over the fence."

"I know," I say. "But, we're entitled to be here. We're not going to run."

The officer is talking to her partner.

"Where's Beth?"

"Gone to get your grandparents."

I'll have to go over the broadcast plan with Davis. The officers are still talking.

"There must be something we can do," says Davis.

"No. Please, don't. I need you and Beth to stay here. We need you for the broadcast."

"The broadcast! You can't go with them. You should run."

"No. It will be okay. You and Beth can do it. All you need to do is to tell them that Kala is no kidnapper. Tell them that Dana is no thief and that they were going to cut off her hand with an axe or something. Tell them about the Island of Contemplation and—" I'm interrupted by the retuning patrol officer.

"You can have twenty minutes."

"One hour," I say.

She looks back towards her car. "You can have twenty-five minutes and that's it."

"Okay, twenty-five minutes. You can escort us to the Dream Council office. We'll return the patrol car we borrowed."

"No, you'll be coming in with us."

"We'll be with you. You have two cars. You can escort us."

The officer looks at me. I feel slightly sorry for her, having this annoying boy trying to negotiate everything.

"I'll radio that one in," says the officer.

"All right. We'll be ready in thirty minutes."

"Twenty-five," she says. "And don't you try anything."

"Don't worry. We're not going anywhere."

***

"What's going on?" asks Kala, in a sleepy voice, and lying very cutely in my bed. Now she's pulling my arm into her. I like that.

"It's the Dream Patrol," I say regretfully.

"Here?"

"They're taking us in. We've only got twenty-five minutes."

"I don't want to go."

"I know. We've just got time for breakfast with Davis," I say, although I'm thinking how much I'd like to nestle back into bed.

I actually can't resist. I jump in and take hold of Kala. Her naked skin is soft, warm and stirring. I want to be with her for every one of the twenty or so remaining minutes. I know that I shouldn't though. I'm no longer a kid. I've got to be responsible, for Kala and me, and for everyone else.

"We've got to get up," I whisper.

"I know."

"I love you," I say.

"I love you, too," she says and adds, "I love you with apple and cinnamon."

I can't help but smile and cuddle her once more. That's my Kala. We're about to be arrested and she loves me with apple and cinnamon.

We really need to get ready. I want to talk to Davis, Beth too, if she's back in time. I'm aware that I smell bad but there's no time for a shower. At least I can have clean clothes from my cupboard. I grab a pair of clean underpants, a pair of grey pants and a green t-shirt, and I hand Kala a pair of my underpants and a grey t-shirt. She smiles approvingly.

Davis is seated at the dining table. He's laid out fruit and cereal for us. I guess we have fifteen minutes left.

"Beth?" I ask.

"I don't think she'll get back in time."

That's a shame, although Davis is ready with a pen and paper.

"The education report is your cue. You and Beth can talk freely and you won't be cut off. You need to tell them about what you know about Kala and Dana, and the Island of Contemplation."

"Tell me exactly what we need to say," says Davis.

"Firstly, you tell them who you are and that I am your son. Tell them that what Krakus says is a lie. I wasn't kidnapped from Norden. It was my choice to go to the South. I went willingly."

"Got it."

"Then tell them that Dana did not steal the printing press. It was a set up. Tell them that Dana is Danata, the daughter of Zennuta, and the leader of the South, and that if she had not escaped, Krakus would have had one of his Dream Patrol officers cut off her hand.

"Tell them that dream justice is a lie and there is no Island of Contemplation. It is just a prison farm outside Norden where people work for Krakus, producing things for him that he knows people would not dream for."

"Okay," says Davis, writing furiously. "What else?"

"Tell them that there are over a thousand people in the South. They just want to live in peace. Their concern is that Norden keeps moving further south and has now reached the edge of their farmland. The people in the South are just farmers who want to live in peace."

"Yes."

"Tell them that tonight the people of the South will deliver fruit to every house in Norden. It is Southern grown fruit. The Southerners want the people of Norden to try this fruit and note the rich and authentic taste of it. They want you to understand that by dreaming up your food you have lost the knowledge of how wonderful real food can taste."

"Tell them that it is not just about the food. Tell them that dream work is stopping the people from experiencing diversity and trying new and real things. Everything in Norden is the same: the cars, the houses, the roads, the schools and even the playgrounds.

"Worst of all though is that Norden doesn't give its citizens freedom of thought or choice and future generations will not know what it means to be free, to have an idea and to see it through, to struggle, to help each other, and to succeed. That is what the people in the South have and they want the people of Norden to join them if they so wish.

"Young people should have a choice. They may choose to go to the South and have a different kind of passage as I did or they may choose a Norden passage.

"Tell them that the Southern people want a truce. People who want to continue the dream work can stay in Norden and live as they are now. Alternatively, those who want to try the South can do so. All we seek is the freedom of choice."

"And Krakus?" asks Davis. "What should we say about him?"

"Tell them that Krakus, like everyone else, will have a choice. He is welcome in the South."

Davis laughs. "Surely you can't see Krakus as a farmer?"

"I don't know. I suppose he could have some kind of advising role. That kind of thing isn't for us to decide. I just want to be back on the farm with Kala. We've got so much more to learn. We haven't even harvested a crop yet. I'd like to learn to cook well and how to fix things around the farm. I also want to trap that pesky rabbit.

"From what I have seen, the trouble seems to be that the people who want to be leaders don't make good leaders."

"How about we share the role?" suggests Kala. "We could have some kind of leadership roster."

"Great idea," I say. "Let's start with a joint council between the South and Norden. The council can sort all that out."

"Good," says Davis. "Anything else?"

"What are we asking them to do tomorrow?" asks Kala.

"Oh, yes. Tomorrow! Tomorrow we want them to dream for us. We want them to show their support for the change by dreaming up a water truck in Norden Square."

"A water truck?"

"Yes. We'll use it to move the spring water."

"Do you really think they will dream that for you?"

"Yes," says Kala. "They will if you tell them how much we need it."

"You know about the rust," I add. "We need that spring water."

There's a knock at the door. Our time must be up.

"Is that it?" whispers Davis.

"That will have to do. The rest is up to you and Beth. You can add anything you think will help."

Davis folds the notes and puts them in his pocket. "You two should have eaten something," he says.

I grab a pear. Kala takes a banana and we go to the door. The patrol officer has been fair. I don't want to annoy her.

"We'll just say our goodbyes," I say, leaving the door open.

Davis holds me tightly, then gently farewells me. "Dream well, my son," he says.

"Dream well, my father," I say. "Tell Beth that I love her."

"Dream well, my daughter," says Davis to Kala.

"Dream well, my father."

***

Driving between the two patrol cars is difficult. They're barely giving us any room.

"I'm surprised they let us take the car," I say.

"I suppose it saved them having to get it," says Kala. "Why did you ask for it?"

"I just didn't want it to be left at my parents. They could have been set up with it and arrested."

"Sometimes you worry too much."

She's right …

"Kala."

"What is it?"

"I've been thinking about what's going to happen after today. Everything is changing so quickly."

"Are you okay?"

"I'm worried about you. You always think that everything is going to work out. Are you going to be happy going back to the farm with me? Is being on the farm going to be enough for you?"

"Wow. You have been thinking. Don't worry, Tomas. The way I see it, everything has already changed. We have your parents on our side. We have my parents, and now we have Dana and Harrop. I can't wait to be on the farm again and to wake up with you each day, and discover new things and explore the possibilities that we have for each day.

"We'll have our own family. We won't just be farmers. We'll be part of whatever happens from now on. Norden and the South are coming together. Nothing will stop that now."

I hope she's right. Perhaps, I'm a bit daft for worrying so much.

"Thank you," I say, moving my hand to her leg. "That's exactly what I wanted to hear. Let's get today done and go back to our farm."

"Okay," she says, squeezing my hand.

What Kala said about having a family surprised me. She's never said anything like that before. A few months ago, it would have been silly talk. Now though, it's something for our future.

The patrol car ahead of us turns the corner and onto the road of the Dream Council office.

"Are you sure we shouldn't make a run for it?" I say. "We could go back to the hot spring," I add, winking.

"But your people need you," jokes Kala.

***

I'm thinking more seriously when we reach the Dream Council office.

"Is that Anita and Leroy's car?" asks Kala, noticing the Southern car parked at the front.

"Yes, and they're still stuck in that holding room. Oh, and by the way, one thing I should mention is that when we're in there, wherever we are, be aware that the Dream Patrol will be listening to us. We should assume they're watching us too. We'll have to be careful with what we say."

"Got it," says Kala.

We're escorted to the front door. At the reception desk we're met by Square Hair and his standard-haired partner.

The other patrol officers hand us over to them. Square Hair doesn't look happy.

"Get yerself caught did ya?" he says.

"I missed my friends," I say.

"Well, they're right where ya left 'em."

***

"Tomas," says Anita before greeting me.

"And Kala," says Leroy.

We have a kind of group hug that lingers.

"We were worried about you," says Anita.

"Are you okay?" I ask.

"Yes, we're fine," says Leroy. "What happened? Where did you go?"

"I'm not sure what to say," I whisper, pointing at the door. "Give us a minute."

I sit on the couch. Kala sits beside me.

"What do you think?" I whisper.

"I guess we just say that everything is okay," says Kala.

"Everything is okay," I say, loudly.

"Dana?" asks Anita.

"Okay," we both say concurrently.

It seems cruel that we can't say more.

"Tomorrow we can tell you everything," I whisper.

"I think I understand," says Anita.

"Good," I say.

"So, what should we talk about?" asks Kala.

"Have they treated you well?" I ask.

"They gave us some of that dream food," says Anita.

"Tasteless," adds Leroy.

"Did they let you go to the toilet?" I ask.

"It took a while. The officer with the square hair said no twice. It was his partner who eventually let me go. I hoped it would give me a clue on where you went. I learned nothing."

"I just went, got Kala, and brought her back here," I joke.

"You might have told us," says Leroy.

His comment has a slight edge to it. I don't blame him.

"I'm sorry. It wasn't something I planned. Can we leave it there?"

"Yes," says Anita.

"Thanks."

"What else happened?" asks Kala.

"Nothing. We slept the night on the couch."

Kala and I had a better night, I note, but we can't say anything about that. I put my hand on Kala's leg and we exchange a knowing glance.

"Why are we here?" asks Leroy loudly. "What are they going to do with us?"

He's obviously frustrated. I don't answer. I look at the roof, thinking of what to say. Krakus is going to present us as the enemy in the broadcast. If he gets the chance he'll accuse us of violence. Thankfully though, the law and order section of the broadcast is after Beth's education report. Krakus doesn't know it, but he won't get to say anything tonight.

I think through what might happen. After the broadcast, Krakus will be furious. The thing we really need to do is convince him to release us. That's going to be tough.

"We are being held without cause," I say loudly, towards the possible listeners. "They should let us go."

"I am no kidnapper," adds Kala.

"We are just farmers," says Anita.

Now they'll know that we know they are listening.

25. Pre-broadcast

I'm watching the door, expecting that Square Hair will come for us any minute now. Krakus has us here for some reason: to parade us on the broadcast, to get more information from us or perhaps just to enjoy our recapture. I'm guessing that any moment we're going to find out more about that.

Leroy has been quiet. Maybe he's still annoyed about the way I left without him or it could be that he's just sick of being in this room. Anita is faring better. She taught Kala a slowly sung song about mending torn clothes. It sounds like it's something from the old times. They pretend to sew as they sing. I wonder what the listening patrol officers made of that.

I hear a sound. Footsteps? No, it's nothing.

***

There's another sound. And now, the door opens! Square Hair looks directly at me. I bet he's annoyed by the attention we're getting. This is it. We'll soon find out what Krakus has planned for us.

We're led back along the corridor and into the same room where we met with Krakus yesterday.

"What's going on?" I ask.

"Wait 'ere," says Square Hair.

"Another meeting with Krakus?" asks Leroy.

I nod in agreement.

We enter the room. The door closes behind us.

"What now?" asks Leroy.

"All we can do is wait," answers Anita.

And wait we do. It's been over fifteen minutes. He's doing this deliberately. I can see Leroy getting edgy. I want to tell him to relax and that Krakus is just messing with us, but I don't. I'd just be acknowledging the situation. I'm not going to give that to the listening ears.

We're all watching the heavy wooden door with the ornately carved border. If only we had something else to do. Unfortunately, the only thing I can think of is that sewing song. It sounds sad, but that seems appropriate now. I'm sick of watching that door.

"Can you teach me the song?" I ask.

Anita smiles. "You want to learn the sewing song?"

"Yes, why not?"

"Start with your needle and thread," says Kala, holding her right hand thumb and index finger together. "And here are the pants you're mending," she says, holding her upturned left hand flat in front of her.

"And we start the song."

Kala sings while pretending to sew:

"We sit in our beds;
With our needle and threads;
We smile as we greet;
Because we're happy to meet;
The holes of our life."

Anita takes over:

"We forgive our cuts;

And our dusty, dirty ruts;
It's the price that we pay;
To make our sweet hay;
This is the way that we live our lives."

They sing it so slowly that they sound like old women lamenting the memories of their lives.

Both Kala and Anita join together for the next bit:
"Feel our touch;"
"We care so much," I add, remembering it from earlier.
"And we sing in rhyme;
Enjoying this time;
This is how we mend our life."
"Now, back to the fields," the three of us continue.
"To our wheat and our meal;
We'll sing another song;
And be back before long;
For this is the way of our lives."

The three of us laugh. Leroy looks at us like we're mad.

"Can I try the whole song?" I ask. This will nicely counter Krakus' waiting game.

"Okay," agrees Anita, amused.

"You lead," says Kala.

And I start by holding the imaginary needle and thread ...

After we've sung the song three times, Leroy comes around and joins us for our fourth go. It must be the mending power of the song, I jest (internally).

"Again," says Kala, and we've got our needles ready.

Then I hear a *click* and a *creak*. It's the wooden door opening. Krakus enters silently, stopping just short of the table. Square Hair is standing proudly behind him.

"Welcome back," says Krakus, looking at me.

I don't respond.

"Did you enjoy driving our patrol car?"

"Yes, we did."

I instantly regret my comment. I shouldn't be agreeing with this man.

"I'm glad you liked it. You'll soon get to see it again on the broadcast."

My mind races. That's why they let us bring it back! The patrol officer must have called it in. They had permission to let us drive. I should have thought of that! I'm a little annoyed with myself. Luckily though, if all goes well, it won't matter what Krakus has planned.

Anita and Leroy are looking at me, surprised.

"We just borrowed the car. And, as you know, we returned it."

"The people will see that you stole the car. And we will tell them about the violence at the farm."

"Tell them what you want," says Kala.

Krakus turns his milky white gaze to Kala. "I will, my dear. The people will be told what you have done. You will soon have your trial."

This concerns me. If the plan fails, we'll be stuck here. "You're holding us without reason," I say. "You are to release us now."

"You will be tried for theft of the patrol car. Kala will be tried for kidnapping. I will release your two friends tomorrow. They have committed no crimes. Now though, you will be my guests for the broadcast. I've arranged for you to have a very good view of us showing the people what you have done."

I hesitate in replying. This will either go very well or very badly for us. Krakus doesn't wait for a response. I watch him leave through the heavy wooden door.

"In ya go," says Square Hair and we're ushered through to a large room that's set up for broadcasting.

The quadrant and the adjacent projection square are exactly the same design as the ones at my parents' house. Everything else in the room is constructed from timber. The wall on the far side has stars engraved in the wood, aligned in the form of a galaxy. All the woodwork has a shiny, clear coating and I have to admit, it's beautiful. I see Leroy admiring the workmanship.

Including us and Square Hair, there are fourteen people in the room. There's a patrol officer in each corner and four others who wear a plain grey uniform that I've never seen before. Within the broadcast pyramid, Krakus calmly occupies an oversized wooden seat with rounded bulbs at the end of each arm rest. He's busy, reading papers and making notes.

A Dream Passage

Square Hair shows us to a three-tiered stand of ornately decorated wooden seats on the left. We sit in the second row.

The broadcast must be about to start. I feel my heart pulsing blood through my arms and I have a dull ache in my stomach. All I can do now is take hold of Kala's hand. I kiss her fingers for luck. The next half hour will impact our future. Kala returns my kiss and gives me a smile. Knowing Kala, she'll be confident.

The funny thing is that there's nothing for us to do. The plan is in place and it will succeed or fail. It's all up to our parents: Kala's parents to intercept the broadcast, and my parents to present the arguments. I'm warmed by the idea that they're doing this for us and there's an irony to Krakus giving us this fantastic view.

Anita and Leroy are holding hands. Leroy seems more settled now that we have some action. They've been assured of release tomorrow. I wonder though, whether Krakus will honour that if the broadcast goes our way.

Krakus, seated, slowly reaches down, placing his notes on the floor next to his chair. He rises and glares at me as he presses the button on his wristband, activating the orange light on top of the metallic silver broadcast quadrant. It must be six p.m.

26. The broadcast

Krakus is staring towards the camera unit. Simultaneously, his bald head and milky white eyes are being both captured and projected onto the white screen beside the communication quadrant. I'm not sure whether to watch Krakus in person or his projected image.

He sits there in his big chair, glaring at his audience. This time, it seems like he's pausing and staring longer than he ever has before.

"Welcome to this broadcast," he says in his slow and measured voice. "I welcome you as honest, decent people who, like me, wish to live in peace."

He looks at me. What's he doing?

"Today will be a special broadcast."

Special broadcast! What about the broadcast schedule? Are Paros and Neros prepared for this? Will my parents be ready for this?

"Today, we will address the growing problem of the aggressive and unlawful behaviour of the people from the South.

"Today, we will be showing you—"

Suddenly, the projection crackles and stops. Something is happening!

And there she is. It's my mother! Her face is there, projected onto the white screen beside the broadcast quadrant.

"What's going on?" asks Krakus, stunned.

A Dream Passage

"It must be the camera feed," says a grey-suited woman from beside the communication quadrant. "We'll get the technical people onto it," she adds, moving towards one of the wooden doors.

The grey-suited people seem to be Krakus' personal staff.

I sit and watch, amazed, tightly holding Kala's hand and pleasantly aware that the technical people for this broadcast are Paros and Neros. They won't be fixing this problem!

"Hello. My name is Beth," says Beth.

"What's she doing?" yells Krakus. "It's not time for education!"

"You will recognise me from the education section of the broadcast," says Beth. "Today, my husband and I have a special broadcast for you."

That's clever. It's going to look like this is the organised broadcast. Wait until you hear the content, Krakus, I think smugly.

"We're going to tell you about the people from the South. We will tell you what is going on in the South and also, what is happening here in Norden."

I know this was the plan, but now that it's really happening I can scarcely believe it.

"I'll start by telling you about my son, Tomas. A few months ago, he turned sixteen. Like the other children of his age, he was doing what we expected of him. He was going to school, learning how to dream well and preparing for his passage.

"The thing about Tomas is that he is a thinker. He has a mind of his own and he likes to question things. He sometimes questioned the dream movement. He was also interested in old times. He'd ask us about it whenever he could, but we were afraid to tell him. The only people who would talk about it with him were his grandparents.

"Tomas had a girlfriend, Kala, who is a lot like him. They both had thoughts and dreams of their own, and it wasn't long before they were both labelled as undisciplined dreamers. As you know, we make it very difficult for them to be together.

"As the time of his passage ceremony neared, I could see the look in Tomas' face change. I could see how worried he was. He didn't want to take the passage. But, I had no other option for him. My husband, Davis, and I literally walked our son towards his expected life path, to his passage and a life of dream work.

"On the day of Tomas' passage ceremony, I saw despair in his eyes, and then surrender. He wore the ceremonial dress and he went with us to the nearby stream where he was to join the other children.

"It was there that something unexpected happened. After he boarded his canoe, we saw that the other occupant was his girlfriend, Kala.

"Krakus told you that my son was kidnapped but that is not true. My son had a choice. He boarded that canoe with Kala and they chose to leave Norden and to live in the South. I know this is the truth. I am his mother.

Now I will tell you about the other lies that you have been told ...”

Beth is speaking so well!

"This is an outrage," yells Krakus, staring angrily towards me. "Stop this broadcast now!"

It's not clear who he is talking to. The grey-suited woman has not come back. I shrug my shoulders and return my gaze to Beth.

"To start with, I'll tell you about the woman, Dana, who was accused of stealing the printing press. Dana is no thief. She is Danata, the daughter of Zennuta, and the leader of the South. If she had not escaped, Krakus would have had one of his Dream Patrol officers cut off her hand.

"That's right. The dream work that we do for justice is a lie. Many of us knew this already. The dream work system that Zennuta set up was not like this. It never allowed for punishment or harm to any person."

I didn't know that—it wasn't covered at school.

"Dream justice is a hoax and there is no Island of Contemplation either. All we have are prison farms, and the workers on those farms work to give Krakus things he would not ask you to dream of.

"Another of the lies is about the numbers in the South. We have been told many times that there are only a hundred people living in the South but that is not the case. They have over a thousand people.

"Tomas has always been an honest boy. We've always been proud of that. But when I heard what he said about the

numbers in the South, I have to admit that I didn't believe
him. I wondered why Krakus would lie about something like
that.

"The whole thing troubled me. I had to know who was
lying, so I decided to look at the Dream Council files. I found
not one record that stated the actual number of people in the
South. What I did find though, was a Southern Schools Plan
that Krakus had our education section prepare. That plan was
designed for one purpose. It was to be implemented
immediately following the takeover of the Southern Parts.
Yes, takeover of the South!

"The plan I found was for more than five schools, each
with capacity for over a hundred students. That's five
hundred children under sixteen who are living in the South!

"I'm sorry for not believing you, Tomas. You are no liar.
There are more than a thousand people in the South and
Krakus has been planning a takeover and an occupation."

I'm not shocked by Beth's revelation but I am surprised by
the detail of Krakus' planning. He's sitting there, unmoved,
seemingly detached from what is being said.

"I'll now hand over to my husband, Davis, who will tell
you some more about the South."

Davis enters the quadrant. At the edge of the camera view,
I see my father give my mother a kiss. And she hugs him
warmly.

Again, I can't believe this. Davis has never presented
before.

"Hello. My name is Davis and I am Tomas' father. I too, know that Tomas was not kidnapped. My son is an honest boy and his girlfriend, Kala, is no kidnapper.

"The people in the South want to live in peace. Their concern is that Norden keeps moving further and further south. Our roads and houses are approaching the edge of their farmland. The other issue they have is disease in their wheat. This is treatable with spring water from the hot spring just outside Norden. But Krakus and his Dream Patrol officers captured two of the group from the South who came to collect the spring water.

"After that a delegation from the South, including my son, came to see Krakus. Their aim was to negotiate a truce with the Krakus, and an agreement to access the spring water. Krakus would not negotiate and he is now holding these Southern representatives at the Dream Council office."

"You won't get away with this," says Krakus, fuming.

"Tonight is a special night," continues Davis. "Tonight, the people from the South will share their food with us. They will deliver their fruit to every one of our houses. They ask that we eat their fruit and compare it with our dream food. They want to show us what we have lost by using our dream work for everything we do.

"When you taste their fruit, you will understand the way that our consensus driven dream work is taking away our experience of diversity, the real and the new. Everything we have in Norden is bland like our fruit. Our houses, our cars, our roads, our playgrounds and our schools are all the same. They're boring and tasteless.

"Don't be concerned. The Southerners don't want to take over. All they're asking for is honesty, respect and the freedom for every person to choose where they live and what work they do. You may choose to continue with your dream work or you may choose to live in the South. You can take your passage here in Norden or you can have a different kind of passage in the South.

"They propose that we have some sort of joint council to work out a new arrangement between the South and Norden. We can discuss that further in another broadcast. For now, though, we ask you to be aware of the lies that you have been told by Krakus. We ask that you respect our Southern neighbours and welcome them to Norden tonight. Taste their fruit and think about the problems of our dream work.

"There is one last thing that you can do tonight. We want you to set aside your normal dream work and dream of a peace offering. The entire dream movement started with an apple that we dreamed would appear in Norden Square. Tonight, we will have fruit delivered to us. In return, if you choose to, you can dream of something that will help our Southern friends. Dream of a water truck, a thousand-litre stainless steel water truck, to appear at Norden Square at six a.m. The Southerners will use the truck to move the spring water to their crops. If you dream up this truck, it will be a gesture of peace. I think we owe the people of the South that, after all the lies and false accusations.

"The final thing we have is a message for Krakus."

Beth joins Davis and they're holding hands.

Davis continues, "The people of the South have told me that they will forgive you. You can have the same freedom and choice as everyone else."

"You can even join them in the South," adds Beth. "If that is what you choose. For now, though, we ask that you release our son, Tomas, his girlfriend, Kala and the other Southerners you're holding."

"Yes!" yells Leroy, standing. Anita joins him, standing and they're holding each other.

I want to stand, but I can't. I want to say something, but I've no words. My body feels heavy and the weight of it is holding me on my seat. I guess I'm just relieved. The truth is there for everyone who wants to know it. It's now up to the people of Norden.

I haven't let go of Kala's hand. She's turned and is looking at me.

"Everything has changed," she says. "You did it."

"We did it," I reply, falling into her, but keeping one eye on Krakus, who was standing, watching us silently, but now he's turned.

"My office," he says to a man in grey. "Holding room," he yells to Square Hair. Now he's leaving through the other wooden door.

I stand to hug Kala properly and then we join Anita and Leroy. Leroy hugs me and follows with the formal touch of heads, and all four of us end up standing with our arms around each other, balancing between two rows of seats.

"Your parents did well," says Anita to me.

"Yes, they did," I reply proudly. "And they did it for us."

"This way," interrupts Square Hair.

"And Paros and Neros," I add. "They did it too."

"Yes, they did," says Kala, smiling at me. "I told you everything would be okay."

27. A long night

We're again in the holding room. The four of us have now caught up on everything we couldn't talk about before. Leroy apologised when I told him what happened when I went to the toilet. He said he was sorry for being annoyed with me. I said it was perfectly understandable that he was annoyed.

Now that our celebration has subsided, I have two things on my mind. The first is what Krakus will do. He's not going to take this easily. He's going to fight us in some way. The question is how? He could try to stop the fruit delivery. He might even succeed.

The other thing he'll be doing is securing the broadcast for tomorrow. That will mean action against Paros and Neros. It could mean action against my parents too. And he could do something to us.

"What's wrong?" asks Kala, taking my hand.

"I'm worried about our parents. I hope they're safe."

"I know. I'm worried for them tonight. Tomorrow though, everything will be different."

"We've just got to get through tonight."

"We could try to escape?" suggests Kala.

"They've got patrol officers on the door … and they won't fall for the same thing as last time."

"We could work on the patrol officers," notes Kala.

"We could try that. That officer with the square haircut is no Harrop, though."

"We could try."

That's my Kala—always positive. We could try it. The problem is that we've been talking loudly. They'll already know what we're doing.

A feeling in my stomach reminds me of something else. We haven't eaten since this morning. They didn't give us any lunch. It's now past dinner time.

"How about we ask for something to eat?"

"Yes, I'm starving," says Leroy.

"Have you eaten anything today?" I ask.

"Not since breakfast," says Anita.

That Krakus! He'll do anything he can to weaken us. I start walking towards the door.

"I'll do it," says Leroy, jumping ahead of me.

"Okay," I laugh. "Don't worry, I'm not going anywhere."

Square Hair answers the door. "What do ya want now?"

"Could we get something to eat?" asks Leroy. "We haven't eaten since breakfast."

"How 'bout some of ya fruit?" says the officer. "If it makes it here."

"The fruit's for you," says Leroy. "Could we get something now?"

"I'll see if we is allowed to give ya somethin'"

"Do you ever take a break?" I ask.

"Not when there's work to do. I'll have me break when you lot are back at ya farms."

And he closes the door. There's no way he's going to let us go.

A Dream Passage

***

It must be after ten p.m. now. Kala, Anita and I are sitting on the couch. Leroy is lying on the floor with his arm across his eyes to shut out the light. They gave us fish and vegetables. I was so hungry I scoffed it down. I felt much better after that.

"They should be delivering the fruit now," says Leroy.

"I hope so," I say.

I imagine Hollis standing watch with his rifle as Tallis and Scratcher make the deliveries. "Hollis will get it done," I add. "He won't let anything stop him."

"Let's just hope that there are no incidents," says Anita.

I must be tired. Anita is right. If there's any sort of confrontation, it could easily go wrong. Hollis just needs to hold back for one more night. I hope he understands just how important tonight is.

"Don't worry," says Kala. "They'll have Dana and Harrop with them. They'll be okay."

I really hope so. I move to the floor, lying in the same way as Leroy. It's a hard floor, but I'm tired now. Hopefully I can sleep.

Kala nestles in front of me and gives me a grin before pulling my arm around her. "Dream well, my love," she says.

"Dream well, my love," I return wearily.

I'm still worried about Hollis. He just has to hold it together for tonight.

28. Awakening

I open my eyes to the unnatural light of the holding room. It's annoying. I'd like a bit more sleep.

I vaguely remember a dream involving Kala and a rabbit. I begin to recall it, but my thoughts are interrupted by voices. I'd forgotten where I was. It's an argument, but I can't work out what they're saying.

Now Kala is waking. "What is it?" she asks.

"They're arguing about something."

The door to our holding room opens suddenly and we watch the standard-hair officer walk backwards through the door, towards us with his stun gun drawn. How strange.

Now we see Square Hair standing beyond the door jam, facing us, also with his stun gun drawn. Both officers are standing, glaring at each other.

Square Hair has his finger on his stun gun trigger. He looks to be thinking; deciding whether to stun Standard Hair. It's his own partner! Standard Hair is also poised to shoot, but he looks anxious.

Square Hair moves, slowly reaching his left arm across his body and taking hold of the door handle. *Whack!* He pulled the door and stepped back, slamming the door shut.

Standard Hair slumps in relief, dropping his gun.

I think about going for his gun but decide against it. "What's going on?" I ask.

Standard Hair doesn't answer. After a minute, he reaches over, collects his gun and places it in his holster. "Your friends are here," he says. "Out the front."

"What's the argument?" asks Kala.

"Krakus ordered us to take you to the farm. We're supposed to take you out the back door. I said I wouldn't do it."

"And now you're with us," notes Kala.

"Well … I'm in here," he says reluctantly.

"You'll be okay," says Kala. "You're with us now."

He doesn't seem to take any comfort. "No," he says. "Brivis will be back. He'll be back with more patrol officers."

"What can we do?" asks Leroy.

"Let's just stay here," says Anita. "We don't want a fight."

"What time is it?" I ask.

"Five-forty-five," says the officer.

That means fifteen minutes until the break of the curfew. We'll know then if they dreamed for us. Anita is right. We can't get involved in any argument now. We just need fifteen minutes.

"Are we being watched?" I whisper to the officer.

"No. They're listening."

"We'll go with them," I say in a normal voice. "Tell them we'll go with them."

Leroy raises his eyebrows. Anita nods.

"We'll go as soon as we've had breakfast," I add loudly. I walk towards the door with the intention of knocking.

"I've got this," says Kala. "He won't stun me," she adds in a whisper.

"Okay," I say, but I'm nervous. I don't want them to separate us. I stand behind Kala as she knocks.

"What is it?" says a voice.

"Open the door," says Kala.

There's a pause, but then the door opens. It's not Square Hair (Brivis) though. It's another officer, a male that I haven't seen before.

"What do you want?"

"Tell Krakus that we'll go to the farm," says Kala. "We'll just need to eat before we go. Can we have our breakfast now?"

"Breakfast? You want to eat now?"

"Yes, we're hungry."

"All right. I'll ask about something to eat. You stay there." He closes the door.

"Well done," I whisper.

"Are we really going with them?" asks Leroy, whispering.

"Yes," I say loudly, giving him a wink. It doesn't seem to satisfy him and he's now looking at Anita who hasn't moved from the couch.

"It's okay," she mouths.

We're all silent for a few minutes.

"What's your name?" Kala asks the standard haired officer.

"Remy."

"I'm Kala. And this is Tomas, Anita, and Leroy."

"It's no use. Brivis will be back any minute."

"With breakfast?" adds Kala.

All of us except Remy laugh.

"With more officers," says Remy. "I'm in trouble."

"No, you're not," says Anita. "Things are different now. You have choices. You can come with us or you can stay in Norden. It's your choice."

She's right. We have our friends out front waiting for us. The fruit delivery must have been a success. Now is the time to convince people that things have changed.

"What's the name of the other officer?" I ask. "The one at the door."

"Victa."

"Is he okay?" I ask. "I mean, is he a fair man?"

Remy gives me a questioning look.

"Is he reasonable like you or is he more like Brivis?"

"Like me, I guess. But he's a good officer. He'll follow his orders."

"What made you change your mind?"

"The broadcast. It was what your parents said about having a choice. I have children. I want them to have a choice."

"Six a.m.," interrupts Anita.

Six a.m.! The dream work for the night will be done. I wonder if we got the water truck.

I knock on the door again.

"What is it?" asks Victa through the door.

"It's after six. Is there any breakfast for us?" I yell.

The door opens slowly. Victa stands back from the door with his stun gun pointing at me.

"There's nothing to eat," he says quietly. "Brivis is coming to take you to the farm."

"The people have voted," I say loudly. "They've dreamed for change. It's time to give up and let us go."

He doesn't reply.

"The people out front won't leave without us," I say quietly. "I'm afraid of what will happen if you don't let us go now. There could be violence."

"It's up to you, Victa," whispers Kala. "You can let us go."

"Let them go," adds Remy, nodding.

I signal Anita and Leroy to come to the door.

"This is it," I whisper to Victa. "All you need to do is leave the door open."

I slowly edge my way through the door, closely watching Victa as I move.

"What are you doing?" yells a voice from the left.

"Go," I yell, ushering Anita, Kala and then Leroy through the door and to the right. I follow, with Remy behind me.

Brivis and the other officers must be close. As I'm moving, I glimpse an officer thirty metres away, drawing a stun gun. What is the range of those things?

"Go!" I yell again. I'm running and expecting to feel the jolt of the gun at any moment. Time is moving slowly as we run towards the first door. I hear the thud of a gun discharge. They're firing!

Anita reaches the door. I'm glad to see it swing open, but there's another thud. I'm surprised that I'm still moving. At the door, I glance back. There are two fallen bodies on the ground. They must have been stunned. The other officers are passing them! One of the two must be Victa. I keep running, urging the others to keep going. The other must be Remy. Poor Remy!

We're now past the desk that was occupied by the curly haired officer. There's no one there now. The front door is just ahead. We're nearly there. I hear another thud but we're still moving. Leroy reaches the door first. It opens!

All four of us are safely out of the building, but we can't relax. There are people ahead. I slow to check the others. Kala is with me. Leroy and Anita are just ahead of us.

Now, I see there's actually two groups of people in front of us. To the left, I recognise the Southerners. I see Hollis, Seamus, Scratcher and Tallis among the twenty or so people. Hollis and Scratcher have rifles. I don't see Dana or Harrop.

On the right are a group of patrol officers. There are at least ten of them, all with their stun guns pointed at the Southerners. I want to greet Hollis and tell him how happy I am to see him, but it's clearly not the right time for that. He's looking stressed.

"What's going on?" I ask.

Hollis doesn't answer.

"They're wantin' to arrest us," says Seamus.

"For what?" I ask.

"They doesn't even know. They is just following their orders."

This is bad. I'm not sure who I should try to placate: Hollis and Scratcher with their rifles or the Dream Patrol with their stun guns.

"What now?" I ask Kala.

"To the middle," she says, moving between the two groups. I follow behind her. She must have an idea. She sits and I follow.

"The song," she says. "The sewing song," she adds, holding up her hand as if it holds a needle.

I'm not sure about this. Kala and I, sitting between rifles and stun guns, singing an old song about mending clothes. Hollis is going to think we're mad. The patrol officers are standing in a semi-circle glaring at us. They could take us at any time. What are they waiting for?

Kala starts the song. I fumble my imaginary needle, but pick it up. I start to sing, nervously mumbling the tune. Kala, though, is focused, singing from her heart. Her eyes say to me, 'Trust me' and at that moment, the first sunbeams of the day turn Kala's blue eyes to turquoise and her blondish-brown hair golden. She looks just like the way she did in our dream.

Kala is sitting and singing with her pretend needle and thread. I'm silent—captivated. The only doubt I have now is whether this is real. Could I have been stunned already?

"Silence," says a voice from behind the patrol officers.

Kala stops singing. My dream seems to have broken. Now I see Krakus walking towards us. Brivis is among the two groups of five officers on either side of Krakus. With the other patrol officers, that's at least twenty officers and twenty stun guns. That's enough fire power to beat our two Southern rifles.

Krakus' walk is self-assured. He's acting as if nothing has changed. I notice the sunlight causing him to squint. He seems angry and he's looking at me.

"Tell them to put their guns down," he says to me.

I look at Hollis. I could ask him and Scratcher to drop their rifles. They won't listen to me, though. Hollis will want action. He'll want to show Norden that we're not going to take any more bullying.

I look at Kala. She's already looking at me. I need to stop this, but how? All I had was my plan. My plan was that people of Norden would eat the fruit and understand the choices that they were missing. Everything was supposed to have changed. Why aren't things different?

Kala nods to me. The problem is that Hollis and Krakus aren't getting the change. They're stuck. Somehow, I've got to show them that things are different. I have to get in between them somehow and show them something new.

I slowly get up. I can do this. I have to. I slowly walk towards Krakus. The Dream Patrol are watching with their guns primed. Surely I'll feel a jolt from one of those any moment now.

I'm surprised that I make it as far as Krakus. I'm right in front of his shiny, bald head. I go even closer, expecting him to back away, but he doesn't.

That's close enough. I extend my arms out either side of his shoulders. My hands crinkle into his loose-fitting clothes and through to his skin and I feel his bony body. It's actually reassuring in a strange way. He is human: just a man, like I am.

I pull him towards me, positioning my head for the greeting. And I have it, his bare forehead touching mine for a moment. I even feel his two hands grasp my shoulders.

"Everything is different now," I whisper.

"Dream well," he says.

I don't get it. Why did he say that?

As we separate, there's a loud cheer from the Southern group behind me. I turn and there, illuminated by the sun, is a giant silver, glistening water tanker, and sitting in the front seat are Dana and Harrop.

I look at Kala and her golden hair. This really is something from a dream.

"Stun them!" says Krakus, suddenly. "Stun them all."

This is madness. Hollis has his rifle aimed at Krakus.

"Noooo!" I yell, covering Krakus as quickly as I can. I brace myself, expecting a gunshot, but there is none. I slowly turn around, ensuring that I stay in front of Krakus.

"Guns down, Hollis," I say. "You too, Scratcher."

No one says anything. No one is moving. There's a long silence that I don't know how to break.

"Guns down!" says Kala, glaring at Hollis.

Slowly, Hollis lowers his rifle. Scratcher soon follows. I move my gaze to Brivis, who's glaring at me.

"Down, Brivis," I say.

Brivis looks at Krakus, then back at me, then slowly lowers his gun.

The other officers follow, placing their stun guns on the ground, one by one. I nod to each of them as they do it. The last officer lowers his gun. This is fantastic.

"Everything is different now," I announce, directing my voice to Krakus.

Everything really is different now. I'm elated, but not certain.

"Dana," I say strongly, half requesting, part demanding. I need her now. I'm relieved when I see her out of the tanker and walking towards me.

"This is Dana, daughter of Zennuta and leader of the South."

I bow my head in respect to Dana. Kala understands immediately and bows too. Harrop and Anita follow, as do the others from of the South.

Dana bows in return. "Thank you, Tomas," she says, standing next to me.

"Thank you, everyone," continues Dana. "Last night you made your choice. You have chosen to be free. As Tomas' parents said, every one of you will be free to live as you choose. You can live here in Norden or live in the South. We will have a joint council and live in peace.

"For now, we need you to maintain your dream work. We will give you more information on tonight's broadcast. Please go home now. Leave in peace and tell everyone you know what has happened here. Tell them that everything is different now."

"What about Krakus?" yells Scratcher.

"Krakus, like everyone else, is free to go."

"Dream well," says Dana, bowing to the crowd.

"Dream well," we all say.

That's it! We did it!

"We did it!" I say hugging Kala.

We're quickly joined by Dana and Harrop, Anita and Leroy, Seamus, Hollis and Scratcher.

"You did it," says Dana.

"We all did this," I say, and I look to Kala, who's glowing with joy.

It all started with Kala and her belief in us. Nothing would have happened without that. Then it was Paros and Neros and their support for us. Dana took us into her home. Seamus lent us his car. Grandmata and Grandpata thought of the hot spring. Anita and Leroy tested the spring water. Harrop would not let Dana lose her hand. Beth and Davis gave us their support and spoke so well on the broadcast. The farmers gave their fruit. Hollis ensured the fruit was delivered and stood up for the South. And in the end, it was the Dream Patrol who put their stun guns down.

29. Birds singing

Something is moving in my face. It's tickling my cheek.

"No," I moan. "Not now." I want more time with Kala.

It's persistent, though. It's in my face, licking me again. I open my eyes and there he is, little Spike, looking at me optimistically.

"Good morning, little one," I say, patting and forgiving. I can't be angry at him. He's happy and enthusiastic and ready for his morning walk.

I take a moment to focus on my dream. It was me and Kala, lying on our mound at the park. How long ago that was. I was nearly sixteen. I remember Kala, illuminated by sun rays. Her golden hair flowing to her shoulder and she was smiling her confident and knowing smile. It was her look that said to me, "Don't worry, everything will work out."

And she was right. Things did work out. The South and Norden became one. People had a choice of where and how they lived. I think our world became better.

Spike barks as I edge myself towards a sitting position on the bed. I don't move as easy as I did back then. They tell me I'm eighty-eight years old. That's too old, I think, and I wonder (again) why I've lasted this long.

I open the door for Spike. He hurriedly runs out towards the vegetable garden, hopeful of catching a rabbit off guard. His optimism is unfounded. The rabbits know him well. I'm sure they wait for him every morning, using his run as their cue to return to their burrows for their morning rest.

I walk past the vegetable garden to the shed where I open the door for the cows and chickens. It's one of the few chores I do these days.

I review the crops. The wheat stems look strong and healthy. There's no sign of disease. I think we'll have a good crop this season. That wasn't the case every year. Still, we managed to get through.

I start my walk along the path to what was Seamus' farm. Sometimes I go as far as the house. It's very different now, brightly painted in blue paint. Seamus would never have had that. Rachus and Milo have done a good job with it. They even use Seamus' old flour mill.

My thoughts return to my dream. For a moment, I see Kala's face rising with the sun above the wheat.

"Sorry, Spikey," I say. "I won't walk far today."

Back at the farmhouse, I begin my routine. I boil the kettle for tea. When it's sunny, I take my tea to the veranda. I sit there on my chair and enjoy the sunshine. That's where I think about Kala.

The kettle begins to whistle. I take it off the heat, pour the water into the teapot and add a little rosemary.

A floorboard creaks. I know what that means. "Good morning, sunshine," I say.

And there she is, running into my legs, hugging my knees. "How were your dreams?" I ask.

She stands, silently looking up to me and smiling. She's not much of a talker in the morning and that's okay with me. My great-granddaughter, at age four, can do whatever she likes. I take the teapot and my cup outside. Little Dana follows me with her cup and sits on the chair next to mine. She likes to copy me. I'll give her a little tea when it cools.

"Bird," she says, pointing at a colourful bird that has landed on the grass in front of the veranda.

"It's a rainbow parrot," I say. They're often here in the morning. I watch them and think about the dream with the parrots in the trees that Kala and I shared so many times.

"It's talking," says little Dana.

The little bird is clearly talking. It chirps and winks and flutters its wings.

"What's it saying?" I ask.

"It's happy to be free."

I can't believe it. It's exactly what the bird in the dream said.

"What else is it saying?"

"Says it's time to go," says Dana, in a matter-of-fact way.

I'm about to say 'wait', but it's too late. The little parrot has taken off. I watch it as it passes over the wheat field, sparkling in the rays of the early morning sun.

What it said: 'Time to go.' Could that be a message for me?

I feel for my pendant, but it isn't there. Sometimes I forget how I gave it to our daughter, Dana, long ago. She wore it well. Now it's with my grandson, Hari, who is the father of this little Dana. He could have done many things. He tried a few of them, even working in Norden for a while. In the end, he chose to come here and take over this farm. That was after Kala passed, two years ago.

Now, again, I'm thinking of Kala and looking forward to dreaming together. Everything is possible in my dreams. I can see Beth and Davis, Paros and Neros, Seamus, Dana and Harrop. One time I even saw Hollis.

There's more of my life in those dreams than there is here right now. That parrot is right. It really is time for me to go. It's time for me to be with Kala again.

Thank you

This story started with the concept of collective thought and the idea that real things can happen when sufficient people believe in a cause.

Adding testament to this theory, I was fortunate to have wonderful people assist me with the dream work that produced this story.

Special thanks to Glenda Savill and Paul Pajalic for tenacious readings of early drafts, to Paul Berry who wanted to know what happened next, to Tessa Woollett who was concerned about the driving and to Julian Ballard for his ellipsis assistance.

Much gratitude also to Margarita Martinez for her thorough editing and thoughts on the structure of the beginning and to Elizabeth Bennett for her exceptional edits and exclamation rationalisation.

Finally, thank you for reading this story. I hope that it inspires you to dream well. Sweet dreams.

J.D.E. Savill

www.ingramcontent.com/pod-product-compliance
Lightning Source LLC
Chambersburg PA
CBHW051134120726
47905CB00005B/1544